D0423904

THE COUNTRY HOUSE

JOHN GALSWORTHY

THE COUNTRY HOUSE

ALAN SUTTON
1987

Alan Sutton Publishing
30 Brunswick Road
Gloucester GL1 1JJ

First published 1907

Copyright © in this edition 1987
Alan Sutton Publishing Limited

British Library Cataloguing in Publication Data

Galsworthy, John, *1867–1933*
    The country house.
    I. Title
    823′.912 [F]   PR6013.A5

ISBN 0–86299–352–0

Cover picture: detail from English Landscape with a House
by Heywood Hardy.
Roy Miles Fine Paintings, London.
Photograph: Bridgeman Art Library

Printed in Great Britain
by The Guernsey Press Company Limited,
Guernsey, Channel Islands.

BIOGRAPHICAL NOTE

In November 1932 John Galsworthy was awarded the Nobel Prize for Literature. He was one of the most impressive and most prolific writers of the first half of the twentieth century: not only did he produce the longest family saga in English Literature, but he also wrote ten other novels, many short stories and essays, and he attained a reputation as a dramatist with some twenty plays to his name.

His family history and early life provide an unlikely background for an outstanding literary figure. His father, grandson of a Devon farmer, was a solicitor and property investor, a wealthy business man in the City, while his mother was descended from a family of needlemakers from Redditch in the Worcestershire Midlands. John, the second of four children, was born on 14 August 1867, in Kingston. Later that year the family moved to Coombe in Surrey, where they lived for the next twenty years in a series of large houses, built to their father's specifications. John attended school at Saugeen in Bournemouth before going to Harrow when he was fourteen. There he was better known for his appearance and his sporting ability than for any artistic potential. A fellow student's view might have been of 'A very nice fellow, without much push, the best dressed boy in the school . . .' (H.V. Marrot). Nevertheless, he was head of his house, and his house master wrote of him when he left as an 'ideal head without exagger-ation.' From Harrow he went to New College, Oxford, where he lived the life of a wealthy and fashionable under-graduate, more interested in horses and clothes than academic achievement. However, he satisfied the examiners at matricul-ation and went on to read law, which he must have studied thoroughly since he narrowly missed gaining first class honours. He was called to the Bar in Lincoln's Inn Fields in 1890. He had no professional ambitions and although the succeeding years saw considerable personal development, he made little progress in his legal career. He travelled widely, to Canada, Australia, Africa, Russia and France, and he met thoughtful and serious-minded people: Georg Sauter, a German artist; the stimulating and lively large Sanderson family from Elstree, and the mariner, Joseph Conrad. While he was living in London he started exploring some of the deprived areas and was appalled by the poverty-stricken sub-culture of tramps, prostitutes and n'er-do-wells, which he found existing alongside his own wealthy middle class. The effect of these experiences was to make him think seriously about his role in life. In 1894, in a letter to Monica Sanderson, he wrote:

> I do wish I had the gift of writing, I really think that is the nicest way of making money going, only it isn't really the writing so much as the thoughts that one wants, and, when you feel like a very shallow pond with no nice cool deep pools with queer and pleasant things at the bottom, what's the good. I suppose one could cultivate writing, but one can't cultivate clear depths and quaint plants.

This first admission of interest in writing reveals a natural facility for self-expression, the makings of a good style. What remained to be developed during the following years was technique and an imaginative interpretation of experience.

In 1895 he met and fell in love with Ada Galsworthy, unhappily married to a cousin. She encouraged him to start writing, and was to be his literary confidante throughout his writing career. In 1897 a first collection of short stories, *From the Four Winds*, based on his travel experiences, was published privately under the pseudonym of John Sinjohn. Two novels followed, *Jocelyn* in 1898 and *The Island Pharisees* in 1904. None of these early works made much impression, but *The Man of Property*, published in 1906, was an instant success. It was a satirical study of the materialism of wealthy middle class Londoners, and had been written and much revised during the first two years of Galsworthy's married life with Ada. It owed much to the guidance of Edward Garnett, reader and critic, who was Galsworthy's mentor for several years. It was followed in the same year by *The Silver Box*, which immediately established Galsworthy as a talented playwright. During the seven months between the writing and the production of *The Silver Box*, he worked on a novel which was intended to be called *Danaë*, and to be a thematic development of *The Man of Property*, but which became in the writing a satire about the country gentry, renamed *The Country House*. Published in 1907, it was considered as good or better than *The Man of Property* by readers and critics alike and may be his most successful novel apart from the *Forsyte Chronicles*. His reputation as a writer of merit confirmed, Galsworthy continued his study of English society with two more novels: *Fraternity* (1909), intended to reveal the lack of practicality of the cultured intellectual coterie in London, and *The Patrician* (1911) a study of the English aristocracy.

Between the publication of *The Country House* and *Fraternity*, Galsworthy had written a series of sketches about the London poor, which were published in a volume called *A Commentary*, and which caused some angry political reaction. This was certainly Galsworthy's intention, and over the years he was to support, financially and with the written word, many causes, including the abolition of play censorship, industrial injustices, women's suffrage, divorce law reform, prison reform, use of aeroplanes in war, slum clearance and many aspects of animal protection. His play, *Justice*, about the torments of solitary confinement, was a resounding success and certainly made an impression on Winston Churchill, then Home Secretary, responsible for prison reform. After putting through a series of prison reforms, including the reduction of solitary confinement, he wrote to Galsworthy, who had managed a public campaign for reform, as well as writing the play, 'there can be no question that your admirable play bore a most important part in creating the atmosphere of sympathy and interest which is so noticeable upon this subject at the present time.'

By this time Galsworthy was a wealthy man in his own right. He was generous, and regularly gave away half of his annual income. He and Ada lived in London and Wingstone, Devon, and travelled abroad every year. He was devoted to Ada, whom he was often nursing, since she was a victim of many minor ailments. At first ostracised by many of their former acquaintances after Ada's divorce, Galsworthy's circle of literary friends grew to include, besides Garnett and Conrad, Gilbert Murray, Granville-Barker, E.V. Lucas, H.G. Wells, Barrie and Thomas Hardy. In the years immediately before the war, he produced only one full-length novel: *The Dark Flower* (1913), a departure from his previous satirical mode, being a study of three types of male–female relationship, all of which he himself had probably experienced. Later when war broke out he hurried to finish *The Freelands* (1916), the proceeds of which, and much more, he gave to help the war effort. For several months he and Ada worked at a French military hospital, at Die, near Valence. In 1917 he declined a knighthood, because he felt that 'between Letters and such honours there is and should be no such liaison.' In July of the following year he was declared unfit for military service, which liberated him from a war-long feeling of guilt, and a few weeks later he had an inspired idea: to develop the story of *The Man of Property* into a trilogy about the Forsyte family.

The next year *In Chancery* appeared and, in 1920, *To Let* completed the tremendously successful *Forsyte Saga*, based on characters and incidents in the Galsworthy family, but existing in a special world of the author's creation. For relaxation from the rigours of writing novels, Galsworthy wrote plays, and they were usually successful. Such a one was *Skin Game*, written and produced in 1919, which was the first of a number of box office successes to be produced during the next ten years. In 1921 he became president of the P.E.N. Club, formed to encourage international friendship among writers. He was a committed and active president for the remaining twelve years of his life. Five years later he and Ada moved into their last country home, Bury House, Surrey, where they lived with their nephew, Rudolf Sauter and his wife. Here Galsworthy completed two more trilogies: *A Modern Comedy*, completed in 1928, which, with *The Forsyte Saga*, formed *The Forsyte Chronicles*, and *End of the Chapter*, about the Charwell family, published in its entirety only after the author's death.

Galsworthy was awarded the Order of Merit in 1929, and three years later his international fame was confirmed when he won the Nobel Prize, with £9000, which, characteristically, he gave away, to establish a trust fund for the P.E.N. Club. Unfortunately he was already in declining health and unable to collect his award in person. He was suffering from a brain tumour and his condition rapidly deteriorated through the winter months of 1932–3. He died in his Hampstead home, Grove Lodge, on 31 January 1933 and his ashes were scattered on Bury Hill in the following March.

SHEILA MICHELL

TO
W. H. HUDSON
FOR LOVE OF
'THE PURPLE LAND'
AND ALL HIS OTHER BOOKS

'. . . 'tis an unweeded garden'

HAMLET.

CONTENTS

PART I

PART II

PART III

PART I

CHAPTER I

A PARTY AT WORSTED SKEYNES

THE year was 1891, the month October, the day Monday.
In the dark outside the railway-station at Worsted
Skeynes Mr. Horace Pendyce's omnibus, his brougham,
his luggage-cart, monopolized space. The face of Mr.
Horace Pendyce's coachman monopolized the light of
the solitary station lantern. Rosy-gilled, with fat close-
clipped grey whiskers and inscrutably pursed lips, it
presided high up in the easterly air like an emblem of
the feudal system. On the platform within, Mr. Horace
Pendyce's first footman and second groom in long livery
coats with silver buttons, their appearance slightly
relieved by the rakish cock of their top-hats, awaited
the arrival of the 6.15.

The first footman took from his pocket a half-sheet
of stamped and crested notepaper covered with Mr.
Horace Pendyce's small and precise calligraphy. He
read from it in a nasal, derisive voice:

'Hon. Geoff. and Mrs. Winlow, blue room and dress;
maid, small drab. Mr. George, white room. Mrs. Jaspar
Bellew, gold. The captain, red. General Pendyce, pink
room; valet, back attic. That's the lot.'

The groom, a red-cheeked youth, paid no attention.

'If this here Ambler of Mr. George's wins on Wednesday,' he said, 'it's as good as five pounds in my pocket.
Who does for Mr. George?'

'James, of course.'

The groom whistled.

'I 'll try an' get his loadin' to-morrow. Are you on, Tom?'

The footman answered:

'Here 's another over the page. Green room, right wing—that Foxleigh; he 's no good. "Take all you can and give nothing" sort! But can't he shoot just! That 's why they ask him!'

From behind a screen of dark trees the train ran in.

Down the platform came the first passengers—two cattlemen with long sticks, slouching by in their frieze coats, diffusing an odour of beast and black tobacco; then a couple, and single figures, keeping as far apart as possible, the guests of Mr. Horace Pendyce. Slowly they came out one by one into the loom of the carriages, and stood with their eyes fixed carefully before them, as though afraid they might recognize each other. A tall man in a fur coat, whose tall wife carried a small bag of silver and shagreen, spoke to the coachman:

'How are you, Benson? Mr. George says Captain Pendyce told him he wouldn't be down till the 9.30. I suppose we 'd better——'

Like a breeze tuning through the frigid silence of a fog, a high, clear voice was heard:

'Oh, thanks; I 'll go up in the brougham.'

Followed by the first footman carrying her wraps, and muffled in a white veil, through which the Hon. Geoffrey Winlow's leisurely gaze caught the gleam of eyes, a lady stepped forward, and with a backward glance vanished into the brougham. Her head appeared again behind the swathe of gauze.

'There 's plenty of room, George.'

George Pendyce walked quickly forward, and disappeared beside her. There was a crunch of wheels; the brougham rolled away.

The Hon. Geoffrey Winlow raised his face again.

'Who was that, Benson?'

The coachman leaned over confidentially, holding his podgy white-gloved hand outspread on a level with the Hon. Geoffrey's hat.

'Mrs. Jaspar Bellew, sir. Captain Bellew's lady, of the Firs.'

'But I thought they weren't——'

'No, sir; they're not, sir.'

'Ah!'

A calm rarefied voice was heard from the door of the omnibus:

'Now, Geoff!'

The Hon. Geoffrey Winlow followed his wife, Mr. Foxleigh, and General Pendyce into the omnibus, and again Mrs. Winlow's voice was heard:

'Oh, do you mind my maid? Get in, Tookson!'

Mr. Horace Pendyce's mansion, white and long and low, standing well within its acres, had come into the possession of his great-great-great-grandfather through an alliance with the last of the Worsteds. Originally a fine property let in smallish holdings to tenants who, having no attention bestowed on them, did very well and paid excellent rents, it was now farmed on model lines at a slight loss. At stated intervals Mr. Pendyce imported a new kind of cow, or partridge, and built a wing to the schools. His income was fortunately independent of this estate. He was in complete accord with the rector and the sanitary authorities, and not infrequently complained that his tenants did not stay on the land. His wife was a Totteridge, and his coverts admirable. He had been, needless to say, an eldest son. It was his individual conviction that individualism had ruined England, and he had set himself deliberately to eradicate this vice from the character of his tenants. By substituting for their individualism his own tastes, plans, and sentiments, one might almost say his own individualism, and losing money thereby, he had gone far to demonstrate his pet theory that the higher the individualism the more sterile the life of the community. If, however, the matter was thus put to him he grew both garrulous and angry, for he considered himself not an individualist, but what he called a 'Tory Communist.' In connection with his agricultural interests he was naturally a Fair Trader; a tax on corn, he knew, would make all the difference in the world to the prosperity of England. As he often said: 'A tax of three or four shillings on corn, and I should be farming my estate at a profit.'

Mr. Pendyce had other peculiarities, in which he was not too individual. He was averse to any change in the existing order of things, made lists of everything, and was never really so happy as when talking of himself or his estate. He had a black spaniel dog called John, with a long nose and longer ears, whom he had bred himself till the creature was not happy out of his sight.

In appearance Mr. Pendyce was rather of the old school, upright and active, with thin side-whiskers, to which, however, for some years past he had added moustaches which drooped and were now grizzled. He wore large cravats and square-tailed coats. He did not smoke.

At the head of his dining-table loaded with flowers and plate, he sat between the Hon. Mrs. Winlow and Mrs. Jaspar Bellew, nor could he have desired more striking and contrasted supporters. Equally tall, full-figured, and comely, Nature had fixed between these two women a gulf which Mr. Pendyce, a man of spare

figure, tried in vain to fill. The composure peculiar to
the ashen type of the British aristocracy wintered per-
manently on Mrs. Winlow's features like the smile of a
frosty day. Expressionless to a degree, they at once
convinced the spectator that she was a woman of the
best breeding. Had an expression ever arisen upon
these features, it is impossible to say what might have
been the consequences. She had followed her nurse's
adjuration: 'Lor, Miss Truda, never you make a face!
You might grow so!' Never since that day had Gertrude Winlow, an Honourable in her own right and
in that of her husband, made a face, not even, it is
believed, when her son was born. And then to find on
the other side of Mr. Pendyce that puzzling Mrs. Bellew
with the green-grey eyes, at which the best people of
her own sex looked with instinctive disapproval! A
woman in her position should avoid anything conspicuous, and Nature had given her a too-striking
appearance. People said that when, the year before
last, she had separated from Captain Bellew, and left
the Firs, it was simply because they were tired of one
another. They said, too, that it looked as if she were
encouraging the attentions of George, Mr. Pendyce's
eldest son.

Lady Malden had remarked to Mrs. Winlow in the
drawing-room before dinner:

'What *is* it about that Mrs. Bellew? *I* never liked
her. A woman situated as she is ought to be more
careful. I don't understand her being asked here at all,
with her husband still at the Firs, only just over the way.
Besides, she's very hard up. She doesn't even attempt
to disguise it. I call her almost an adventuress.'

Mrs. Winlow had answered:

'But she's some sort of cousin to Mrs. Pendyce.

The Pendyces are related to everybody! It's so boring.
One never knows——'

Lady Malden replied:

'Did you know her when she was living down here?
I dislike those hard-riding women. She and her husband were perfectly reckless. One heard of nothing
else but what she had jumped and how she had jumped
it; and she bets and goes racing. If George Pendyce is
not in love with her, I'm very much mistaken. He's
been seeing far too much of her in town. She's one of
those women that men are always hanging about!'

At the head of his dinner-table, where before each
guest was placed a menu carefully written in his eldest
daughter's handwriting, Horace Pendyce supped his
soup.

'This soup,' he said to Mrs. Bellew, 'reminds me of
your dear old father; he was extraordinarily fond of it.
I had a great respect for your father—a wonderful
man! I always said he was the most determined man
I'd met since my own dear father, and *he* was the most
obstinate man in the three kingdoms!'

He frequently made use of the expression 'in the
three kingdoms,' which sometimes preceded a statement that his grandmother was descended from Richard
III, while his grandfather came down from the Cornish
giants, one of whom, he would say with a disparaging
smile, had once thrown a cow over a wall.

'Your father was too much of an individualist, Mrs.
Bellew. I have a lot of experience of individualism in
the management of my estate, and I find that an
individualist is never contented. My tenants have
everything they want, but it's impossible to satisfy them.
There's a fellow called Peacock, now, a most pig-headed,
narrow-minded chap. I don't give in to him, of course.

If he had his way, he 'd go back to the old days, farm the land in his own fashion. He wants to buy it from me. Old vicious system of yeoman farming. Says his grandfather had it. He 's that sort of man. I hate individualism; it 's ruining England. You won't find better cottages or better farm-buildings anywhere than on my estate. I go in for centralization. I dare say you know what I call myself—a "Tory Communist." To my mind, that 's the party of the future. Now, your father's motto was: "Every man for himself!" On the land that would never do. Landlord and tenant must work together. You 'll come over to Newmarket with us on Wednesday? George has a very fine horse running in the Rutlandshire—a very fine horse. He doesn't bet, I 'm glad to say. If there 's one thing I hate more than another, it 's gambling!'

Mrs. Bellew gave him a sidelong glance, and a little ironical smile peeped out on her full red lips. But Mr. Pendyce had been called away to his soup. When he was ready to resume the conversation she was talking to his son, and the squire, frowning, turned to the Hon. Mrs. Winlow. *Her* attention was automatic, complete, monosyllabic; she did not appear to fatigue herself by an over-sympathetic comprehension, nor was she subservient. Mr. Pendyce found her a competent listener.

'The country is changing,' he said, 'changing every day. Country houses are not what they were. A great responsibility rests on us landlords. If *we* go, the whole thing goes.'

What, indeed, could be more delightful than this country-house life of Mr. Pendyce; its perfect cleanliness, its busy leisure, its combination of fresh air and scented warmth, its complete intellectual repose, its

essential and professional aloofness from suffering of
any kind, and its soup—emblematically and above all,
its soup—made from the rich remains of pampered
beasts?

Mr. Pendyce thought this life the one right life;
those who lived it the only right people. He considered
it a *duty* to live this life, with its simple, healthy, yet
luxurious curriculum, surrounded by creatures bred for
his own devouring, surrounded, as it were, by a sea of
soup! And that people should go on existing by the
million in the towns, preying on each other, and getting
continually out of work, with all those other depress-
ing concomitants of an awkward state, distressed him.
While suburban life, that living in little rows of slate-
roofed houses so lamentably similar that no man of
individual taste could bear to see them, he much disliked. Yet, in spite of his strong prejudice in favour of
country-house life, he was not a rich man, his income
barely exceeding ten thousand a year.

The first shooting-party of the season, devoted to
spinneys and the outlying coverts, had been, as usual,
made to synchronize with the last Newmarket meeting,
for Newmarket was within an uncomfortable distance
of Worsted Skeynes; and though Mr. Pendyce had a
horror of gaming, he liked to figure there and pass for
a man interested in sport for sport's sake, and he was
really rather proud of the fact that his son had picked
up so good a horse as the Ambler promised to be for so
little money, and was racing him for pure sport.

The guests had been carefully chosen. On Mrs.
Winlow's right was Thomas Brandwhite (of Brown
and Brandwhite), who had a position in the financial
world which could not well be ignored, two places in
the country, and a yacht. His long, lined face, with very

heavy moustaches, wore habitually a peevish look. He had retired from his firm, and now only sat on the boards of several companies. Next to him was Mrs. Hussell Barter, with that touching look to be seen on the faces of many English ladies, that look of women who are always doing their duty, their rather painful duty; whose eyes, above cheeks creased and withered, once rose-leaf hued, now over-coloured by strong weather, are starry and anxious; whose speech is simple, sympathetic, direct, a little shy, a little hopeless, yet always hopeful; who are ever surrounded by children, invalids, old people, all looking to them for support; who have never known the luxury of breaking down —of these was Mrs. Hussell Barter, the wife of the Reverend Hussell Barter, who would shoot to-morrow, but would not attend the race-meeting on the Wednesday. On her other hand was Gilbert Foxleigh, a lean-flanked man with a long, narrow head, strong white teeth, and hollow, thirsting eyes. He came of a county family of Foxleighs, and was one of six brothers, invaluable to the owners of coverts or young, half-broken horses in days when, as a Foxleigh would put it, 'hardly a Johnny of the lot could shoot or ride for nuts.' There was no species of beast, bird, or fish that he could not and did not destroy with equal skill and enjoyment. The only thing against him was his income, which was very small. He had taken in Mrs. Brandwhite, to whom, however, he talked but little, leaving her to General Pendyce, her neighbour on the other side.

Had he been born a year before his brother, instead of a year after, Charles Pendyce would naturally have owned Worsted Skeynes, and Horace would have gone into the army instead. As it was, having almost

imperceptibly become a major-general, he had retired,
taking with him his pension.   The third brother, had he
chosen to be born, would have gone into the Church,
where a living awaited him; he had elected otherwise,
and the living had passed perforce to a collateral
branch.   Between Horace and Charles, seen from
behind, it was difficult to distinguish.   Both were spare,
both erect, with the least inclination to bottle shoulders,
but Charles Pendyce brushed his hair, both before and
behind, away from a central parting, and about the
back of his still active knees there was a look of feeble-
ness.   Seen from the front they could readily be differ-
entiated, for the general's whiskers broadened down his
cheeks till they reached his moustaches, and there was
in his face and manner a sort of formal, though discontented, effacement, as of an individualist who has
all his life been part of a system, from which he has
issued at last, unconscious indeed of his loss, but with
a vague sense of injury.   He had never married, feeling
it to be comparatively useless, owing to Horace having
gained that year on him at the start, and he lived with
a valet close to his club in Pall Mall.

In Lady Malden, whom he had taken in to dinner,
Worsted Skeynes entertained a good woman and a
personality, whose teas to working men in the London
season were famous.   No working man who had attended
them had ever gone away without a wholesome respect
for his hostess.   She was indeed a woman who permitted no liberties to be taken with her in any walk
of life.   The daughter of a rural dean, she appeared
at her best when seated, having rather short legs.
Her face was well-coloured, her mouth firm and rather
wide, her nose well-shaped, her hair dark.   She spoke
in a decided voice, and did not mince her words.   It

was to her that her husband, Sir James, owed his
reactionary principles on the subject of woman.

Round the corner at the end of the table the Hon.
Geoffrey Winlow was telling his hostess of the Balkan
Provinces, from a tour in which he had just returned.
His face, of the Norman type, with regular, handsome
features, had a leisurely and capable expression. His
manner was easy and pleasant; only at times it became
apparent that his ideas were in perfect order, so that
he would naturally not care to be corrected. His father,
Lord Montrossor, whose seat was at Coldingham, six
miles away, would ultimately yield to him his place
in the House of Lords.

And next to him sat Mrs. Pendyce. A portrait of
this lady hung over the sideboard at the end of the room,
and though it had been painted by a fashionable painter,
it had caught a gleam of that 'something' still in her
face these twenty years later. She was not young, her
dark hair was going grey; but she was not old, for she
had been married at nineteen and was still only fifty-
two. Her face was rather long and very pale, and her
eyebrows arched and dark and always slightly raised.
Her eyes were dark grey, sometimes almost black, for
the pupils dilated when she was moved; her lips were
the least thing parted, and the expression of those lips
and eyes was of a rather touching gentleness, of a rather
touching expectancy. And yet all this was not the
'something'; *that* was rather the outward sign of an
inborn sense that she had no need to ask for things,
of an instinctive faith that she had already had them.
By that 'something,' and by her long, transparent
hands, men could tell that she had been a Totteridge.
And her voice, which was rather slow, with a little, not
unpleasant, trick of speech, and her eyelids by second

nature just a trifle lowered, confirmed this impression. Over her bosom, which hid the heart of a lady, rose and fell a piece of wonderful old lace.

Round the corner again Sir James Malden and Bee Pendyce (the eldest daughter) were talking of horses and hunting—Bee seldom from choice spoke of anything else. Her face was pleasant and good, yet not quite pretty, and this little fact seemed to have entered into her very nature, making her shy and ever willing to do things for others.

Sir James had small grey whiskers and a carved, keen visage. He came of an old Kentish family which had migrated to Cambridgeshire; his coverts were exceptionally fine; he was also a justice of the peace, a colonel of Yeomanry, a keen churchman, and much feared by poachers. He held the reactionary views already mentioned, being a little afraid of Lady Malden.

Beyond Miss Pendyce sat the Reverend Hussell Barter, who would shoot to-morrow, but would not attend the race-meeting on Wednesday.

The Rector of Worsted Skeynes was not tall, and his head had been rendered somewhat bald by thought. His broad face, of very straight build from the top of the forehead to the base of the chin, was well-coloured, clean-shaven, and of a shape that may be seen in portraits of the Georgian era. His cheeks were full and folded, his lower lip had a habit of protruding, and his eyebrows jutted out above his full, light eyes. His manner was authoritative, and he articulated his words in a voice to which long service in the pulpit had imparted remarkable carrying-power—in fact, when engaged in private conversation, it was with difficulty that he was not overheard. Perhaps even in confidential matters he was not unwilling that what he said should

bear fruit. In some ways, indeed, he was typical. Uncertainty, hesitation, toleration—except of such opinions
as he held—he did not like. Imagination he distrusted.
He found his duty in life very clear, and other people's
perhaps clearer, and he did not encourage his parish-
ioners to think for themselves. The habit seemed to
him a dangerous one. He was outspoken in his opinions,
and when he had occasion to find fault, spoke of the
offender as 'a man of no character,' 'a fellow like
that,' with such a ring of conviction that his audience
could not but be convinced of the immorality of that
person. He had a bluff jolly way of speaking, and was
popular in his parish—a good cricketer, a still better
fisherman, a fair shot, though, as he said, he could not
really afford time for shooting. While disclaiming
interference in secular matters, he watched the ten-
dencies of his flock from a sound point of view, and
especially encouraged them to support the existing
order of things—the British Empire and the English
Church. His cure was hereditary, and he fortunately
possessed some private means, for he had a large family.
His partner at dinner was Norah, the younger of the
two Pendyce girls, who had a round, open face, and a
more decided manner than her sister Bee.

Her brother George, the eldest son, sat on her right.
George was of middle height, with a red-brown, clean-
shaved face and solid jaw. His eyes were grey; he
had firm lips, and darkish, carefully brushed hair, a
little thin on the top, but with that peculiar gloss seen
on the hair of some men about town. His clothes were
unostentatiously perfect. Such men may be seen in
Piccadilly at any hour of the day or night. He had been
intended for the Guards, but had failed to pass the
necessary examination, through no fault of his own,

owing to a constitutional inability to spell. Had he
been his younger brother Gerald, he would probably
have fulfilled the Pendyce tradition and passed into the
army as a matter of course. And had Gerald (now
Captain Pendyce) been George the elder son, he might
possibly have failed. George lived at his club in town
on an allowance of six hundred a year, and sat a great
deal in a bay-window reading Ruff's *Guide to the Turf*.

He raised his eyes from the menu and looked stealthily
round. Helen Bellew was talking to his father, her
white shoulder turned a little away. George was
proud of his composure, but there was a strange longing
in his face. She gave, indeed, just excuse for people to
consider her too good-looking for the position in which
she was placed. Her figure was tall and supple and
full, and now that she no longer hunted was getting
fuller. Her hair, looped back in loose bands across a
broad low brow, had a peculiar soft lustre. There was
a touch of sensuality about her lips. The face was too
broad across the brow and cheekbones, but the eyes
were magnificent — ice-grey, sometimes almost green,
always luminous, and set in with dark lashes.

There was something pathetic in George's gaze, as
of a man forced to look against his will.

It had been going on all that past summer, and still
he did not know where he stood. Sometimes she
seemed fond of him, sometimes treated him as though
he had no chance. That which he had begun as a game
was now deadly earnest. And this in itself was tragic.
That comfortable ease of spirit which is the breath of
life was taken away; he could think of nothing but her.
Was she one of those women who feed on men's admiration, and give them no return? Was she only waiting
to make her conquest more secure? These riddles he

asked of her face a hundred times, lying awake in the dark. To George Pendyce, a man of the world, unaccustomed to privation, whose simple creed was 'Live and enjoy,' there was something terrible about a longing which never left him for a moment, which he could not help any more than he could help eating, the end of which he could not see. He had known her when she lived at the Firs, he had known her in the hunting-field, but his passion was only of last summer's date. It had sprung suddenly out of a flirtation started at a dance.

A man about town does not psychologize himself; he accepts his condition with touching simplicity. He is hungry; he must be fed. He is thirsty; he must drink. Why he is hungry, when he became hungry, these inquiries are beside the mark. No ethical aspect of the matter troubled him; the attainment of a married woman, not living with her husband, did not impinge upon his creed. What would come after, though full of unpleasant possibilities, he left to the future. His real disquiet, far nearer, far more primitive and simple, was the feeling of drifting helplessly in a current so strong that he could not keep his feet.

'Ah, yes; a bad case. Dreadful thing for the Sweetenhams! That young fellow's been obliged to give up the army. Can't think what old Sweetenham was about. He must have known his son was hit. I should say Bethany himself was the only one in the dark. There's no doubt Lady Rose was to blame!' Mr. Pendyce was speaking.

Mrs. Bellew smiled.

'My sympathies are all with Lady Rose. What do you say, George?'

George frowned.

'I always thought,' he said, 'that Bethany was an ass.'

'George,' said Mr. Pendyce, 'is immoral. All young men are immoral. I notice it more and more. You 've given up your hunting, I hear.'

Mrs. Bellew sighed.

'One can't hunt on next to nothing!'

'Ah, you live in London. London spoils everybody. People don't take the interest in hunting and farming they used to. I can't get George here at all. Not that I 'm a believer in apron-strings. Young men will be young men!'

Thus summing up the laws of Nature, the squire resumed his knife and fork.

But neither Mrs. Bellew nor George followed his example; the one sat with her eyes fixed on her plate and a faint smile playing on her lips, the other sat without a smile, and his eyes, in which there was such a deep resentful longing, looked from his father to Mrs. Bellew, and from Mrs. Bellew to his mother. And as though down that vista of faces and fruits and flowers a secret current had been set flowing, Mrs. Pendyce nodded gently to her son.

CHAPTER II

THE COVERT SHOOT

AT the head of the breakfast-table sat Mr. Pendyce, eating methodically. He was somewhat silent, as became a man who has just read family prayers; but about that silence, and the pile of half-opened letters on his right, was a hint of autocracy.

'Be informal—do what you like, dress as you like, sit where you like, eat what you like, drink tea or coffee, but——' Each glance of his eyes, each sentence of his sparing, semi-genial talk, seemed to repeat that 'but.'

At the foot of the breakfast-table sat Mrs. Pendyce behind a silver urn which emitted a gentle steam. Her hands worked without ceasing amongst cups, and while they worked her lips worked too in spasmodic utterances that never had any reference to herself. Pushed a little to her left and entirely neglected, lay a piece of dry toast on a small white plate. Twice she took it up, buttered a bit of it, and put it down again. Once she rested, and her eyes, which fell on Mrs. Bellew, seemed to say: 'How very charming you look, my dear!' Then, taking up the sugar-tongs, she began again.

On the long sideboard covered with a white cloth reposed a number of edibles only to be found amongst that portion of the community which breeds creatures for its own devouring. At one end of this row of viands was a large game pie with a triangular gap in the pastry;

at the other, on two oval dishes, lay four cold part-ridges in various stages of decomposition. Behind them a silver basket of openwork design was occupied by three bunches of black, one bunch of white grapes, and a silver grape-cutter, which performed no function (it was so blunt), but had once belonged to a Totteridge and wore their crest.

No servants were in the room, but the side-door was now and again opened, and something brought in, and this suggested that behind the door persons were collected, only waiting to be called upon. It was, in fact, as though Mr. Pendyce had said: 'A butler and two footmen at least could hand you things, but this is a simple country house.'

At times a male guest rose, napkin in hand, and said to a lady: 'Can I get you anything from the sideboard?' Being refused, he went and filled his own plate. Three dogs — two fox-terriers and a decrepit Skye — circled round uneasily, smelling at the visitors' napkins. And there went up a hum of talk in which sentences like these could be distinguished: 'Rippin' stand that, by the wood. D' you remember your rocketin' woodcock last year, Jerry?' 'And the dear old squire never touched a feather! Did you, squire?' 'Dick—Dick! Bad dog! —come and do your tricks. Trust—trust! Paid for! Isn't he rather a darling?'

On Mr. Pendyce's foot, or by the side of his chair, whence he could see what was being eaten, sat the spaniel John, and now and then Mr. Pendyce, taking a small portion of something between his finger and thumb, would say:

'John!—Make a good breakfast, Sir James; I always say a half-breakfasted man is no good!'

And Mrs. Pendyce, her eyebrows lifted, would look

anxiously up and down the table, murmuring: 'Another cup, dear; let me see—are you sugar?'

When all had finished a silence fell, as if each sought to get away from what he had been eating, as if each felt he had been engaged in an unworthy practice; then Mr. Pendyce, finishing his last grape, wiped his mouth.

'You've a quarter of an hour, gentlemen; we start at ten-fifteen.'

Mrs. Pendyce, left seated with a vague, ironical smile, ate one mouthful of her buttered toast, now very old and leathery, gave the rest to 'the dear dogs,' and called:

'George! You want a new shooting tie, dear boy; that green one's quite faded. I've been meaning to get some silks down for ages. Have you had any news of your horse this morning?'

'Yes, Blacksmith says he's fit as a fiddle.'

'I do so hope he'll win that race for you. Your Uncle Hubert once lost four thousand pounds over the Rutlandshire. I remember perfectly; my father had to pay it. I'm so glad you don't bet, dear boy!'

'My dear mother, I do bet.'

'Oh, George, I hope not much! For goodness' sake, don't tell your father; he's like all the Pendyces, can't bear a risk.'

'My dear mother, I'm not likely to; but, as a matter of fact, there is no risk. I stand to win a lot of money to nothing.'

'But, George, is that right?'

'Of course it's all right.'

'Oh, well, I don't understand.' Mrs. Pendyce dropped her eyes, a flush came into her white cheeks; she looked up again and said quickly: 'George, I *should* like just a little bet on your horse—a *real* bet, say about a sovereign.'

George Pendyce's creed permitted the show of no emotion. He smiled.

'All right, mother, I 'll put it on for you. It 'll be about eight to one.'

'Does that mean that if he wins I shall get eight?'

George nodded.

Mrs. Pendyce looked abstractedly at his tie.

'I think it might be two sovereigns; one seems very little to lose, because I do so want him to win. Isn't Helen Bellew perfectly charming this morning! It 's delightful to see a woman look her best in the morning.'

George turned, to hide the colour in his cheeks.

'She looks fresh enough, certainly.'

Mrs. Pendyce glanced up at him; there was a touch of quizzicality in one of her lifted eyebrows.

'I mustn't keep you, dear; you 'll be late for the shooting.'

Mr. Pendyce, a sportsman of the old school, who still kept pointers, which, in the teeth of modern fashion, he was unable to employ, set his face against the use of two guns.

'Any man,' he would say, 'who cares to shoot at Worsted Skeynes must do with one gun, as my dear old father had to do before me. He 'll get a good day's sport — no barndoor birds' (for he encouraged his pheasants to remain lean, that they might fly the better), 'but don't let him expect one of these battues—sheer butchery, I call them.'

He was excessively fond of birds—it was, in fact, his hobby, and he had collected under glass cases a prodigious number of specimens of those species which are in danger of becoming extinct, having really, in some Pendycean sort of way, a feeling that by this practice he was doing them a good turn, championing them, as it were, to a world that would soon be unable to look upon them in the flesh. He wished, too, that his collection should become an integral part of the estate, and be passed on to his son, and his son's son after him.

'Look at this Dartford warbler,' he would say; 'beautiful little creature—getting rarer every day. I had the greatest difficulty in procuring this specimen. You wouldn't believe me if I told you what I had to pay for him!'

Some of his unique birds he had shot himself, having in his youth made expeditions to foreign countries solely with this object, but the great majority he had been compelled to purchase. In his library were row upon row of books carefully arranged and bearing on this fascinating subject; and his collection of rare, almost extinct, birds' eggs was one of the finest in the 'three kingdoms.' One egg especially he would point to with pride as the last obtainable of that particular breed. 'This was procured,' he would say, 'by my dear old gillie Angus out of the bird's very nest. There was just the single egg. The species,' he added, tenderly handling the delicate, porcelain-like oval in his brown hand covered with very fine, blackish hairs, 'is now extinct.' He was, in fact, a true bird-lover, strongly condemning cockneys, or rough, ignorant persons who, with no collections of their own, wantonly destroyed kingfishers, or scarce birds of any sort, out of pure stupidity. 'I would have them flogged,' he would say, for he believed that no such bird should be killed except on commission, and for choice—barring such extreme cases as that Dartford warbler—in some

foreign country or remoter part of the British Isles.
It was indeed illustrative of Mr. Pendyce's character
and whole point of view that whenever a rare, winged
stranger appeared on his own estate it was talked of as
an event, and preserved alive with the greatest care,
in the hope that it might breed and be handed down
with the property; but if it were personally known to
belong to Mr. Fuller or Lord Quarryman, whose estates
abutted on Worsted Skeynes, and there was grave and
imminent danger of its going back, it was promptly
shot and stuffed, that it might not be lost to posterity.
An encounter with another landowner having the same
hobby, of whom there were several in his neighbourhood,
would upset him for a week, making him strangely
morose, and he would at once redouble his efforts to add
something rarer than ever to his own collection.

His arrangements for shooting were precisely conceived. Little slips of paper with the names of the
'guns' written thereon were placed in a hat, and one
by one drawn out again, and this he always did himself.
Behind the right wing of the house he held a review of
the beaters, who filed before him out of the yard, each
with a long stick in his hand, and no expression on his
face. Five minutes of directions to the keeper, and
then the guns started, carrying their own weapons and a
sufficiency of cartridges for the first drive in the old way.

A misty radiance clung over the grass as the sun
dried the heavy dew; the thrushes hopped and ran
and hid themselves, the rooks cawed peacefully in the
old elms. At an angle the game cart, constructed on
Mr. Pendyce's own pattern, and drawn by a hairy
horse in charge of an aged man, made its way slowly
to the end of the first beat.

George lagged behind, his hands deep in his pockets,

drinking in the joy of the tranquil day, the soft bird sounds, so clear and friendly, that chorus of wild life. The scent of the coverts stole to him, and he thought:

'What a ripping day for shooting!'

The squire, wearing a suit carefully coloured so that no bird should see him, leather leggings, and a cloth helmet of his own devising, ventilated by many little holes, came up to his son; and the spaniel John, who had a passion for the collection of birds almost equal to his master's, came up too.

'You're end gun, George,' he said; 'you'll get a nice high bird!'

George felt the ground with his feet, and blew a speck of dust off his barrels, and the smell of the oil sent a delicious tremor darting through him. Everything, even Helen Bellew, was forgotten. Then in the silence rose a far-off clamour; a cock pheasant, skimming low, his plumage silken in the sun, dived out of the green and golden spinney, curled to the right, and was lost in undergrowth. Some pigeons passed over at a great height. The tap-tap of sticks beating against trees began; then with a fitful rushing noise a pheasant came straight out. George threw up his gun and pulled. The bird stopped in mid-air, jerked forward, and fell headlong into the grass sods with a thud. In the sunlight the dead bird lay, and a smirk of triumph played on George's lips. He was feeling the joy of life.

During his covert shoots the squire had the habit of recording his impressions in a mental note-book. He put special marks against such as missed, or shot birds behind the waist, or placed lead in them to the detriment of their market value, or broke only one leg of a hare at a time, causing the animal to cry like a tortured

child, which some men do not like; or such as, anxious
for fame, claimed dead creatures that they had not
shot, or peopled the next beat with imaginary slain, or
too frequently 'wiped an important neighbour's eye,'
or shot too many beaters in the legs. Against this
evidence, however, he unconsciously weighed the more
undeniable social facts, such as the title of Winlow's
father; Sir James Malden's coverts, which must also
presently be shot; Thomas Brandwhite's position in
the financial world; General Pendyce's relationship to
himself; and the importance of the English Church.
Against Foxleigh alone he could put no marks. The
fellow destroyed everything that came within reach
with utter precision, and this was perhaps fortunate,
for Foxleigh had neither title, coverts, position, nor
cloth! And the squire weighed one thing else besides
—the pleasure of giving them all a good day's sport, for
his heart was kind.

The sun had fallen well behind the home wood
when the guns stood waiting for the last drive of the
day. From the keeper's cottage in the hollow, where
late threads of crimson clung in the brown network of
Virginia creeper, rose a mist of wood smoke, dispersed
upon the breeze. Sound there was none, only that
faint stir—the far, far callings of men and beasts and
birds—that never quite dies of a country evening. High
above the wood some startled pigeons were still wheeling, no other life in sight; but a gleam of sunlight
stole down the side of the covert and laid a burnish on
the turned leaves till the whole wood seemed quivering
with magic. Out of that quivering wood a wounded
rabbit had stolen and was dying. It lay on its side on
the slope of a tussock of grass, its hind legs drawn under
it, its forelegs raised like the hands of a praying child.

Motionless as death, all its remaining life was centred in its black soft eyes. Uncomplaining, ungrudging, unknowing, with that poor soft wandering eye, it was going back to Mother Earth. There Foxleigh, too, some day must go. asking of Nature why she had murdered him.

CHAPTER III

THE BLISSFUL HOUR

It was the hour between tea and dinner, when the spirit of the country house was resting, conscious of its virtue, half asleep.

Having bathed and changed, George Pendyce took his betting-book into the smoking-room. In a nook devoted to literature, protected from draught and intrusion by a high leather screen, he sat down in an arm-chair and fell into a doze.

With legs crossed, his chin resting on one hand, his comely figure relaxed, he exhaled a fragrance of soap, as though in this perfect peace his soul were giving off its natural odour. His spirit, on the borderland of dreams, trembled with those faint stirrings of chivalry and aspiration, the outcome of physical well-being after a long day in the open air, the outcome of security from all that is unpleasant and fraught with danger. He was awakened by voices.

'George is not a bad shot!'

'Gave a shocking exhibition at the last stand; Mrs. Bellew was with him. They were going over him like smoke; he couldn't touch a feather.'

It was Winlow's voice. A silence, then Thomas Brandwhite's:

'A mistake, the ladies coming out. I never will have them myself. What do you say, Sir James?'

'Bad principle—very bad!'

A laugh—Thomas Brandwhite's laugh, the laugh of a man never quite sure of himself.

'That fellow Bellew is a cracked chap. They call him the "desperate character" about here. Drinks like a fish, and rides like the devil. *She* used to go pretty hard, too. I 've noticed there 's always a couple like that in a hunting country. Did you ever see him? Thin, high-shouldered, white-faced chap, with little dark eyes and a red moustache.'

'She 's still a young woman?'

'Thirty or thirty-two.'

'How was it they didn't get on?'

The sound of a match being struck.

'Case of the kettle and the pot.'

'It 's easy to see she 's fond of admiration. Love of admiration plays old Harry with women!'

Winlow's leisurely tones again:

'There was a child, I believe, and it died. And after that—I know there was some story; you never could get to the bottom of it. Bellew chucked his regiment in consequence. She 's subject to moods, they say, when nothing 's exciting enough; must skate on thin ice, must have a man skating after her. If the poor devil weighs more than she does, in he goes.'

'That 's like her father, old Cheriton. I knew him at the club—one of the old sort of squires; married his second wife at sixty and buried her at eighty. Old "Claret and Piquet," they called him; had more children under the rose than any man in Devonshire. I saw him playing half-crown points the week before he died. It 's in the blood. What 's George's weight?—ah, ha!'

'It 's no laughing matter, Brandwhite. There 's time for a hundred up before dinner if you care for a game, Winlow?'

The sound of chairs drawn back, of footsteps, and the closing of a door. George was alone again, a spot of red in either of his cheeks. Those vague stirrings of chivalry and aspiration were gone, and gone that sense of well-earned ease. He got up, came out of his corner, and walked to and fro on the tiger-skin before the fire. He lit a cigarette, threw it away, and lit another.

Skating on thin ice! That would not stop him! Their gossip would not stop him, nor their sneers; they would but send him on the faster!

He threw away the second cigarette. It was strange for him to go to the drawing-room at this hour of the day, but he went.

Opening the door quietly, he saw the long, pleasant room lighted with tall oil-lamps, and Mrs. Bellew seated at the piano, singing. The tea things were still on a table at one end, but every one had finished. As far away as might be, in the embrasure of the bay-window, General Pendyce and Bee were playing chess. Grouped in the centre of the room, by one of the lamps, Lady Malden, Mrs. Winlow, and Mrs. Brandwhite had turned their faces towards the piano, and a sort of slight unwillingness or surprise showed on those faces, a sort of 'We were having a most interesting talk; I don't think we ought to have been stopped' expression.

Before the fire, with his long legs outstretched, stood Gerald Pendyce. And a little apart, her dark eyes fixed on the singer, and a piece of embroidery in her lap, sat Mrs. Pendyce, on the edge of whose skirt lay Roy, the old Skye terrier.

> But had I wist, before I kist,
>   That love had been sae ill to win;
> I had lockt my heart in a case of gowd
>   And pinn'd it with a siller pin. . . .

O waly waly, but love be bonny
A little time while it is new,
But when 'tis auld, it waxeth cauld
And fades awa' like morning dew.

This was the song George heard, trembling and dying to the chords of the fine piano that was a little out of tune.

He gazed at the singer, and though he was not musical, there came a look into his eyes that he quickly hid away.

A slight murmur occurred in the centre of the room, and from the fire-place Gerald called out: 'Thanks; that's rippin'!'

The voice of General Pendyce rose in the bay-window: 'Check!'

Mrs. Pendyce, taking up her embroidery, on which a tear had dropped, said gently:

'Thank you, dear; most charming!'

Mrs. Bellew left the piano, and sat down beside her. George moved into the bay-window. He knew nothing of chess—indeed, he could not stand the game; but from here, without attracting attention, he could watch Mrs. Bellew.

The air was drowsy and sweet-scented; a log of cedar-wood had just been put on the fire; the voices of his mother and Mrs. Bellew, talking of what he could not hear, the voices of Lady Malden, Mrs. Brandwhite, and Gerald, discussing some neighbours, of Mrs. Winlow dissenting or assenting in turn, all mingled in a comfortable, sleepy sound, clipped now and then by the voice of General Pendyce calling: 'Check!' and of Bee saying: 'Oh, uncle!'

A feeling of rage rose in George. Why should they all be so comfortable and cosy while this perpetual fire was burning in himself? And he fastened his moody eyes on her who was keeping him thus dancing to her pipes.

He made an awkward movement which shook the chess-table. The general said behind him: 'Look out, George! What—what!'

George went up to his mother.

'Let 's have a look at that, mother.'

Mrs. Pendyce leaned back in her chair and handed up her work with a smile of pleased surprise.

'My dear boy, you won't understand it a bit. It 's for the front of my new frock.'

George took the piece of work. He did not understand it, but turning and twisting it he could breathe the warmth of the woman he loved. In bending over the embroidery he touched Mrs. Bellew's shoulder; it was not drawn away, a faint pressure seemed to answer his own. His mother's voice recalled him:

'Oh, my needle, dear! It 's so sweet of you, but perhaps——'

George handed back the embroidery. Mrs. Pendyce received it with a grateful look. It was the first time he had ever shown an interest in her work.

Mrs. Bellew had taken up a palm-leaf fan to screen her face from the fire. She said slowly:

'If we win to-morrow I 'll embroider you something, George.'

'And if we lose?'

Mrs. Bellew raised her eyes, and involuntarily George moved so that his mother could not see the sort of slow mesmerism that was in them.

'If we lose,' she said, 'I shall sink into the earth. We must win, George.'

He gave an uneasy little laugh, and glanced quickly at his mother. Mrs. Pendyce had begun to draw her needle in and out with a half-startled look on her face.

'That 's a most haunting little song you sang, dear,' she said.

Mrs. Bellew answered: 'The words are so true, aren't they?'

George felt her eyes on him, and tried to look at her, but those half-smiling, half-threatening eyes seemed to twist and turn him about as his hands had twisted and turned about his mother's embroidery. Again across Mrs. Pendyce's face flitted that half-startled look.

Suddenly General Pendyce's voice was heard saying very loud:

'Stale? Nonsense, Bee, nonsense! Why, damme, so it is!'

A hum of voices from the centre of the room covered up that outburst, and Gerald, stepping to the hearth, threw another cedar log upon the fire. The smoke came out in a puff.

Mrs. Pendyce leaned back in her chair smiling, and wrinkling her fine, thin nose.

'Delicious!' she said, but her eyes did not leave her son's face, and in them was still that vague alarm.

CHAPTER IV

THE HAPPY HUNTING-GROUND

OF all the places where, by a judicious admixture of whip and spur, oats and whisky, horses are caused to place one leg before another with unnecessary rapidity, in order that men may exchange little pieces of metal with the greater freedom, Newmarket Heath is 'the topmost, and merriest, and best.'

This museum of the state of flux—the secret reason of horse-racing being to afford an example of perpetual motion (no proper racing-man having ever been found to regard either gains or losses in the light of an accomplished fact)—this museum of the state of flux has a climate unrivalled for the production of the British temperament.

Not without a due proportion of that essential formative of character, east wind, it has at once the hottest sun, the coldest blizzards, the wettest rain, of any place of its size in the 'three kingdoms.' It tends—in advance even of the City of London—to the nurture and improvement of individualism, to that desirable 'I'll see you d——d' state of mind which is the proud objective of every Englishman, and especially of every country gentleman. In a word—a mother to the self-reliant secretiveness which defies intrusion and forms an integral part in the Christianity of this country—Newmarket Heath is beyond all others the happy hunting-ground of the landed classes.

In the paddock half an hour before the Rutlandshire Handicap was to be run numbers of racing-men were gathered in little knots of two and three, describing to each other with every precaution the points of strength in the horses they had laid against, the points of weakness in the horses they had backed, or vice versa, together with the latest discrepancies of their trainers and jockeys. At the far end George Pendyce, his trainer Blacksmith, and his jockey Swells, were talking in low tones. Many people have observed with surprise the close-buttoned secrecy of all who have to do with horses. It is no matter for wonder. The horse is one of those generous and somewhat careless animals that, if not taken firmly from the first, will surely give itself away. Essential to a man who has to do with horses is a complete closeness of physiognomy, otherwise the animal will never know what is expected of him. The more that is expected of him, the closer must be the expression of his friends, or a grave fiasco may have to be deplored.

It was for these reasons that George's face wore more than its habitual composure, and the faces of his trainer and his jockey were alert, determined, and expressionless. Blacksmith, a little man, had in his hand a short notched cane, with which, contrary to expectation, he did not switch his legs. His eyelids drooped over his shrewd eyes, his upper lip advanced over the lower, and he wore no hair on his face. The jockey Swells's pinched-up countenance, with jutting eyebrows and practically no cheeks, had under George's racing-cap of 'peacock blue' a subfusc hue like that of old furniture.

The Ambler had been bought out of the stud of Colonel Dorking, a man opposed on high grounds to

the racing of two-year-olds, and at the age of three
had never run.   Showing more than a suspicion of form
in one or two home trials, he ran a bye in the Fane
Stakes, when obviously not up to the mark, and was
then withdrawn from the public gaze.   The stable had
from the start kept its eye on the Rutlandshire Handicap,
and no sooner was Goodwood over than the commission was placed in the hands of Barney's, well known
for their power to enlist at the most appropriate moment
the sympathy of the public in a horse's favour.   Almost
coincidentally with the completion of the stable commission it was found that the public were determined
to support the Ambler at any price over seven to one.
Barney's at once proceeded judiciously to lay off the
stable money, and this having been done, George
found that he stood to win four thousand pounds to
nothing.   If he had now chosen to bet this sum against
the horse at the then current price of eight to one, it
is obvious that he could have made an absolute certainty
of five hundred pounds, and the horse need never even
have started.   But George, who would have been glad
enough of such a sum, was not the man to do this sort
of thing.   It was against the tenets of his creed.   He
believed, too, in his horse, and had enough of the
Totteridge in him to like a race for a race's sake.   Even
when beaten there was enjoyment to be had out of the
imperturbability with which he could take that beating,
out of a sense of superiority to men not quite so sports-
manlike as himself.

'Come and see the nag saddled,' he said to his brother
Gerald.

In one of the long line of boxes the Ambler was
awaiting his toilette, a dark-brown horse, about sixteen
hands, with well-placed shoulders, straight hocks, a

small head, and what is known as a rat-tail. But of all
his features, the most remarkable was his eye. In the
depths of that full, soft eye was an almost uncanny
gleam, and when he turned it, half-circled by a moon of
white, and gave bystanders that look of strange comprehension, they felt that he saw to the bottom of all
this that was going on around him. He was still but
three years old, and had not yet attained the age when
people apply to action the fruits of understanding;
yet there was little doubt that as he advanced in years
he would manifest his disapproval of a system whereby
men made money at his expense. And with that eye
half-circled by the moon he looked at George, and in
silence George looked back at him, strangely baffled
by the horse's long, soft, wild gaze. On this heart
beating deep within its warm, dark satin sheath, on
the spirit gazing through that soft, wild eye, too much
was hanging, and he turned away.

'Mount, jockeys!'

Through the crowd of hard-looking, hatted, muffled,
two-legged men, those four-legged creatures in their
chestnut, bay, and brown, and satin nakedness, most
beautiful in all the world, filed proudly past, as though
going forth to death. The last vanished through the
gate, the crowd dispersed.

Down by the rails of Tattersall's George stood
alone. He had screwed himself into a corner, whence
he could watch through his long glasses that gay-
coloured shifting wheel at the end of the mile and
more of turf. At this moment, so pregnant with
the future, he could not bear the company of his
fellows.

'They 're off!'

He looked no longer, but hunched his shoulders,

holding his elbows stiff, that none might see what he was feeling. Behind him a man said:

'The favourite's beat. What's that in blue on the rails?'

Out by himself on the far rails, out by himself, sweeping along like a home-coming bird, was the Ambler. And George's heart leaped, as a fish leaps of a summer evening out of a dark pool.

'They'll never catch him. The Ambler wins! It's a walk-over! The Ambler!'

Silence amidst the shouting throng, George thought: 'My horse! my horse!' and tears of pure emotion sprang into his eyes. For a full minute he stood quite still; then, instinctively adjusting hat and tie, made his way calmly to the paddock. He left it to his trainer to lead the Ambler back, and joined him at the weighing-room.

The little jockey was seated, nursing his saddle, negligent and saturnine, awaiting the words: 'All right.'

Blacksmith said quietly:

'Well, sir, we've pulled it off. Four lengths. I've told Swells he does no more riding for me. There's a gold-mine given away. What on earth was he about to come in by himself like that? We shan't get into the "City" now under nine stone. It's enough to make a man cry!'

And, looking at his trainer, George saw the little man's lips quiver.

In his stall, streaked with sweat, his hind-legs out-stretched, fretting under the ministrations of the groom, the Ambler stayed the whisking of his head to look at his owner, and once more George met that long, proud, soft glance. He laid his gloved hand on the horse's lather-flecked neck. The Ambler tossed his head and turned it away.

George came out into the open, and made his way towards the stand. His trainer's words had instilled a drop of poison into his cup. 'A gold-mine given away!'

He went up to Swells. On his lips were the words: 'What made you give the show away like that?' He did not speak them, for in his soul he felt it would not become him to ask his jockey why he had not dissembled and won by a length. But the little jockey understood at once.

'Mr. Blacksmith's been at me, sir. You take my tip: he's a queer one, that 'orse. I thought it best to let him run his own race. Mark my words, *he knows what's what*. When they're like that, they're best let alone.'

A voice behind him said:

'Well, George, congratulate you! Not the way I should have ridden the race myself. He should have lain off to the distance. Remarkable turn of speed, that horse. There's no riding nowadays!'

The squire and General Pendyce were standing there. Erect and slim, unlike and yet so very much alike, the eyes of both of them seemed saying:

'I shall differ from you; there are no two opinions about it. I shall differ from you!'

Behind them stood Mrs. Bellew. Her eyes could not keep still under their lashes, and their light and colour changed continually. George walked on slowly at her side. There was a look of triumph and softness about her; the colour kept deepening in her cheeks, her figure swayed. They did not look at each other.

Against the paddock railings stood a man in riding-

clothes, of spare figure, with a horseman's square, high
shoulders, and thin long legs a trifle bowed. His
narrow, thin-lipped, freckled face, with close-cropped
sandy hair and clipped red moustache, was of a strange
dead pallor. He followed the figures of George and his
companion with little fiery dark-brown eyes, in which
devils seemed to dance. Someone tapped him on the
arm.

'Hallo, Bellew! had a good race?'

'Devil take you, no! Come and have a drink?'

Still without looking at each other, George and Mrs.
Bellew walked towards the gate.

'I don't want to see any more,' she said. 'I should
like to get away at once.'

'We'll go after this race,' said George. 'There's
nothing running in the last.'

At the back of the grand stand, in the midst of all
the hurrying crowd, he stopped.

'Helen?' he said.

Mrs. Bellew raised her eyes and looked full into his.

Long and cross-country is the drive from Royston
railway station to Worsted Skeynes. To George Pendyce, driving the dog-cart, with Helen Bellew beside
him, it seemed but a minute—that strange minute
when the heaven is opened and a vision shows between.
To some men that vision comes but once, to some men
many times. It comes after long winter, when the
blossom hangs; it comes after parched summer, when
the leaves are going gold; and of what hues it is painted
—of frost-white and fire, of wine and purple, of moun-
tain flowers, or the shadowy green of still deep pools
—the seer alone can tell. But this is certain—the
vision steals from him who looks on it all images of
other things, all sense of law, of order, of the living

past, and the living present. It is the future, fair-scented, singing, jewelled, as when suddenly between high banks a bough of apple blossom hangs quivering in the wind loud with the song of bees.

George Pendyce gazed before him at this vision over the grey mare's back, and she who sat beside him muffled in her fur was touching his arm with hers. And back to them the second groom, hugging himself above the road that slipped away beneath, saw another kind of vision, for he had won five pounds, and his eyes were closed. And the grey mare saw a vision of her warm light stall, and the oats dropping between her manger bars, and fled with light hoofs along the lanes where the side-lamps shot two moving gleams over dark beech hedges that rustled crisply in the north-east wind. Again and again she sneezed in the pleasure of that homeward flight, and the light foam of her nostrils flicked the faces of those behind. And they sat silent, thrilling at the touch of each other's arms, their cheeks glowing in the windy darkness, their eyes shining and fixed before them.

The second groom awoke suddenly from his dream.

'If I owned that 'orse, like Mr. George, and had such a topper as this 'ere Mrs. Bellew beside me, would I be sittin' there without a word?'

CHAPTER V

MRS. PENDYCE believed in the practice of assembling
county society for the purpose of inducing it to dance,
a hardy enterprise in a county where the souls, and
incidentally the feet, of the inhabitants were shaped
for more solid pursuits. Men were her chief difficulty,
for in spite of really national discouragement, it was
rare to find a girl who was not 'fond of dancing.'

'Ah, dancing; I did so love it! Oh, *poor* Cecil Tharp!'
And with a queer little smile she pointed to a strapping red-faced youth dancing with her daughter. 'He
nearly trips Bee up every minute, and he hugs her so,
as if he were afraid of falling on his head. Oh, dear,
what a bump! It's lucky she's so nice and solid.
I like to see the dear boy. Here come George and Helen
Bellew. Poor George is not quite up to her form, but
he's better than most of them. Doesn't she look lovely
this evening?'

Lady Malden raised her glasses to her eyes by the
aid of a tortoiseshell handle.

'Yes, but she's one of those women you never can
look at without seeing that she has a—a—body. She's
too—too—d' you see what I mean? It's almost—
almost like a Frenchwoman!'

Mrs. Bellew had passed so close that the skirt of her
sea-green dress brushed their feet with a swish, and a
scent as of a flower-bed was wafted from it. Mrs.
Pendyce wrinkled her nose.

'Much nicer. Her figure's so delicious,' she said.

Lady Malden pondered.

'She's a dangerous woman. James quite agrees with me.'

Mrs. Pendyce raised her eyebrows; there was a touch of scorn in that gentle gesture.

'She's a very distant cousin of mine,' she said. 'Her father was quite a wonderful man. It's an old Devonshire family. The Cheritons of Bovey are mentioned in Twisdom. I like young people to enjoy themselves.'

A smile illumined softly the fine wrinkles round her eyes. Beneath her lavender satin bodice, with strips of black velvet banding it at intervals, her heart was beating faster than usual. She was thinking of a night in her youth, when her old playfellow, young Trefane of the Blues, danced with her nearly all the evening, and of how at her window she saw the sun rise, and gently wept because she was married to Horace Pendyce.

'I always feel sorry for a woman who can dance as she does. I should have liked to have got some men from town, but Horace will only have the county people. It's not fair to the girls. It isn't so much their dancing, as their conversation—all about the first meet, and yesterday's cubbing, and to-morrow's covert-shooting, and their fox-terriers (though I'm awfully fond of the dear dogs), and then that new golf course. Really, it's quite distressing to me at times.' Again Mrs. Pendyce looked out into the room with her patient smile, and two little lines of wrinkles formed across her forehead between the regular arching of her eyebrows that were still dark brown. 'They don't seem able to be gay. I feel they don't really care about it. They're only just

waiting till to-morrow morning, so that they can go
out and kill something. Even Bee's like that!'

Mrs. Pendyce was not exaggerating. The guests at
Worsted Skeynes on the night of the Rutlandshire
Handicap were nearly all county people, from the Hon.
Gertrude Winlow, revolving like a faintly coloured
statue, to young Tharp, with his clean face and his fair
bullety head, who danced as though he were riding at a
bullfinch. In a niche old Lord Quarryman, the Master
of the Gaddesdon, could be discerned in conversation
with Sir James Malden and the Reverend Hussell Barter.

Mrs. Pendyce said:

'Your husband and Lord Quarryman are talking of
poachers; I can tell that by the look of their hands.
I can't help sympathizing a little with poachers.'

Lady Malden dropped her eyeglasses.

'James takes a very just view of them,' she said.
'It's such an insidious offence. The more insidious the
offence the more important it is to check it. It seems
hard to punish people for stealing bread or turnips,
though one must, of course; but I've no sympathy with
poachers. So many of them do it for sheer love of sport!'

Mrs. Pendyce answered:

'That's Captain Maydew dancing with her now. He
is a good dancer. Don't their steps fit? Don't they
look happy? I *do* like people to enjoy themselves!
There is such a dreadful lot of unnecessary sadness and
suffering in the world. I think it's really all because
people won't make allowances for each other.'

Lady Malden looked at her sideways, pursing her
lips; but Mrs. Pendyce, by race a Totteridge, continued
to smile. She had been born unconscious of her neighbour's scrutinies.

'Helen Bellew,' she said, 'was such a lovely girl.

Her grandfather was my mother's cousin. What does that make her? Anyway, my cousin, Gregory Vigil, is her first cousin once removed—the Hampshire Vigils. Do you know him?'

Lady Malden answered:

'Gregory Vigil? The man with a lot of greyish hair? I've had to do with him in the S.R.W.C.'

But Mrs. Pendyce was dancing mentally.

'Such a good fellow! What is that—the——?'

Lady Malden gave her a sharp look.

'Society for the Rescue of Women and Children, of course. Surely you know about that?'

Mrs. Pendyce continued to smile.

'Ah, yes, that is nice! What a beautiful figure she has! It's so refreshing. I envy a woman with a figure like that; it looks as if it would never grow old. "Society for the Regeneration of Women"? Gregory's so good about that sort of thing. But he never seems quite successful, have you noticed? There was a woman he was very interested in this spring. I think she drank.'

'They all do,' said Lady Malden; 'it's the curse of the day.'

Mrs. Pendyce wrinkled her forehead.

'Most of the Totteridges,' she said, 'were great drinkers. They ruined their constitutions. Do you know Jaspar Bellew?'

'No.'

'It's such a pity he drinks. He came to dinner here once, and I'm afraid he must have come intoxicated. He took me in; his little eyes quite burned me up. He drove his dog-cart into a ditch on the way home. That sort of thing gets about so. It's such a pity. He's quite interesting. Horace can't stand him.'

The music of the waltz had ceased. Lady Malden

put her glasses to her eyes. From close beside them George and Mrs. Bellew passed by. They moved on out of hearing, but the breeze of her fan had touched the arching hair on Lady Malden's forehead, the down on her upper lip.

'Why isn't she with her husband?' she asked abruptly.

Mrs. Pendyce lifted her brows.

'Do you concern yourself to ask that which a well-bred woman leaves unanswered?' she seemed to say, and a flush coloured her cheeks.

Lady Malden winced, but, as though it were forced through her mouth by some explosion in her soul, she said:

'You have only to look and see how dangerous she is!'

The colour in Mrs. Pendyce's cheeks deepened to a blush like a girl's.

'Every man,' she said, 'is in love with Helen Bellew. She's so tremendously alive. My Cousin Gregory has been in love with her for years, though he *is* her guardian or trustee, or whatever they call them now. It's quite romantic. If I were a man I should be in love with her myself.' The flush vanished and left her cheeks to their true colour, that of a faded rose.

Once more she was listening to the voice of young Trefane: 'Ah, Margery, I love you!'—to her own half-whispered answer: 'Poor boy!' Once more she was looking back through that forest of her life where she had wandered so long, and where every tree was Horace Pendyce.

'What a pity one can't always be young!' she said.

Through the conservatory door, wide open to the lawn, a full moon flooded the country with pale gold light, and in that light the branches of the cedar trees seemed printed black on the grey-blue paper of the

sky; all was cold, still witchery out there, and not very
far away an owl was hooting.

The Reverend Hussell Barter, about to enter the
conservatory for a breath of air, was arrested by the
sight of a couple half-hidden by a bushy plant; side
by side they were looking at the moonlight, and he
knew them for Mrs. Bellew and George Pendyce.
Before he could either enter or retire, he saw George
seize her in his arms. She seemed to bend her head
back, then bring her face to his. The moonlight fell on
it, and on the full, white curve of her neck. The Rector
of Worsted Skeynes saw, too, that her eyes were closed,
her lips parted.

CHAPTER VI

INFLUENCE OF THE REVEREND HUSSELL BARTER

ALONG the walls of the smoking-room, above a leather dado, were prints of horsemen in night-shirts and night-caps, or horsemen in red coats and top hats, with words underneath such as:

'Yeoicks!' says Thruster; 'Yeoicks!' says Dick.
'My word! these d——d Quornites shall now see the trick!'

Two pairs of antlers surmounted the hearth, mementoes of Mr. Pendyce's deer-forest, Strathbegally, now given up, where, with the assistance of his dear old gillie Angus McBane, he had secured the heads of these monarchs of the glen. Between them was the print of a personage in trousers, with a rifle under his arm and a smile on his lips, while two large deerhounds worried a dying stag, and a lady approached him on a pony.

The squire and Sir James Malden had retired; the remaining guests were seated round the fire. Gerald Pendyce stood at a side-table, on which was a tray of decanters, glasses, and mineral water.

'Who's for a dhrop of the craythur? A wee dhrop of the craythur? Rector, a dhrop of the craythur? George, a dhrop——'

George shook his head. A smile was on his lips, and that smile had in it a quality of remoteness, as though it belonged to another sphere, and had strayed on to the lips of this man of the world against his will. He seemed trying to conquer it, to twist his face into its habitual shape, but, like the spirit of a strange force, the smile broke through. It had mastered him, his thoughts, his habits, and his creed; he was stripped of fashion, as on a thirsty noon a man stands stripped for a cool plunge from which he hardly cares if he come up again.

And this smile, not by intrinsic merit, but by virtue of its strangeness, attracted the eye of each man in the room; so, in a crowd, the most foreign-looking face will draw all glances.

The Reverend Hussell Barter with a frown watched that smile, and strange thoughts chased through his mind.

'Uncle Charles, a dhrop of the craythur—a wee dhrop of the craythur?'

General Pendyce caressed his whisker.

'The least touch,' he said, 'the least touch! I hear that our friend Sir Percival is going to stand again.'

Mr. Barter rose and placed his back before the fire.

'Outrageous!' he said. 'He ought to be told at once that we can't have him.'

The Hon. Geoffrey Winlow answered from his chair:

'If he puts up, he 'll get in; they can't afford to lose him.' And with a leisurely puff of smoke: 'I must say, sir, I don't quite see what it has to do with his public life.'

Mr. Barter thrust forth his lower lip.

'An impenitent man,' he said.

'But a woman like that! What chance has a fellow if she once gets hold of him?'

'When I was stationed at Halifax,' began General Pendyce, 'she was the belle of the place——'

Again Mr. Barter thrust out his lower lip.

'Don't let 's talk of her—the jade!' Then suddenly to George: 'Let 's hear your opinion, George. Dreaming of your victories, eh?' And the tone of his voice was peculiar.

But George got up.

'I'm too sleepy,' he said; 'good night.' Curtly nodding, he left the room.

Outside the door stood a dark oak table covered with silver candlesticks; a single candle burned thereon, and made a thin gold path in the velvet blackness. George lighted his candle, and a second gold path leaped out in front; up this he began to ascend. He carried his candle at the level of his breast, and the light shone sideways and up over his white shirt-front and the comely, bulldog face above it. It shone, too, into his eyes, grey and slightly bloodshot, as though their surfaces concealed passions violently struggling for expression. At the turning platform of the stairs he paused. In darkness above and in darkness below the country house was still; all the little life of its day, its petty sounds, movements, comings, goings, its very breathing, seemed to have fallen into sleep. The forces of its life had gathered into that pool of light where George stood listening. The beating of his heart was the only sound; in that small sound was all the pulse of this great slumbering space. He stood there long, motionless, listening to the beating of his heart, like a man fallen into a trance. Then floating up through the darkness came the echo of a laugh. George started. 'The d——d parson!' he muttered, and turned up the stairs again; but now he moved like a man with a purpose, and held his candle high so that the light fell far out into the darkness. He went beyond his own room, and stood still again. The light of the candle showed the blood flushing his forehead, beating and pulsing in the veins at the side of his temples; showed,

too, his lips quivering, his shaking hand. He stretched
out that hand and touched the handle of a door; then
stood again like a man of stone, listening for the laugh.
He raised the candle, and it shone into every nook;
his throat clicked, as though he found it hard to
swallow. . . .

It was at Barnard Scrolls, the next station to Worsted
Skeynes, on the following afternoon, that a young man
entered a first-class compartment of the 3.10 train to
town. The young man wore a Newmarket coat, natty
white gloves, and carried an eyeglass. His face was
well coloured, his chestnut moustache well brushed, and
his blue eyes with their loving expression seemed to
say: 'Look at me—come, look at me—can any one be
better fed?' His valise and hat-box, of the best leather,
bore the inscription: 'E. Maydew, 8th Lancers.'

There was a lady leaning back in a corner, wrapped
to the chin in a fur garment, and the young man,
encountering through his eyeglass her cool, ironical
glance, dropped it and held out his hand.

'Ah, Mrs. Bellew, great pleasure t' see you again so
soon. You goin' up to town? Jolly dance last night,
wasn't it? Dear old sort, the squire, and Mrs. Pendyce
such an awf'ly nice woman.'

Mrs. Bellew took his hand, and leaned back again in
her corner. She was rather paler than usual, but it
became her, and Captain Maydew thought he had never
seen so charming a creature.

'Got a week's leave, thank goodness. Most awf'ly
slow time of year. Cubbin' 's pretty well over, an' we
don't open till the first.'

He turned to the window. There in the sunlight
the hedgerows ran golden and brown away from the

clouds of trailing train smoke. Young Maydew shook his head at their beauty.

'The country's still very blind,' he said. 'Awful pity you've given up your huntin'.'

Mrs. Bellew did not trouble to answer, and it was just that certainty over herself, the cool assurance of a woman who has known the world, her calm, almost negligent eyes, that fascinated this young man. He looked at her quite shyly.

'I suppose you will become my slave,' those eyes seemed to say, 'but I can't help you, really.'

'Did you back George's horse? I had an awf'ly good race. I was at school with George. Charmin' fellow, old George.'

In Mrs. Bellew's eyes something seemed to stir down in the depths, but young Maydew was looking at his glove. The handle of the carriage had left a mark that saddened him.

'You know him well, I suppose, old George?'

'Very well.'

'Some fellows, if they have a good thing, keep it so jolly dark. You fond of racin', Mrs. Bellew?'

'Passionately.'

'So am I.' And his eyes continued: 'It's ripping to like what you like,' for, hypnotized, they could not tear themselves away from that creamy face, with its full lips and the clear, faintly smiling eyes above the high collar of white fur.

At the terminus his services were refused, and rather crestfallen, with his hat raised, he watched her walk away. But soon, in his cab, his face regained its normal look, his eyes seemed saying to the little mirror: 'Look at me—come, look at me—can any one be better fed?'

CHAPTER VII

SABBATH AT WORSTED SKEYNES

In the white morning-room which served for her boudoir
Mrs. Pendyce sat with an opened letter in her lap.
It was her practice to sit there on Sunday mornings for
an hour before she went to her room adjoining to put
on her hat for church. It was her pleasure during that
hour to do nothing but sit at the window, open if the
weather permitted, and look over the home paddock
and the squat spire of the village church rising among a
group of elms. It is not known what she thought about
at those times, unless of the countless Sunday mornings
she had sat there with her hands in her lap waiting to
be roused at 10.45 by the squire's entrance and his
'Now, my dear, you'll be late!' She had sat there till
her hair, once dark brown, was turning grey; she
would sit there until it was white. One day she would
sit there no longer, and, as likely as not, Mr. Pendyce,
still well preserved, would enter and say: 'Now, my
dear, you'll be late!' having for the moment forgotten.

But this was all to be expected, nothing out of the
common; the same thing was happening in hundreds
of country houses throughout the 'three kingdoms,'
and women were sitting waiting for their hair to turn
white, who, long before, at the altar of a fashionable
church, had parted with their imaginations and all the
changes and chances of this mortal life.

Round her chair 'the dear dogs' lay—this was their

practice too, and now and again the Skye (he was getting very old) would put out a long tongue and lick her little pointed shoe. For Mrs. Pendyce had been a pretty woman, and her feet were as small as ever.

Beside her on a spindly table stood a china bowl filled with dried rose leaves, whereon had been scattered an essence smelling like sweetbrier, whose secret she had learned from her mother in the old Warwickshire home of the Totteridges, long since sold to Mr. Abraham Brightman. Mrs. Pendyce, born in the year 1840, loved sweet perfumes, and was not ashamed of using them.

The Indian summer sun was soft and bright; and wistful, soft, and bright were Mrs. Pendyce's eyes, fixed on the letter in her lap. She turned it over and began to read again. A wrinkle visited her brow. It was not often that a letter demanding decision or involving responsibility came to her hands past the kind and just censorship of Horace Pendyce. Many matters were under her control, but were not, so to speak, connected with the outer world. Thus ran the letter:

'S.R.W.C., HANOVER SQUARE,
    '1st November 1891.

'DEAR MARGERY,

'I want to see you and talk something over, so I'm running down on Sunday afternoon. There is a train of sorts. Any loft will do for me to sleep in if your house is full, as it may be, I suppose, at this time of year. On second thoughts I will tell you what I want to see you about. You know, of course, that since her father died I am Helen Bellew's only guardian. Her present position is one in which no woman should be placed; I am convinced it ought to be put an end to. That man Bellew deserves no consideration. I cannot

write of him coolly, so I won't write at all. It is two
years now since they separated, entirely, as I consider,
through his fault. The law has placed her in a cruel and
helpless position all this time; but now, thank God, I
believe we can move for a divorce. You know me well
enough to realize what I have gone through before
coming to this conclusion. Heaven knows if I could
hit on some other way in which her future could be
safeguarded, I would take it in preference to this, which
is most repugnant; but I cannot. You are the only
woman I can rely on to be interested in her, and I must
see Bellew. Let not the fat and just Benson and his
estimable horses be disturbed on my account; I will
walk up and carry my toothbrush.

> 'Affectionately your cousin,
> 'GREGORY VIGIL.'

Mrs. Pendyce smiled. She saw no joke, but she knew
from the wording of the last sentence that Gregory saw
one, and she liked to give it a welcome; so smiling and
wrinkling her forehead, she mused over the letter. Her
thoughts wandered. The last scandal — Lady Rose
Bethany's divorce—had upset the whole county, and
even now one had to be careful what one said. Horace
would not like the idea of another divorce-suit, and
that so close to Worsted Skeynes. When Helen left on
Thursday he had said:

'I'm not sorry she's gone. Her position is a queer
one. People don't like it. The Maldens were quite——'

And Mrs. Pendyce remembered with a glow at her
heart how she had broken in:

'Ellen Malden is too bourgeoise for anything!'

Nor had Mr. Pendyce's look of displeasure effaced the
comfort of that word.

Poor Horace! The children took after him, except
George, who took after her brother Hubert. The dear
boy had gone back to his club on Friday—the day after
Helen and the others went. She wished he could have
stayed. She wished—— The wrinkle deepened on her
brow. Too much London was bad for him! Too
much—— Her fancy flew to the London which she
saw now only for three weeks in June and July, for the
sake of the girls, just when her garden was at its best,
and when really things were such a whirl that she never
knew whether she was asleep or awake. It was not like
London at all—not like that London under spring
skies, or in early winter lamplight, where all the passers-
by seemed so interesting, living all sorts of strange and
eager lives, with strange and eager pleasures, running
all sorts of risks, hungry sometimes, homeless even—*so*
fascinating, *so* unlike——

'Now, my dear, you'll be late!'

Mr. Pendyce, in his Norfolk jacket, which he was on
his way to change for a black coat, passed through the
room, followed by the spaniel John. He turned at the
door, and the spaniel John turned too.

'I hope to goodness Barter 'll be short this morning.
I want to talk to old Fox about that new chaff-cutter.'

Round their mistress the three terriers raised their
heads; the aged Skye gave forth a gentle growl. Mrs.
Pendyce leaned over and stroked his nose.

'Roy, Roy, how *can* you, dear?'

Mr. Pendyce said:

'The old dog's losing all his teeth; he'll have to be
put away.'

His wife flushed painfully.

'Oh, no, Horace—oh, no!'

The squire coughed.

'We must think of the dog!' he said.

Mrs. Pendyce rose, and crumpling the letter nervously, followed him from the room.

A narrow path led through the home paddock towards the church, and along it the household were making their way. The maids in feathers hurried along guiltily by twos and threes; the butler followed slowly by himself. A footman and a groom came next, leaving trails of pomatum in the air. Presently General Pendyce, in a high square-topped bowler hat, carrying a malacca cane, and Prayer Book, appeared walking between Bee and Norah, also carrying Prayer Books, with fox-terriers by their sides. Lastly, the squire in a high hat, six or seven paces in advance of his wife, in a small velvet toque.

The rooks had ceased their wheeling and their cawing; the five-minutes bell, with its jerky, toneless tolling, alone broke the Sunday hush. An old horse, not yet taken up from grass, stood motionless, resting a hindleg, with his face turned towards the footpath. Within the churchyard wicket the rector, firm and square, a low-crowned hat tilted up on his bald forehead, was talking to a deaf old cottager. He raised his hat and nodded to the ladies; then, leaving his remark unfinished, disappeared within the vestry. At the organ Mrs. Barter was drawing out stops in readiness to play her husband into church, and her eyes, half-shining and half-anxious, were fixed intently on the vestry door.

The squire and Mrs. Pendyce, now almost abreast, came down the aisle and took their seats beside their daughters and the general in the first pew on the left. It was high and cushioned. They knelt down on tall red hassocks. Mrs. Pendyce remained over a minute

buried in thought; Mr. Pendyce rose sooner, and looking down, kicked the hassock that had been put too
near the seat.   Fixing his glasses on his nose, he consulted a worn old Bible, then rising, walked to the
lectern and began to find the Lessons.   The bell ceased;
a wheezing, growling noise was heard.   Mrs. Barter
had begun to play; the rector, in a white surplice, was
coming in.   Mr. Pendyce, with his back turned, continued to find the Lessons.   The service began.

Through a plain glass window high up in the right-
hand aisle the sun shot a gleam athwart the Pendyces'
pew.   It found its last resting-place on Mrs. Barter's
face, showing her soft crumpled cheeks painfully
flushed, the lines on her forehead, and those shining
eyes, eager and anxious, travelling ever from her husband
to her music and back again.   At the least fold or
frown on his face the music seemed to quiver, as to
some spasm in the player's soul.   In the Pendyces' pew
the two girls sang loudly and with a certain sweetness.
Mr. Pendyce, too, sang, and once or twice he looked in
surprise at his brother, as though he were not making
a creditable noise.   Mrs. Pendyce did not sing, but her
lips moved, and her eyes followed the millions of little
dust atoms dancing in the long slanting sunbeam.   Its
gold path canted slowly from her, then, as by magic,
vanished.   Mrs. Pendyce let her eyes fall.   Something
had fled from her soul with the sunbeam; her lips
moved no more.

The squire sang two loud notes, spoke three, sang
two again; the Psalms ceased.   He left his seat, and
placing his hands on the lectern's sides, leaned forward
and began to read the Lesson.   He read the story of
Abraham and Lot, and of their flocks and herds, and
how they could not dwell together, and as he read,

hypnotized by the sound of his own voice, he was
thinking:

'This Lesson is well read by me, Horace Pendyce.
I am Horace Pendyce — Horace Pendyce.   Amen,
Horace Pendyce!'

And in the first pew on the left Mrs. Pendyce fixed
her eyes upon him, for this was her habit and she
thought how, when the spring came again, she would
run up to town alone, and stay at Green's Hotel, where
she had always stayed with her father when a girl.
George had promised to look after her, and take her
round the theatres.   And forgetting that she had thought
this every autumn for the last ten years, she gently
smiled and nodded.   Mr. Pendyce said:

'"And I will make thy seed as the dust of the earth;
so that if a man can number the dust of the earth, then
shall thy seed also be numbered.   Arise, walk through
the land in the length of it and in the breadth of it;
for I will give it unto thee.   Then Abram removed his
tent, and came and dwelt in the plain of Mamre, which
is in Hebron, and built there an altar unto the Lord."
Here endeth the first Lesson.'

The sun, reaching the second window, again shot a
gold pathway athwart the church; again the millions
of dust atoms danced, and the service went on.

There came a hush.   The spaniel John, crouched close
to the ground outside, poked his long black nose under
the churchyard gate; the fox-terriers, seated patient
in the grass, pricked their ears.   A voice speaking on
one note broke the hush.   The spaniel John sighed, the
fox-terriers dropped their ears, and lay down heavily
against each other.   The rector had begun to preach.
He preached on fruitfulness, and in the first right-hand
pew six of his children at once began to fidget.   Mrs.

Barter, sideways and unsupported on her seat, kept her
starry eyes fixed on his cheek; a line of perplexity
furrowed her brow. Now and again she moved as
though her back ached. The rector quartered his
congregation with his gaze, lest any amongst them should
incline to sleep. He spoke in a loud-sounding voice.

God—he said—wished men to be fruitful, intended
them to be fruitful, commanded them to be fruitful.
God—he said—made men, and made the earth; He
made man to be fruitful in the earth; He made man
neither to question nor answer nor argue: He made
him to be fruitful and possess the land. As they had
heard in that beautiful Lesson this morning, God had
set bounds, the bounds of marriage, within which man
should multiply; within those bounds it was his duty to
multiply, and that exceedingly—even as Abraham multi-
plied. In these days dangers, pitfalls, snares, were
rife; in these days men went about and openly, un-
ashamedly advocated shameful doctrines. Let them
beware. It would be his sacred duty to exclude such
men from within the precincts of that parish entrusted
to his care by God. In the language of their greatest
poet: 'Such men were dangerous' — dangerous to
Christianity, dangerous to their country, and to national
life. They were not brought into this world to follow
sinful inclination, to obey their mortal reason. God
demanded sacrifices of men. Patriotism demanded
sacrifices of men, it demanded that they should curb
their inclinations and desires. It demanded of them
their first duty as men and Christians, the duty of being
fruitful and multiplying, in order that they might till
this fruitful earth, not selfishly, not for themselves
alone. It demanded of them the duty of multiplying
in order that they and their children might be equipped

to smite the enemies of their queen and country, and uphold the name of England in whatever quarrel, against all who rashly sought to drag her flag in the dust.

The squire opened his eyes and looked at his watch. Folding his arms, he coughed, for he was thinking of the chaff-cutter. Beside him Mrs. Pendyce, with her eyes on the altar, smiled as if in sleep. She was thinking: 'Skyward's in Bond Street used to have lovely lace. Perhaps in the spring I could—— Or there was Goblin's, their *point de Venise*——'

Behind them, four rows back, an aged cottage woman, as upright as a girl, sat with a rapt expression on her carved old face. She never moved, her eyes seemed drinking in the movements of the rector's lips, her whole being seemed hanging on his words. It is true her dim eyes saw nothing but a blur, her poor deaf ears could not hear one word, but she sat at the angle she was used to, and thought of nothing at all. And perhaps it was better so, for she was near her end.

Outside the churchyard, in the sun-warmed grass, the fox-terriers lay one against the other, pretending to shiver, with their small bright eyes fixed on the church door, and the rubbery nostrils of the spaniel John worked ever busily beneath the wicket gate.

CHAPTER VIII

GREGORY VIGIL PROPOSES

ABOUT three o'clock that afternoon a tall man walked up the avenue at Worsted Skeynes, in one hand carrying his hat, in the other a small brown bag. He stopped now and then, and took deep breaths, expanding the nostrils of his straight nose. He had a fine head, with wings of grizzled hair. His clothes were loose, his stride was springy. Standing in the middle of the drive, taking those long breaths, with his moist blue eyes upon the sky, he excited the attention of a robin, who ran out of a rhododendron to see, and when he had passed began to whistle. Gregory Vigil turned, and screwed up his humorous lips, and, except that he was completely lacking in *embonpoint*, he had a certain resemblance to this bird, which is supposed to be peculiarly British.

He asked for Mrs. Pendyce in a high, light voice, very pleasant to the ear, and was at once shown to the white morning-room.

She greeted him affectionately, like many women who have grown used to hearing from their husbands the formula: 'Oh, *your* people!'—she had a strong feeling for her kith and kin.

'You know, Grig,' she said, when her cousin was seated, 'your letter was rather disturbing. Her separation from Captain Bellew has caused such a lot of talk about here. Yes; it's very common, I know, that sort of thing, but Horace is so——! All the squires

and parsons and county people we get about here are
just the same. Of course, I 'm very fond of her, she 's
so charming to look at; but, Gregory, I really don't
dislike her husband. He 's a desperate sort of person—
I think that 's rather refreshing; and you know I *do*
think she 's a little like him in that!'

The blood rushed up into Gregory Vigil's forehead;
he put his hand to his head, and said:

'Like him? Like that man? Is a rose like an
artichoke?'

Mrs. Pendyce went on:

'I enjoyed having her here immensely. It 's the first
time she 's been here since she left the Firs. How long
is that? Two years? But you know, Grig, the Maldens
were quite upset about her. Do you think a divorce
is really necessary?'

Gregory Vigil answered: 'I 'm afraid it is.'

Mrs. Pendyce met her cousin's gaze serenely; if
anything, her brows were uplifted more than usual;
but, as at the stirring of secret trouble, her fingers
began to twine and twist. Before her rose a vision of
George and Mrs. Bellew side by side. It was a vague
maternal feeling, an instinctive fear. She stilled her
fingers, let her eyelids droop, and said:

'Of course, dear Grig, if I can help you in any way—
Horace does so dislike anything to do with the papers.'

Gregory Vigil drew in his breath.

'The papers!' he said. 'How hateful it is! To think
that our civilization should allow women to be cast to
the dogs! Understand, Margery, I 'm thinking of her.
In this matter I 'm not capable of considering anything
else.'

Mrs. Pendyce murmured: 'Of course, dear Grig, I
quite understand.'

'Her position is odious; a woman should not have to live like that, exposed to every one's foul gossip.'

'But, dear Grig, I don't think she minds; she seemed to me in such excellent spirits.'

Gregory ran his fingers through his hair.

'Nobody understands her,' he said; 'she 's so plucky!'

Mrs. Pendyce stole a glance at him, and a little ironical smile flickered over her face.

'No one can look at her without seeing her spirit. But, Grig, perhaps you don't quite understand her either!'

Gregory Vigil put his hand to his head.

'I must open the window a moment,' he said.

Again Mrs. Pendyce's fingers began twisting, again she stilled them.

'We were quite a large party last week, and now there 's only Charles. Even George has gone back; he 'll be so sorry to have missed you!'

Gregory neither turned nor answered, and a wistful look came into Mrs. Pendyce's face.

'It was so nice for the dear boy to win that race! I 'm afraid he bets rather! It 's such a comfort Horace doesn't know.'

Still Gregory did not speak.

Mrs. Pendyce's face lost its anxious look, and gained a sort of gentle admiration.

'Dear Grig,' she said, 'where do you go about your hair? It *is* so nice and long and wavy!'

Gregory turned with a blush.

'I 've been wanting to get it cut for ages. Do you really mean, Margery, that your husband can't realize the position she 's placed in?'

Mrs. Pendyce fixed her eyes on her lap.

'You see, Grig,' she began, 'she was here a good deal

before she left the Firs, and, of course, she 's related
to me—though it 's very distant. With those horrid
cases, you never know what will happen. Horace is
certain to say that she ought to go back to her husband;
or, if that 's impossible, he 'll say she ought to think of
society. Lady Rose Bethany's case has shaken everybody, and Horace *is* nervous. I don't know how it is,
there 's a great feeling amongst people about here
against women asserting themselves. You should hear
Mr. Barter and Sir James Malden, and dozens of others;
the funny thing is that the women take their side. Of
course, it seems odd to me, because so many of the
Totteridges ran away, or did something funny. I can't
help sympathizing with her, but I have to think of—
of—— In the country, you don't know how things
that people do get about before they 've done them!
There 's only that and hunting to talk of.'

Gregory Vigil clutched at his head.

'Well, if this is what chivalry has come to, thank God
I 'm not a squire!'

Mrs. Pendyce's eyes flickered.

'Ah!' she said, 'I 've thought like that so often.'

Gregory broke the silence.

'I can't help the customs of the country. My duty 's
plain. There 's nobody else to look after her.'

Mrs. Pendyce sighed, and, rising from her chair, said:
'Very well, dear Grig; do let us go and have some tea.'

Tea at Worsted Skeynes was served in the hall on
Sundays, and was usually attended by the rector and
his wife. Young Cecil Tharp had walked over with his
dog, which could be heard whimpering faintly outside
the front door.

General Pendyce, with his knees crossed and the tips
of his fingers pressed together, was leaning back in his

chair and staring at the wall. The squire, who held his
latest bird's-egg in his hand, was showing its spots
to the rector.

In a corner by a harmonium, on which no one ever
played, Norah talked of the village hockey club to
Mrs. Barter, who sat with her eyes fixed on her husband.
On the other side of the fire Bee and young Tharp,
whose chairs seemed very close together, spoke of their
horses in low tones, stealing shy glances at each other.
The light was failing, the wood logs crackled, and now
and then over the cosy hum of talk there fell short,
drowsy silences—silences of sheer warmth and comfort,
like the silence of the spaniel John asleep against his
master's boot.

'Well,' said Gregory softly, 'I must go and see this
man.'

'Is it really necessary, Grig, to see him at all? I
mean—if you 've made up your mind——'

Gregory ran his hand through his hair.

'It 's only fair, I think!' And crossing the hall, he
let himself out so quietly that no one but Mrs. Pendyce
noticed he had gone.

An hour and a half later, near the railway station,
on the road from the village back to Worsted Skeynes,
Mr. Pendyce and his daughter Bee were returning from
their Sunday visit to their old butler, Bigson. The
squire was talking.

'He 's failing, Bee—dear old Bigson 's failing. I can't
hear what he says, he mumbles so; and he forgets.
Fancy his forgetting that I was at Oxford. But we don't
get servants like him nowadays. That chap we 've got
now is a sleepy fellow. Sleepy! he 's—— What 's that
in the road? They 've no business to be coming at
that pace. Who is it? I can't see.'

Down the middle of the dark road a dog-cart was approaching at top speed. Bee seized her father's arm and pulled it vigorously, for Mr. Pendyce was standing stock-still in disapproval. The dog-cart passed within a foot of him and vanished, swinging round into the station. Mr. Pendyce turned in his tracks.

'Who was that? Disgraceful! On Sunday, too! The fellow must be drunk; he nearly ran over my legs. Did you see, Bee, he nearly ran over——'

Bee answered:

'It was Captain Bellew, father; I saw his face.'

'Bellew? That drunken fellow? I shall summons him. Did you see, Bee, he nearly ran over my——'

'Perhaps he's had bad news,' said Bee. 'There's the train going out now; I do hope he caught it!'

'Bad news! Is that an excuse for driving over me? You hope he *caught* it! I hope he's thrown himself out. The ruffian! I hope he's killed himself.'

In this strain Mr. Pendyce continued until they reached the church. On the way up the aisle they passed Gregory Vigil leaning forward with his elbows on the desk and his hand covering his eyes. . . .

At eleven o'clock that night a man stood outside the door of Mrs. Bellew's flat in Chelsea violently ringing the bell. His face was deathly white, but his little dark eyes sparkled. The door was opened, and Helen Bellew in evening dress stood there holding a candle in her hand.

'Who are you? What do you want?'

The man moved into the light.

'Jaspar! You? What on earth——'

'I want to talk.'

'Talk? Do you know what time it is?'

'Time—there's no such thing. You might give me

a kiss after two years. I 've been drinking, but I 'm not drunk.'

Mrs. Bellew did not kiss him, neither did she draw back her face. No trace of alarm showed in her ice-grey eyes. She said: 'If I let you in, will you promise to say what you want to say quickly, and go away?'

The little brown devils danced in Bellew's face. He nodded. They stood by the hearth in the sitting-room, and on the lips of both came and went a peculiar smile.

It was difficult to contemplate too seriously a person with whom one had lived for years, with whom one had experienced in common the range of human passion, intimacy, and estrangement, who knew all those little daily things that men and women living together know of each other, and with whom in the end, without hatred, but because of one's nature, one had ceased to live. There was nothing for either of them to find out, and with a little smile, like the smile of knowledge itself, Jaspar Bellew and Helen his wife looked at each other.

'Well,' she said again; 'what have you come for?'

Bellew's face had changed. Its expression was furtive; his mouth twitched; a furrow had come between his eyes.

'How—are—you?' he said in a thick, muttering voice.

Mrs. Bellew's clear voice answered:

'Now, Jaspar, what is it that you want?'

The little brown devils leaped up again in Jaspar's face.

'You look very pretty to-night!'

His wife's lips curled.

'I 'm much the same as I always was,' she said.

A violent shudder shook Bellew. He fixed his eyes on the floor a little beyond her to the left; suddenly he raised them. They were quite lifeless.

'I'm perfectly sober,' he murmured thickly; then with startling quickness his eyes began to sparkle again. He came a step nearer.

'You're my wife!' he said.

Mrs. Bellew smiled.

'Come,' she answered, 'you must go!' and she put out her bare arm to push him back. But Bellew recoiled of his own accord; his eyes were fixed again on the floor a little beyond her to the left.

'What's that?' he stammered. 'What's that— that black——?'

The devilry, mockery, admiration, bemusement, had gone out of his face; it was white and calm, and horribly pathetic.

'Don't turn me out,' he stammered; 'don't turn me out!'

Mrs. Bellew looked at him hard; the defiance in her eyes changed to a sort of pity. She took a quick step and put her hand on his shoulder.

'It's all right, old boy—all right!' she said. 'There's nothing there!'

CHAPTER IX

MR. PARAMOR DISPOSES

MRS. PENDYCE, who, in accordance with her husband's wish, still occupied the same room as Mr. Pendyce, chose the ten minutes before he got up to break to him Gregory's decision. The moment was auspicious, for he was only half awake.

'Horace,' she said, and her face looked young and anxious, 'Grig says that Helen Bellew ought not to go on in her present position. Of course, I told him that you'd be annoyed, but Grig says that she can't go on like this, that she simply must divorce Captain Bellew.'

Mr. Pendyce was lying on his back.

'What's that?' he said.

Mrs. Pendyce went on:

'I knew it would worry you; but really'—she fixed her eyes on the ceiling—'I suppose we ought only to think of her.'

The squire sat up.

'What was that,' he said, 'about Bellew?'

Mrs. Pendyce went on in a languid voice and without moving her eyes:

'Don't be angrier than you can help, dear; it *is* so wearing. If Grig says she ought to divorce Captain Bellew, then I'm sure she ought.'

Horace Pendyce subsided on his pillow with a bounce, and he too lay with his eyes fixed on the ceiling.

'Divorce him!' he said—'I should think so! He

ought to be hanged, a fellow like that. I told you last
night he nearly drove over me. Living just as he likes,
setting an example of devilry to the whole neighbourhood! If I hadn't kept my head he 'd have bowled me
over like a ninepin, and Bee into the bargain.'

Mrs. Pendyce sighed.

'It *was* a narrow escape,' she said.

'Divorce him!' resumed Mr. Pendyce — 'I should
think so! She ought to have divorced him long ago.
It was the nearest thing in the world; another foot
and I should have been knocked off my feet!'

Mrs. Pendyce withdrew her glance from the ceiling.

'At first,' she said, 'I wondered whether it was
quite—but I 'm very glad you 've taken it like this.'

'Taken it! I can tell you, Margery, that sort of thing
makes one think. All the time Barter was preaching
last night I was wondering what on earth would have
happened to this estate if — if——' And he looked
round with a frown. 'Even as it is, I barely make the
two ends of it meet. As to George, he 's no more fit
at present to manage it than you are; he 'd make a
loss of thousands.'

'I 'm afraid George is too much in London. That 's
the reason I wondered whether—I 'm afraid he sees too
much of——'

Mrs. Pendyce stopped; a flush suffused her cheeks;
she had pinched herself violently beneath the bed-
clothes.

'George,' said Mr. Pendyce, pursuing his own thoughts,
'has no gumption. He 'd never manage a man like
Peacock—and you encourage him! He ought to marry
and settle down.'

Mrs. Pendyce, the flush dying in her cheeks, said:
'George is very like poor Hubert.'

Horace Pendyce drew his watch from beneath his pillow.

'Ah!' But he refrained from adding, 'Your people!' for Hubert Totteridge had not been dead a year. 'Ten minutes to eight! You keep me talking here; it's time I was in my bath.'

Clad in pyjamas with a very wide blue stripe, grey-eyed, grey-moustached, slim and erect, he paused at the door.

'The girls haven't a scrap of imagination. What do you think Bee said? "I hope he hasn't lost his train." Lost his train! Good God! and I might have —I might have——' The squire did not finish his sentence; no words but what seemed to him violent and extreme would have fulfilled his conception of the danger he had escaped, and it was against his nature and his training to exaggerate a physical risk.

At breakfast he was more cordial than usual to Gregory, who was going up by the first train, for as a rule Mr. Pendyce rather distrusted him, as one would a wife's cousin, especially if he had a sense of humour.

'A very good fellow,' he was wont to say of him, 'but an out-and-out Radical.' It was the only label he could find for Gregory's peculiarities.

Gregory departed without further allusion to the object of his visit. He was driven to the station in a brougham by the first groom, and sat with his hat off and his head at the open window, as if trying to get something blown out of his brain. Indeed, throughout the whole of his journey up to town he looked out of the window, and expressions half humorous and half puzzled played on his face. Like a panorama slowly unrolled, country house after country house, church after church, appeared before his eyes in the autumn sunlight, among the hedgerows and the coverts that were all brown and gold; and far away on the rising uplands the slow ploughman drove, outlined against the sky.

He took a cab from the station to his solicitors' in Lincoln's Inn Fields. He was shown into a room bare of all legal accessories, except a series of Law Reports and a bunch of violets in a glass of fresh water. Edmund Paramor, the senior partner of Paramor and Herring, a clean-shaven man of sixty, with iron-grey hair brushed in a cockscomb off his forehead, greeted him with a smile.

'Ah, Vigil, how are you? Up from the country?'

'From Worsted Skeynes.'

'Horace Pendyce is a client of mine. Well, what can we do for *you*? Your society up a tree?'

Gregory Vigil, in the padded leather chair that had held so many aspirants for comfort, sat a full minute without speaking; and Mr. Paramor, too, after one keen glance at his client that seemed to come from very far down in his soul, sat motionless and grave. There was at that moment something a little similar in the eyes of these two very different men, a look of kindred honesty and aspiration. Gregory spoke at last.

'It's a painful subject to me.'

Mr. Paramor drew a face on his blotting-paper.

'I have come,' went on Gregory, 'about a divorce for my ward.'

'Mrs. Jaspar Bellew?'

'Yes; her position is intolerable.'

Mr. Paramor gave him a searching look.

'Let me see: I think she and her husband have been separated for some time.'

'Yes, for two years.'

'You're acting with her consent, of course?'

'I have spoken to her.'

'You know the law of divorce, I suppose?'

Gregory answered with a painful smile:

'I 'm not very clear about it; I hardly ever look at those cases in the paper. I hate the whole idea.'

Mr. Paramor smiled again, became instantly grave, and said:

'We shall want evidence of certain things. Have you got any evidence?'

Gregory ran his hand through his hair.

'I don't think there 'll be any difficulty,' he said. 'Bellew agrees—they both agree!'

Mr. Paramor stared.

'What 's that to do with it?'

Gregory caught him up.

'Surely, where both parties are anxious, and there 's no opposition, it can't be difficult.'

'Good Lord!' said Mr. Paramor.

'But I 've seen Bellew; I saw him yesterday. I 'm sure I can get him to admit anything you want!'

Mr. Paramor drew his breath between his teeth.

'Did you ever,' he said dryly, 'hear of what 's called collusion?'

Gregory got up and paced the room.

'I don't know that I 've ever heard anything very exact about the thing at all,' he said. 'The whole subject is hateful to me. I regard marriage as sacred, and when, which God forbid, it proves unsacred, it is horrible to think of these formalities. This is a Christian country; we are all flesh and blood. What is this slime, Paramor?'

With this outburst he sank again into the chair, and leaned his head on his hand. And oddly, instead of smiling, Mr. Paramor looked at him with haunting eyes.

'Two unhappy persons must not seem to agree to

be parted,' he said. 'One must be believed to desire
to keep hold of the other, and must pose as an injured
person. There must be evidence of misconduct, and
in this case of cruelty or of desertion. The evidence
must be impartial. This is the law.'

Gregory said without looking up:

'But why?'

Mr. Paramor took his violets out of the water, and
put them to his nose.

'How do you mean—why?'

'I mean, why this underhand, roundabout way?'

Mr. Paramor's face changed with startling speed
from its haunting look back to his smile.

'Well,' he said, 'for the preservation of morality.
What do you suppose?'

'Do you call it moral so to imprison people that
you drive them to sin in order to free themselves?'

Mr. Paramor obliterated the face on his blotting-pad.

'Where's your sense of humour?' he said.

'I see no joke, Paramor.'

Mr. Paramor leaned forward.

'My dear friend,' he said earnestly, 'I don't say for
a minute that our system doesn't cause a great deal of
quite unnecessary suffering; I don't say that it doesn't
need reform. Most lawyers and almost any thinking
man will tell you that it does. But that's a wide
question which doesn't help us here. We'll manage
your business for you, if it can be done. You've made
a bad start, that's all. The first thing is for us to write
to Mrs. Bellew, and ask her to come and see us. We
shall have to get Bellew watched.'

Gregory said:

'That's detestable. Can't it be done without that?'

Mr. Paramor bit his forefinger.

'Not safe,' he said. 'But don't bother; we 'll see to all that.'

Gregory rose and went to the window. He said suddenly:

'I can't bear this underhand work.'

Mr. Paramor smiled.

'Every honest man,' he said, 'feels as you do. But, you see, we must think of the law.'

Gregory burst out again:

'Can no one get a divorce, then, without making beasts or spies of themselves?'

Mr. Paramor said gravely:

'It is difficult, perhaps impossible. You see, the law is based on certain principles.'

'Principles?'

A smile wreathed Mr. Paramor's mouth, but died instantly.

'Ecclesiastical principles, and according to these a person desiring a divorce *ipso facto* loses caste. That they should have to make spies or beasts of themselves is not of grave importance.'

Gregory came back to the table, and again buried his head in his hands.

'Don't joke, please, Paramor,' he said; 'it 's all so painful to me.'

Mr. Paramor's eyes haunted his client's bowed head.

'I 'm not joking,' he said. 'God forbid! Do you read poetry?' And opening a drawer, he took out a book bound in red leather. 'This is a man I 'm fond of:

> Life is mostly froth and bubble;
> Two things stand like stone—
> KINDNESS in another's trouble,
> COURAGE in your own.

That seems to me the sum of all philosophy.'

'Paramor,' said Gregory, 'my ward is very dear to me; she is dearer to me than any woman I know. I am here in a most dreadful dilemma. On the one hand there is this horrible underhand business, with all its publicity; and on the other there is her position—a beautiful woman, fond of gaiety, living alone in this London, where every man's instincts and every woman's tongue look upon her as fair game. It has been brought home to me only too painfully of late. God forgive me! I have even advised her to go back to Bellew, but that seems out of the question. What am I to do?'

Mr. Paramor rose.

'I know,' he said—'I know. My dear friend, I know!' And for a full minute he remained motionless, a little turned from Gregory. 'It will be better,' he said suddenly, 'for her to get rid of him. I'll go and see her myself. We'll spare her all we can. I'll go this afternoon, and let you know the result.'

As though by mutual instinct, they put out their hands, which they shook with averted faces. Then Gregory, seizing his hat, strode out of the room.

He went straight to the rooms of his society in Hanover Square. They were on the top floor, higher than the rooms of any other society in the building—so high, in fact, that from their windows, which began five feet up, you could practically only see the sky.

A girl with sloping shoulders, red cheeks, and dark eyes was working a typewriter in a corner, and sideways to the sky, at a bureau littered with addressed envelopes, unanswered letters, and copies of the society's publications, was seated a grey-haired lady with a long, thin, weather-beaten face and glowing eyes, who was frowning at a page of manuscript.

'Oh, Mr. Vigil,' she said, 'I'm so glad you've come. This paragraph mustn't go as it is. It will never do.'

Gregory took the manuscript and read the paragraph in question.

'This case of Eva Nevill is so horrible that we ask those of our women readers who live in the security, luxury perhaps, peace certainly, of their country homes, what they would have done, finding themselves suddenly in the position of this poor girl—in a great city, without friends, without money, almost without clothes, and exposed to all the craft of one of those fiends in human form who prey upon our womankind. Let each one ask herself: Should I have resisted where she fell?'

'It will never do to send that out,' said the lady again.

'What is the matter with it, Mrs. Shortman?'

'It's too personal. Think of Lady Malden, or most of our subscribers. You can't expect them to imagine themselves like poor Eva. I'm sure they won't like it.'

Gregory clutched at his hair.

'Is it possible they can't stand that?' he said.

'It's only because you've given such horrible details of poor Eva.'

Gregory got up and paced the room.

Mrs. Shortman went on:

'You've not lived in the country for so long, Mr. Vigil, that you don't remember. You see, I know. People don't like to be harrowed. Besides, think how difficult it is for them to imagine themselves in such a position. It'll only shock them, and do our circulation harm.'

Gregory snatched up the page and handed it to the girl who sat at the typewriter in the corner.

'Read that, please, Miss Mallow.'

The girl read without raising her eyes.

'Well, is it what Mrs. Shortman says?'

The girl handed it back with a blush.

'It's perfect, of course, in itself, but I think Mrs. Shortman is right. It might offend some people.'

Gregory went quickly to the window, threw it up, and stood gazing at the sky. Both women looked at his back.

Mrs. Shortman said gently:

'I would only just alter it like this, from after "country homes": "whether they do not pity and forgive this poor girl in a great city, without friends, without money, almost without clothes, and exposed to all the craft of one of those fiends in human form who prey upon our womankind," and just stop there.'

Gregory returned to the table.

'Not "forgive,"' he said, 'not "forgive"!'

Mrs. Shortman raised her pen.

'You don't know,' she said, 'what a strong feeling there is. Mind, it has to go to numbers of parsonages, Mr. Vigil. Our principle has always been to be very careful. And you *have* been plainer than usual in stating the case. It's not as if they really could put themselves in her position; that's impossible. Not one woman in a hundred could, especially among those who live in the country and have never seen life. I'm a squire's daughter myself.'

'And I a parson's,' said Gregory, with a smile.

Mrs. Shortman looked at him reproachfully.

'Joking apart, Mr. Vigil, it's touch and go with our paper as it is; we really can't afford it. I've had lots of letters lately complaining that we put the cases unnecessarily strongly. Here's one:

                       "BOURNEFIELD RECTORY,
'DEAR MADAM,   "1st *November*.

  "While sympathizing with your good work, I am afraid I cannot become a subscriber to your paper while it takes its present form, as I do not feel that it is always fit reading for my girls. I cannot think it either wise or right that they should become acquainted with such dreadful aspects of life, however true they may be.

           "I am, dear madam,
                "Respectfully yours,
                    "WINIFRED TUDDENHAM.

  "PS.—I could never feel sure, too, that my maids would not pick it up, and perhaps take harm."

I had that only this morning.'

Gregory buried his face in his hands, and sitting thus he looked so like a man praying that no one spoke. When he raised his face it was to say:

'Not "forgive," Mrs. Shortman, not "forgive"!'

Mrs. Shortman ran her pen through the word.

'Very well, Mr. Vigil,' she said; 'it 's a risk.'

The sound of the typewriter, which had been hushed, began again from the corner.

'That case of drink, Mr. Vigil—Millicent Porter— I 'm afraid there 's very little hope there.'

Gregory asked:

'What now?'

'Relapsed again; it 's the fifth time.'

Gregory turned his face to the window, and looked at the sky.

'I must go and see her. Just give me her address.'

Mrs. Shortman read from a green book:

'"Mrs. Porter, 2 Bilcock Buildings, Bloomsbury." Mr. Vigil!'

'Yes.'

'Mr. Vigil, I do sometimes wish you would not persevere so long with those hopeless cases; they never seem to come to anything, and your time is *so* valuable.'

'How can I give them up, Mrs. Shortman? There's no choice.'

'But, Mr. Vigil, why is there no choice? You must draw the line somewhere. Do forgive me for saying that I think you sometimes waste your time.'

Gregory turned to the girl at the typewriter.

'Miss Mallow, is Mrs. Shortman right? do I waste my time?'

The girl at the typewriter blushed vividly, and without looking round, said:

'How can I tell, Mr. Vigil? But it does worry one.'

A humorous and perplexed smile passed over Gregory's lips.

'Now I know I shall cure her,' he said. '2 Bilcock Buildings.' And he continued to look at the sky. 'How's your neuralgia, Mrs. Shortman?'

Mrs. Shortman smiled.

'Awful!'

Gregory turned quickly.

'You feel that window, then; I'm so sorry.'

Mrs. Shortman shook her head.

'No, but perhaps Molly does.'

The girl at the typewriter said:

'Oh, no; please, Mr. Vigil, don't shut it for me.'

'Truth and honour?'

'Truth and honour,' replied both women. And all three for a moment sat looking at the sky. Then Mrs. Shortman said:

'You see, you can't get to the root of the evil—that husband of hers.'

Gregory turned.

'Ah,' he said, 'that man! If she could only get rid of him! That ought to have been done long ago, before he drove her to drink like this. Why didn't she, Mrs. Shortman, why didn't she?'

Mrs. Shortman raised her eyes, which had such a peculiar spiritual glow.

'I don't suppose she had the money,' she said; 'and she must have been such a nice woman then. A nice woman doesn't like to divorce——'

Gregory looked at her.

'What, Mrs. Shortman, you too, you too among the Pharisees?'

Mrs. Shortman flushed.

'She wanted to save him,' she said; 'she must have wanted to save him.'

'Then you and I——' But Gregory did not finish, and turned again to the window. Mrs. Shortman, too, biting her lips, looked anxiously at the sky.

Miss Mallow at the typewriter, with a scared face, plied her fingers faster than ever.

Gregory was the first to speak.

'You must please forgive me,' he said gently. 'A personal matter; I forgot myself.'

Mrs. Shortman withdrew her gaze from the sky.

'Oh, Mr. Vigil, if I had known——'

Gregory smiled.

'Don't, don't!' he said; 'we've quite frightened poor Miss Mallow!'

Miss Mallow looked round at him, he looked at her, and all three once more looked at the sky. It was the chief recreation of this little society.

Gregory worked till nearly three, and walked out to a bun-shop, where he lunched off a piece of cake and a cup of coffee. He took an omnibus, and getting on the top, was driven west with a smile on his face and his hat in his hand. He was thinking of Helen Bellew. It had become a habit with him to think of her, the best and most beautiful of her sex—a habit in which he was growing grey, and with which, therefore, he could not part. And those women who saw him with his uncovered head smiled, and thought:

'What a fine-looking man!'

But George Pendyce, who saw him from the window of the Stoics' Club, smiled a different smile; the sight of him was always a little unpleasant to George.

Nature, who had made Gregory Vigil a man, had long found that he had got out of her hands, and was living in celibacy, deprived of the comfort of woman, even of those poor creatures whom he befriended; and Nature, who cannot bear that man should escape her control, avenged herself through his nerves and a habit of blood to the head. Extravagance, she said, I cannot have, and when I made this man I made him quite extravagant enough. For his temperament (not uncommon in a misty climate) had been born seven feet high; and as a man cannot add a cubit to his stature, so neither can he take one off. Gregory could not bear that a yellow man must always remain a yellow man, but trusted by care and attention some day to see him white. There lives no mortal who has not a philosophy as distinct from every other mortal's as his face is different from their faces; but Gregory believed that philosophers unfortunately alien must gain in time a likeness to himself if he were careful to tell them often that they had been mistaken. Other men in this Great Britain had the same belief.

To Gregory's reforming instinct it was a constant

grief that he had been born refined. A natural delicacy *would* interfere and mar his noblest efforts. Hence failures deplored by Mrs. Pendyce to Lady Malden the night they danced at Worsted Skeynes.

He left his bus near to the flat where Mrs. Bellew lived; with reverence he made the tour of the building and back again. He had long fixed a rule, which he never broke, of seeing her only once a fortnight; but to pass her windows he went out of his way most days and nights. And having made this tour, not conscious of having done anything ridiculous, still smiling, and with his hat on his knee, perhaps really happier because he had not seen her, was driven east, once more passing George Pendyce in the bow-window of the Stoics' Club, and once more raising on his face a jeering smile.

He had been back at his rooms in Buckingham Street half an hour when a club commissionaire arrived with Mr. Paramor's promised letter.

He opened it hastily.

'THE NELSON CLUB,
'TRAFALGAR SQUARE.

'MY DEAR VIGIL,

'I 've just come from seeing your ward. An embarrassing complexion is lent to affairs by what took place last night. It appears that after your visit to him yesterday afternoon her husband came up to town, and made his appearance at her flat about eleven o'clock. He was in a condition bordering on delirium tremens, and Mrs. Bellew was obliged to keep him for the night. "I could not," she said to me, "have refused a dog in such a state." The visit lasted until this afternoon—in fact, the man had only just gone when I arrived. It is a piece of irony, of which I must explain to you the importance. I think I told you that the law of divorce is based on certain principles. One of these excludes any forgiveness of offences by the party moving for a divorce. In technical language, any such forgiveness or overlooking is called condonation, and it is a complete bar to further action for the time being. The Court is very jealous of this principle of non-forgiveness, and will regard with grave suspicion *any conduct on the part of the offended party* which might be construed as amounting to condonation. I fear that what your ward tells me will make it altogether inadvisable to apply for a divorce on any evidence that may lie in the past. It is too dangerous. In other words, the Court would almost certainly consider that she has condoned offences so far. Any further offence, however, will in technical language "revive" the past, and under these circumstances, though nothing can be done at present, there may be hope in the future. After seeing your ward, I quite appreciate your anxiety in the matter, though I am *by no means sure* that you are right in advising this divorce. If you remain in the same mind, however, I will give the matter my best personal attention, and my counsel to you is not to worry. This is no matter for a layman, especially not for one who, like you, judges of things rather as they ought to be than as they are.

'I am, my dear Vigil,

'Very sincerely yours,

'EDMUND PARAMOR.

'GREGORY VIGIL, ESQ.

'If you want to see me, I shall be at my club all the evening.—E.P.'

When Gregory had read this note he walked to the window, and stood looking out over the lights on the river. His heart beat furiously, his temples were crimson. He went downstairs, and took a cab to the Nelson Club.

Mr. Paramor, who was about to dine, invited his visitor to join him.

Gregory shook his head.

'No, thanks,' he said; 'I don't feel like dining. What is this, Paramor? Surely there's some mistake? Do you mean to tell me that because she acted like a Christian to that man she is to be punished for it in this way?'

Mr. Paramor bit his finger.

'Don't confuse yourself by dragging in Christianity. Christianity has nothing to do with law.'

'You talked of principles,' said Gregory—'ecclesi- astical——'

'Yes, yes; I meant principles imported from the old ecclesiastical conception of marriage, which held man and wife to be undivorceable. That conception has been abandoned by the law, but the principles still haunt——'

'I don't understand.'

Mr. Paramor said slowly:

'I don't know that any one does. It's our usual muddle. But I know this, Vigil—in such a case as your ward's we must tread very carefully. We must "save face," as the Chinese say. We must pretend we don't want to bring this divorce, but that we have been so injured that we are obliged to come forward. If Bellew says nothing, the judge will have to take what's put before him. But there's always the Queen's Proctor. I don't know if you know anything about him?'

'No,' said Gregory, 'I don't.'

'Well, if he can find out anything against our getting this divorce, he will. It is not my habit to go into Court with a case in which anybody can find out anything.'

'Do you mean to say——'

'I mean to say that she must not ask for a divorce merely because she is miserable, or placed in a position that no woman should be placed in, but only if she has been offended in certain technical ways; and if—by condonation, for instance—she has given the Court technical reason for refusing her a divorce, that divorce will be refused her. To get a divorce, Vigil, you must be as hard as nails and as wary as a cat. Now do you understand?'

Gregory did not answer.

Mr. Paramor looked searchingly and rather pityingly in his face.

'It won't do to go for it at present,' he said. 'Are you still set on this divorce? I told you in my letter that I am not sure you are right.'

'How can you ask me, Paramor? After that man's conduct last night, I am more than ever set on it.'

'Then,' said Mr. Paramor, 'we must keep a sharp eye on Bellew, and hope for the best.'

Gregory held out his hand.

'You spoke of morality,' he said. 'I can't tell you how inexpressibly mean the whole thing seems to me. Good night.'

And, turning rather quickly, he went out.

His mind was confused and his heart torn. He thought of Helen Bellew as of the woman dearest to him in the coils of a great slimy serpent, and

the knowledge that each man and woman unhappily married was, whether by his own, his
partner's, or by no fault at all, in the same
embrace, afforded him no comfort whatsoever. It
was long before he left the windy streets to go
to his home.

CHAPTER X

AT BLAFARD'S

THERE comes now and then to the surface of our modern civilization one of those great and good men who, unconscious, like all great and good men, of the goodness and greatness of their work, leave behind a lasting memorial of themselves before they go bankrupt.

It was so with the founder of the Stoics' Club.

He came to the surface in the year 187–, with nothing in the world but his clothes and an idea. In a single year he had floated the Stoics' Club, made ten thousand pounds, lost more, and gone down again.

The Stoics' Club lived after him by reason of the immortal beauty of his idea. In 1891 it was a strong and corporate body, not perhaps quite so exclusive as it had been, but, on the whole, as smart and aristocratic as any club in London, with the exception of that one or two into which nobody ever got. The idea with which its founder had underpinned the edifice was, like all great ideas, simple, permanent, and perfect—so simple, permanent, and perfect that it seemed amazing no one had ever thought of it before. It was embodied in No. 1 of the members' rules:

'No member of this club shall have any occupation whatsoever.'

Hence the name of a club renowned throughout London for the excellence of its wines and cuisine

Its situation was in Piccadilly, fronting the Green

Park, and through the many windows of its ground-floor smoking-room the public were privileged to see at all hours of the day numbers of Stoics in various attitudes reading the daily papers or gazing out of the window.

Some of them who did not direct companies, grow fruit, or own yachts, wrote a book, or took an interest in a theatre. The greater part eked out existence by racing horses, hunting foxes, and shooting birds. Individuals among them, however, had been known to play the piano and take up the Roman Catholic religion. Many explored the same spots of the Continent year after year at stated seasons. Some belonged to the Yeomanry; others called themselves barristers; once in a way one painted a picture or devoted himself to good works. They were, in fact, of all sorts and temperaments, but their common characteristic was an independent income, often so settled by Providence that they could not in any way get rid of it.

But though the principle of no occupation over-ruled all class distinctions, the Stoics were mainly derived from the landed gentry. An instinct that the spirit of the club was safest with persons of this class guided them in their elections, and eldest sons, who became members almost as a matter of course, lost no time in putting up their younger brothers, thereby keeping the wine as pure as might be, and preserving that fine old country-house flavour which is nowhere so appreciated as in London.

After seeing Gregory pass on the top of a bus, George Pendyce went into the card-room, and as it was still empty, set to contemplation of the pictures on the walls. They were effigies of all those members of the Stoics' Club who from time to time had come under

the notice of a celebrated caricaturist in a celebrated
society paper. Whenever a Stoic appeared, he was at
once cut out, framed, glassed, and hung alongside his
fellows in this room. And George moved from one to
another till he came to the last. It was himself. He
was represented in very perfectly cut clothes, with
slightly crooked elbows, and race-glasses slung across
him. His head, disproportionately large, was surmounted by a black billycock hat with a very flat brim.
The artist had thought long and carefully over the
face. The lips and cheeks and chin were moulded so
as to convey a feeling of the unimaginative joy of life,
but to their shape and complexion was imparted a
suggestion of obstinacy and choler. To the eyes was
given a glazed look, and between them set a little line,
as though their owner were thinking:

'Hard work, hard work! *Noblesse oblige.* I must
keep it going!'

Underneath was written: 'The Ambler.'

George stood long looking at the apotheosis of his
fame. His star was high in the heavens. With the
eye of his mind he saw a long procession of turf triumphs,
a long vista of days and nights, and in them, round
them, of them—Helen Bellew; and by an odd coinci-
dence, as he stood there, the artist's glazed look came
over his eyes, the little line sprang up between them.

He turned at the sound of voices and sank into a
chair. To have been caught thus gazing at himself
would have jarred on his sense of what was right.

It was twenty minutes past seven, when, in evening
dress, he left the club, and took a shillingsworth to
Buckingham Gate. Here he dismissed his cab, and
turned up the large fur collar of his coat. Between the
brim of his opera-hat and the edge of that collar nothing

but his eyes were visible. He waited, compressing his lips, scrutinizing each hansom that went by. In the soft glow of one coming fast he saw a hand raised to the trap. The cab stopped; George stepped out of the shadow and got in. The cab went on, and Mrs. Bellew's arm was pressed against his own.

It was their simple formula for arriving at a restaurant together.

In the third of several little rooms, where the lights were shaded, they sat down at a table in a corner, facing each a wall, and, underneath, her shoe stole out along the floor and touched his patent-leather boot. In their eyes, for all their would-be wariness, a light smouldered which would not be put out. An habitué, sipping claret at a table across the little room, watched them in a mirror, and there came into his old heart a glow of warmth, half ache, half sympathy; a smile of understanding stirred the crow's-feet round his eyes. Its sweetness ebbed, and left a little grin about his shaven lips. Behind the archway in the neighbouring room two waiters met, and in their nods and glances was that same unconscious sympathy, the same conscious grin. And the old habitué thought:

'How long will it last?' . . . 'Waiter, some coffee and my bill!'

He had meant to go to the play, but he lingered instead to look at Mrs. Bellew's white shoulders and bright eyes in the kindly mirror. And he thought:

'Young days at present. Ah, young days!' . . . 'Waiter, a Benedictine!' And hearing her laugh, his old heart ached. 'No one,' he thought, 'will ever laugh like that for me again!' . . . 'Here, waiter, how's this? You've charged me for an ice!' But when the waiter had gone he glanced back into the mirror, and saw them clink their glasses filled with golden bubbling wine, and he thought: 'Wish you good luck! For a flash of those teeth, my dear, I'd give——'

But his eyes fell on the paper flowers adorning his little table—yellow and red and green; hard, lifeless, tawdry. He saw them suddenly as they were, with the dregs of wine in his glass, the spill of gravy on the cloth, the ruin of the nuts that he had eaten. Wheezing and coughing, 'This place is not what it was,' he thought; 'I shan't come here again!'

He struggled into his coat to go, but he looked once more in the mirror, and met their eyes resting on himself. In them he read the careless pity of the young for the old. His eyes answered the reflection of their eyes. 'Wait, wait! It is young days yet! I wish you no harm, my dears!' and limping—for one of his legs was lame—he went away.

But George and his partner sat on, and with every glass of wine the light in their eyes grew brighter. For who was there now in the room to mind? Not a living soul! Only a tall, dark young waiter, a little cross-eyed, who was in consumption; only the little wine-waiter, with a pallid face, and a look as if he suffered. And the whole world seemed of the colour of the wine they had been drinking; but they talked of indifferent things, and only their eyes, bemused and shining, really spoke. The dark young waiter stood apart, unmoving, and his cross-eyed glance, fixed on her shoulders, had all unconsciously the longing of a saint in some holy picture. Unseen, behind the serving screen, the little wine-waiter poured out and drank a glass from a derelict bottle. Through a chink of the red blinds an eye peered in from the chill outside, staring and curious, till its owner passed on in the cold.

It was long after nine when they rose. The dark young waiter laid her cloak upon her with adoring hands. She looked back at him, and in her eyes was an infinite indulgence. 'God knows,' she seemed to say, 'if I could make you happy as well, I would. Why should one suffer? Life is strong and good!'

The young waiter's cross-eyed glance fell before her and he bowed above the money in his hand. Quickly, before them the little wine-waiter hurried to the door, his suffering face screwed into one long smile.

'Good night, madam; good night, sir. Thank you very much!'

And he, too, remained bowed over his hand, and his smile relaxed.

But in the cab George's arm stole round her underneath the cloak, and they were borne on in the stream of hurrying hansoms, carrying couples like themselves, cut off from all but each other's eyes, from all but each other's touch; and with their eyes turned in the half-dark they spoke together in low tones.

PART II

CHAPTER I

GREGORY REOPENS THE CAMPAIGN

At one end of the walled garden which Mr. Pendyce had formed in imitation of that at dear old Strathbegally, was a virgin orchard of pear and cherry trees. They blossomed early, and by the end of the third week in April the last of the cherries had broken into flower. In the long grass, underneath, a wealth of daffodils, jonquils, and narcissi came up year after year, and sunned their yellow stars in the light which dappled through the blossom.

And here Mrs. Pendyce would come, tan gauntlets on her hands, and stand, her face a little flushed with stooping, as though the sight of all that bloom was restful. It was due to her that these old trees escaped year after year the pruning and improvements which the genius of the squire would otherwise have applied. She had been brought up in an old Totteridge tradition that fruit trees should be left to themselves, while her husband, possessed of a grasp of the subject not more than usually behind the times, was all for newer methods. She had fought for those trees. They were as yet the only things she *had* fought for in her married life, and Horace Pendyce still remembered with a discomfort robbed by time of poignancy how she had stood with her back to their bedroom door and said: 'If you cut those poor trees, Horace, I won't live here!' He had at once expressed his determination to have them pruned; but, having put off the action for a day or two, the trees still stood unpruned thirty-three years later. He had even come to feel rather proud of the fact that they continued to bear fruit, and would speak of them thus: 'Queer fancy of my wife's, never been cut. And yet, remarkable thing, they do better than any of the others!'

This spring, when all was so forward, and the cuckoos already in full song, when the scent of young larches in the New Plantation (planted the year of George's birth) was in the air like the perfume of celestial lemons, she came to the orchard more than usual, and her spirit felt the stirring, the old, half-painful yearning for she knew not what, that she had felt so often in her first years at Worsted Skeynes. And sitting there on a green-painted seat under the largest of the cherry trees, she thought even more than her wont of George, as though her son's spirit, vibrating in its first real passion, were calling to her for sympathy.

He had been down so little all that winter, twice for a couple of days' shooting, once for a week-end, when she had thought him looking thinner and rather worn. He had missed Christmas for the first time. With infinite precaution she had asked him casually if he had seen Helen Bellew, and he had answered: 'Oh, yes, I see her once in a way!'

Secretly all through the winter she consulted *The Times* newspaper for mention of George's horse, and was disappointed not to find any. One day, however, in February, discovering him absolutely at the head of several lists of horses with figures after them, she wrote off at once with a joyful heart. Of five lists in which the Ambler's name appeared, there was only one in which he was second. George's answer came in the course of a week or so.

'MY DEAR MOTHER,

'What you saw were the weights for the Spring Handicaps. They've simply done me out of everything. In great haste,

'Your affectionate son,

'GEORGE PENDYCE.'

As the spring approached, the vision of her independent visit to London, which had sustained her throughout the winter, having performed its annual function, grew mistier and mistier, and at last faded away. She ceased even to dream of it, as though it had never been, nor did George remind her, and as usual, she ceased even to wonder whether he would remind her. She thought instead of the season visit, and its scurry of parties, with a sort of languid fluttering. For Worsted Skeynes, and all that Worsted Skeynes stood for, was like a heavy horseman guiding her with iron hands along the narrow lane; she dreamed of throwing him in the open, but the open she never reached.

She woke at seven with her tea, and from seven to eight made little notes on tablets, while on his back Mr. Pendyce snored lightly. She rose at eight. At nine she poured out coffee. From half-past nine to ten she attended to the housekeeper and her birds. From ten to eleven she attended to the gardener and her dress. From eleven to twelve she wrote invitations to persons for whom she did not care, and acceptances to persons who did not care for her; she drew out also and placed in due sequence cheques for Mr. Pendyce's signature; and secured receipts, carefully docketed on the back, within an elastic band; as a rule, also, she received a visit from Mrs. Hussell Barter. From

twelve to one she walked with her and 'the dear dogs'
to the village, where she stood hesitatingly in the
cottage doors of persons who were shy of her. From
half-past one to two she lunched. From two to three
she rested on a sofa in the white morning-room with the
newspaper in her hand, trying to read the Parliamentary
debate, and thinking of other things. From three to
half-past four she went to her dear flowers, from whom
she was liable to be summoned at any moment by the
arrival of callers; or, getting into the carriage, was
driven to some neighbour's mansion, where she sat for
half an hour and came away. At half-past four she
poured out tea. At five she knitted a tie, or socks,
for George or Gerald, and listened with a gentle smile
to what was going on. From six to seven she received
from the squire his impressions of Parliament and things
at large. From seven to seven-thirty she changed to a
black low dress, with old lace about the neck. At
seven-thirty she dined. At a quarter to nine she
listened to Norah playing two waltzes of Chopin's,
and a piece called *Sérénade du Printemps* by Baff, and
to Bee singing *The Mikado*, or the *Saucy Girl*. From
nine to ten-thirty she played a game called piquet,
which her father had taught her, if she could get any
one with whom to play; but as this was seldom, she
played as a rule patience by herself. At ten-thirty
she went to bed. At eleven-thirty punctually the
squire woke her. At one o'clock she went to sleep.
On Mondays she wrote out in her clear Totteridge
hand, with its fine straight strokes, a list of library
books, made up without distinction of all that were
recommended in the *Ladies' Paper* that came weekly
to Worsted Skeynes. Periodically Mr. Pendyce would
hand her a list of his own, compiled out of *The Times*

and the *Field* in the privacy of his study; this she sent too.

Thus was the household supplied with literature unerringly adapted to its needs; nor was it possible for any undesirable book to find its way into the house —not that this would have mattered much to Mrs. Pendyce, for as she often said with gentle regret: 'My dear, I have no time to read.'

This afternoon it was so warm that the bees were all around among the blossoms, and two thrushes, who had built in a yew tree that watched over the Scotch garden, were in a violent flutter because one of their chicks had fallen out of the nest. The mother bird, at the edge of the long orchard grass, was silent, trying by example to still the tiny creature's cheeping, lest it might attract some large or human thing.

Mrs. Pendyce, sitting under the oldest cherry tree, looked for the sound, and when she had located it, picked up the baby bird, and, as she knew the whereabouts of all the nests, put it back into its cradle, to the loud terror and grief of the parent birds. She went back to the bench and sat down again.

She had in her soul something of the terror of the mother thrush. The Maldens had been paying the call that preceded their annual migration to town, and the peculiar glow which Lady Malden had the power of raising had not yet left her cheeks. True, she had the comfort of the thought, 'Ellen Malden is so bourgeoise,' but to-day it did not still her heart.

Accompanied by one pale daughter who never left her, and two pale dogs forced to run all the way, now lying under the carriage with their tongues out, Lady Malden had come and stayed full time; and for three-quarters of that time she had seemed, as it were, labouring under a sense of duty unfulfilled; for the remaining quarter Mrs. Pendyce had laboured under a sense of duty fulfilled.

'My dear,' Lady Malden had said, having told the pale daughter to go into the conservatory, 'I'm the last person in the world to repeat gossip, as you know; but I think it's only right to tell you that I've been hearing things. You see, my boy Fred' (who would ultimately become Sir Frederick Malden) 'belongs to the same club as your son George—the Stoics. All young men belong there of course—I mean, if they're anybody. I'm sorry to say there's no doubt about it; your son has been seen dining at—perhaps I ought not to mention the name—Blafard's, with Mrs. Bellew. I dare say you don't know what sort of a place Blafard's is—a lot of little rooms where people go when they don't want to be seen. I've never been there, of course; but I can imagine it perfectly. And not once, but frequently. I thought I would speak to you, because I do think it's so scandalous of her in her position.'

An azalea in a blue and white pot had stood between them, and in this plant Mrs. Pendyce buried her cheeks and eyes; but when she raised her face her eyebrows were lifted to their utmost limit, her lips trembled with anger.

'Oh,' she said, 'didn't you know? There's nothing in that; it's the latest thing!'

For a moment Lady Malden wavered, then duskily flushed; her temperament and principles had recovered themselves.

'If that,' she said with some dignity, 'is the latest thing, I think it is quite time we were back in town.'

She rose, and as she rose, such was her unfortunate

conformation, it flashed through Mrs. Pendyce's mind:
'Why was I afraid? She's only——' And then as
quickly: 'Poor woman! how can she help her legs
being short?'

But when she was gone, side by side with the pale
daughter, the pale dogs once more running behind
the carriage, Margery Pendyce put her hand to her
heart.

And out here amongst the bees and blossom, where
the blackbirds were improving each minute their new
songs, and the air was so fainting sweet with scents,
her heart would not be stilled, but throbbed as though
danger were coming on herself; and she saw her son as
a little boy again in a dirty holland suit with a straw
hat down the back of his neck, flushed and sturdy as he
came to her from some adventure.

And suddenly a gush of emotion from deep within
her heart and the heart of the spring day, a sense of
being severed from him by a great, remorseless power,
came over her; and taking out a tiny embroidered
handkerchief, she wept. Round her the bees hummed
carelessly, the blossom dropped, the dappled sunlight
covered her with a pattern as of her own fine lace.
From the home farm came the lowing of the cows on
their way to milking, and, strange sound in that well-
ordered home, a distant piping on a penny flute. . . .

'Mother, mother, mo-o-ther!'

Mrs. Pendyce passed her handkerchief across her
eyes, and instinctively obeying the laws of breeding, her
face lost all trace of its emotion. She waited, crumpling
the tiny handkerchief in her gauntleted hand.

'Mother! Oh, there you are! Here's Gregory
Vigil!'

Norah, a fox-terrier on either side, was coming down

the path; behind her, unhatted, showed Gregory's
sanguine face between his wings of grizzled hair.

'I suppose you're going to talk. I'm going over to
the rectory. Ta-ta!'

And preceded by her dogs, Norah went on.

Mrs. Pendyce put out her hand.

'Well, Grig,' she said, 'this is a surprise.'

Gregory seated himself beside her on the bench.

'I've brought you this,' he said. 'I want you to
look at it before I answer.'

Mrs. Pendyce, who vaguely felt that he would want
her to see things as he was seeing them, took a letter
from him with a sinking heart.

'*Private*.
'LINCOLN'S INN FIELDS,
'*21st April* 1892.

'MY DEAR VIGIL,

'I have now secured such evidence as should warrant
our instituting a suit. I've written your ward to that
effect, and am awaiting her instructions. Unfortunately, we have no act of cruelty, and I've been obliged
to draw her attention to the fact that, should her
husband defend the suit, it will be very difficult to
get the Court to accept their separation in the light of
desertion on *his* part—difficult indeed, even if he doesn't
defend the suit. In divorce cases one has to remember
that what has to be kept out is often more important
than what has to be got in, and it would be useful to
know, therefore, whether there is likelihood of opposition. I do not advise any direct approaching of the
husband, but if you are possessed of the information
you might let me know. I hate humbug, my dear
Vigil, and I hate anything underhand, but divorce is

always a dirty business, and while the law is shaped as at present, and the linen washed in public, it will remain impossible for any one, guilty or innocent, and even for us lawyers, to avoid soiling our hands in one way or another. I regret it as much as you do.

'There is a new man writing verse in the *Tertiary*, some of it quite first-rate. You might look at the last number. My blossom this year is magnificent.

'With kind regards, I am,

'Very sincerely yours,

'EDMUND PARAMOR.

'GREGORY VIGIL, ESQ.'

Mrs. Pendyce dropped the letter in her lap, and looked at her cousin.

'He was at Harrow with Horace. I *do* like him. He is one of the very nicest men I know.'

It was clear that she was trying to gain time.

Gregory began pacing up and down.

'Paramor is a man for whom I have the highest respect. I would trust him before any one.'

It was clear that he, too, was trying to gain time.

'Oh, mind my daffodils, *please*!'

Gregory went down on his knees, and raised the bloom that he had trodden on. He then offered it to Mrs. Pendyce. The action was one to which she was so unaccustomed that it struck her as slightly ridiculous.

'My dear Grig, you'll get rheumatism, and spoil that nice suit; the grass comes off so terribly!'

Gregory got up, and looked shamefacedly at his knees.

'The knee is not what it used to be,' he said.

Mrs. Pendyce smiled.

'You should keep your knees for Helen Bellew, Grig. I was always five years older than you.'

Gregory rumpled up his hair.

'Kneeling's out of fashion, but I thought in the country you wouldn't mind!'

'You don't notice things, dear Grig. In the country it's still more out of fashion. You wouldn't find a woman within thirty miles of here who would like a man to kneel to her. We've lost the habit. She would think she was being made fun of. We soon grow out of vanity!'

'In London,' said Gregory, 'I hear all women intend to be men; but in the country I thought——'

'In the country, Grig, all women would like to be men, but they don't dare to try. They trot behind.'

As if she had been guilty of thoughts too insightful, Mrs. Pendyce blushed.

Gregory broke out suddenly:

'I can't bear to think of women like that!'

Again Mrs. Pendyce smiled.

'You see, Grig dear, you are not married.'

'I detest the idea that marriage changes our views, Margery; I loathe it.'

'Mind my daffodils!' murmured Mrs. Pendyce.

She was thinking all the time: 'That dreadful letter! What am I to do?'

And as though he knew her thoughts, Gregory said:

'I shall assume that Bellew will not defend the case. If he has a spark of chivalry in him he will be only too glad to see her free. I will never believe that any man could be such a soulless clod as to wish to keep her bound. I don't pretend to understand the law, but it seems to me that there's only one way for a man to act— and after all Bellew's a gentleman. You'll see that he will act like one!'

Mrs. Pendyce looked at the daffodil in her lap.

'I have only seen him three or four times, but it seemed to me, Grig, that he was a man who might act in one way to-day and another to-morrow. He is so very different from all the men about here.'

'When it comes to the deep things of life,' said Gregory, 'one man is much as another. Is there any man you know who would be so lacking in chivalry as to refuse in these circumstances?'

Mrs. Pendyce looked at him with a confused expression—wonder, admiration, irony, and even fear struggled in her eyes.

'I can think of dozens.'

Gregory clutched his forehead.

'Margery,' he said, 'I hate your cynicism. I don't know where you get it from.'

'I'm so sorry; I didn't mean to be cynical—I didn't, really. I only spoke from what I've seen.'

'Seen?' said Gregory. 'If I were to go by what I saw daily, hourly, in London in the course of my work I should commit suicide within a week.'

'But what else can one go by?'

Without answering, Gregory walked to the edge of the orchard, and stood gazing over the Scotch garden, with his face a little tilted towards the sky. Mrs. Pendyce felt he was grieving that she failed to see whatever it was he saw up there, and she was sorry. He came back, and said:

'We won't discuss it any more.'

Very dubiously she heard those words, but as she could not express the anxiety and doubt torturing her soul, she told him tea was ready. But Gregory would not come in just yet out of the sun.

In the drawing-room Beatrix was already giving tea to young Tharp and the Reverend Hussell Barter. And the sound of these well-known voices restored to Mrs. Pendyce something of her tranquillity. The rector came towards her at once with a tea-cup in his hand.

'My wife has got a headache,' he said. 'She wanted to come over with me, but I made her lie down. Nothing like lying down for a headache. We expect it in June, you know. Let me get you your tea.'

Mrs. Pendyce, already aware even to the day of what he expected in June, sat down, and looked at Mr. Barter with a slight feeling of surprise. He was really a very good fellow; it was nice of him to make his wife lie down! She thought his broad, red-brown face, with its projecting, not unhumorous, lower lip, looked very friendly. Roy, the Skye terrier at her feet, was smelling at the reverend gentleman's legs with a slow movement of his tail.

'The old dog likes me,' said the rector; 'they know a dog-lover when they see one—wonderful creatures, dogs! I'm sometimes tempted to think they may have souls!'

Mrs. Pendyce answered:

'Horace says he's getting too old.'

The dog looked up in her face, and her lip quivered. The rector laughed.

'Don't you worry about that; there's plenty of life in *him*.' And he added unexpectedly: 'I couldn't bear to put a dog away, the friend of man. No, no; let Nature see to that.'

Over at the piano Bee and young Tharp were turning the pages of the *Saucy Girl*; the room was full of the scent of azaleas; and Mr. Barter, astride of a gilt chair, looked almost sympathetic, gazing tenderly at the old Skye.

Mrs. Pendyce felt a sudden yearning to free her mind, a sudden longing to ask a man's advice.

'Oh, Mr. Barter,' she said, 'my cousin, Gregory Vigil, has just brought me some news; it is confidential, please. Helen Bellew is going to sue for a divorce. I wanted to ask you whether you could tell me——' Looking in the rector's face, she stopped.

'A divorce! H'm! Really!'

A chill of terror came over Mrs. Pendyce.

'Of course you will not mention it to any one, not even to Horace. It has nothing to do with us.'

Mr. Barter bowed; his face wore the expression it so often wore in school on Sunday mornings.

'H'm!' he said again.

It flashed through Mrs. Pendyce that this man with the heavy jowl and menacing eyes, who sat so square on that flimsy chair, knew something. It was as though he had answered:

'This is not a matter for women; you will be good enough to leave it to me.'

With the exception of those few words of Lady Malden's, and the recollection of George's face when he had said, 'Oh, yes, I see her now and then,' she had no evidence, no knowledge, nothing to go on; but she knew from some instinctive source that her son was Mrs. Bellew's lover.

So, with terror and a strange hope, she saw Gregory entering the room.

'Perhaps,' she thought, 'he will make Grig stop it.'

She poured out Gregory's tea, followed Bee and Cecil Tharp into the conservatory, and left the two men together.

CHAPTER II

To understand and sympathize with the feelings and
action of the Rector of Worsted Skeynes, one must
consider his origin and the circumstances of his life.

The second son of an old Suffolk family, he had
followed the routine of his house, and having passed
at Oxford through certain examinations, had been
certificated at the age of twenty-four as a man fitted to
impart to persons of both sexes rules of life and conduct
after which they had been groping for twice or thrice
that number of years. His character, never at any
time undecided, was by this fortunate circumstance
crystallized and rendered immune from the necessity
for self-search and spiritual struggle incidental to his
neighbours. Since he was a man neither below nor
above the average, it did not occur to him to criticize or
place himself in opposition to a system which had gone
on so long and was about to do him so much good.
Like all average men, he was a believer in authority,
and none the less because authority placed a large
portion of itself in his hands. It would, indeed, have
been unwarrantable to expect a man of his birth,
breeding, and education to question the machine of
which he was himself a wheel.

He had dropped, therefore, at the age of twenty-six,
insensibly, on the death of an uncle, into the family

living at Worsted Skeynes. He had been there ever
since. It was a constant and natural grief to him that
on his death the living would go neither to his eldest
nor his second son, but to the second son of his elder
brother, the squire. At the age of twenty-seven he had
married Miss Rose Twining, the fifth daughter of a
Huntingdonshire parson, and in less than eighteen
years begotten ten children, and was expecting the
eleventh, all healthy and hearty like himself. A family
group hung over the fire-place in the study, under the
framed and illuminated text, 'Judge not, that ye be
not judged,' which he had chosen as his motto in the
first year of his cure, and never seen any reason to
change. In that family group Mr. Barter sat in the
centre with his dog between his legs; his wife stood
behind him, and on both sides the children spread out
like the wings of a fan or butterfly. The bills of their
schooling were beginning to weigh rather heavily, and
he complained a good deal; but in principle he still
approved of the habit into which he had got, and his
wife never complained of anything.

The study was furnished with studious simplicity;
many a boy had been, not unkindly, caned there, and
in one place the old Turkey carpet was rotted away,
but whether by their tears or by their knees, not even
Mr. Barter knew. In a cabinet on one side of the fire
he kept all his religious books, many of them well worn;
in a cabinet on the other side he kept his bats, to which
he was constantly attending; a fishing-rod and a gun-
case stood modestly in a corner. The archway between
the drawers of his writing-table held a mat for his
bulldog, a prize animal, wont to lie there and guard his
master's legs when he was writing his sermons. Like
those of his dog, the rector's good points were the old

English virtues of obstinacy, courage, intolerance, and humour; his bad points, owing to the circumstances of his life, had never been brought to his notice.

When, therefore, he found himself alone with Gregory Vigil, he approached him as one dog will approach another, and came at once to the matter in hand.

'It's some time since I had the pleasure of meeting you, Mr. Vigil,' he said. 'Mrs. Pendyce has been giving me in confidence the news you've brought down. I'm bound to tell you at once that I'm surprised.'

Gregory made a little movement of recoil, as though his delicacy had received a shock.

'Indeed!' he said, with a sort of quivering coldness.

The rector, quick to note opposition, repeated emphatically:

'More than surprised; in fact, I think there must be some mistake.'

'Indeed?' said Gregory again.

A change came over Mr. Barter's face. It had been grave, but was now heavy and threatening.

'I have to say to you,' he said, 'that somehow—somehow, this divorce must be put a stop to.'

Gregory flushed painfully.

'On what grounds? I am not aware that my ward is a parishioner of yours, Mr. Barter, or that if she were——'

The rector closed in on him, his head thrust forward, his lower lip projecting.

'If she were doing her duty,' he said, 'she would be. I'm not considering her—I'm considering her husband; *he* is a parishioner of mine, and I say this divorce must be stopped.'

Gregory retreated no longer.

'On what grounds?' he said again, trembling all over.

'I 've no wish to enter into particulars,' said Mr. Barter, 'but if you force me to, I shall not hesitate.'

'I regret that I must,' answered Gregory.

'Without mentioning names, then, I say that she is not a fit person to bring a suit for divorce!'

'You say that?' said Gregory. 'You——'

He could not go on.

'You will not move me, Mr. Vigil,' said the rector, with a grim little smile. 'I have my duty to do.'

Gregory recovered possession of himself with an effort.

'You have said that which no one but a clergyman could say with impunity,' he said freezingly. 'Be so good as to explain yourself.'

'My explanation,' said Mr. Barter, 'is what I have seen with my own eyes.'

He raised those eyes to Gregory. Their pupils were contracted to pin-points, the light-grey irises around had a sort of swimming glitter, and round these again the whites were injected with blood.

'If you must know, with my own eyes I 've seen her in that very conservatory over there kissing a man.'

Gregory threw up his hand.

'How dare you!' he whispered.

Again Mr. Barter's humorous under-lip shot out.

'I dare a good deal more than that, Mr. Vigil,' he said, 'as you will find; and I say this to you—stop this divorce, or I 'll stop it myself!'

Gregory turned to the window. When he came back he was outwardly calm.

'You have been guilty of indelicacy,' he said. 'Continue in your delusion, think what you like, do what you like. The matter will go on. Good evening, sir.'

And turning on his heel, he left the room.

Mr. Barter stepped forward. The words, 'You have been guilty of indelicacy,' whirled round his brain till every blood-vessel in his face and neck was swollen to bursting, and with a hoarse sound like that of an animal in pain he pursued Gregory to the door. It was shut in his face. And since on taking Orders he had abandoned for ever the use of bad language, he was very near an apoplectic fit. Suddenly he became aware that Mrs. Pendyce was looking at him from the conservatory door. Her face was painfully white, her eyebrows lifted, and before that look Mr. Barter recovered a measure of self-possession.

'Is anything the matter, Mr. Barter?'

The rector smiled grimly.

'Nothing, nothing,' he said. 'I must ask you to excuse me, that's all. I've a parish matter to attend to.'

When he found himself in the drive, the feeling of vertigo and suffocation passed, but left him unrelieved. He had, in fact, happened on one of those psychological moments which enable a man's true nature to show itself. Accustomed to say of himself bluffly, 'Yes, yes; I've a hot temper, soon over,' he had never, owing to the autocracy of his position, had a chance of knowing the tenacity of his soul. So accustomed and so able for many years to vent displeasure at once, he did not himself know the wealth of his old English spirit, did not know of what an ugly grip he was capable. He did not even know it at this minute, conscious only of a sort of black wonder at this monstrous conduct to a man in his position, doing his simple duty. The more he reflected, the more intolerable did it seem that a woman like this Mrs. Bellew should have the impudence to invoke the law of the land in her favour— a woman who was no better than a common baggage

—a woman he had seen kissing George Pendyce. To
have suggested to Mr. Barter that there was something
pathetic in this black wonder of his, pathetic in the
spectacle of his little soul delivering its little judgments,
stumbling its little way along with such blind certainty
under the huge heavens, amongst millions of organisms
as important as itself, would have astounded him; and
with every step he took the blacker became his wonder,
the more fixed his determination to permit no such abuse
of morality, no such disregard of Hussell Barter.

'You have been guilty of indelicacy!' This indict-
ment had a wriggling sting, and lost no venom from
the fact that he could in no wise have perceived where
the indelicacy of his conduct lay. But he did not try
to perceive it. Against himself, clergyman and gentleman, the monstrosity of the charge was clear. This
was a point of morality. He felt no anger against
George; it was the woman that excited his just wrath.
For so long he had been absolute among women, with
the power, as it were, over them of life and death.
This was flat immorality! He had never approved of
her leaving her husband; he had never approved of her
at all! He turned his steps towards the Firs.

From above the hedges the sleepy cows looked down;
a yaffle laughed a field or two away; in the sycamores,
which had come out before their time, the bees hummed.
Under the smile of the spring the innumerable life of
the fields went carelessly on around that square black
figure ploughing along the lane with head bent down
under a wide-brimmed hat.

George Pendyce, in a fly drawn by an old grey horse,
the only vehicle that frequented the station at Worsted
Skeynes, passed him in the lane, and leaned back to
avoid observation. He had not forgotten the tone of

the rector's voice in the smoking-room on the night of
the dance. George was a man who could remember
as well as another. In the corner of the old fly, that
rattled and smelled of stables and stale tobacco, he
fixed his moody eyes on the driver's back and the ears
of the old grey horse, and never stirred till they set
him down at the hall door.

He went at once to his room, sending word that he
had come for the night. His mother heard the news
with feelings of joy and dread, and she dressed quickly
for dinner that she might see him the sooner. The
squire came into her room just as she was going down.
He had been engaged all day at Sessions, and was in
one of the moods of apprehension as to the future
which but seldom came over him.

'Why didn't you keep Vigil to dinner?' he said. 'I
could have given him things for the night. I wanted
to talk to him about insuring my life; he knows about
that. There'll be a lot of money wanted, to pay my
death-duties. And if the Radicals get in I shouldn't
be surprised if they put them up fifty per cent.'

'I wanted to keep him,' said Mrs. Pendyce, 'but he
went away without saying good-bye.'

'He's an odd fellow!'

For some moments Mr. Pendyce made reflections on
this breach of manners. He had a nice standard of
conduct in all social affairs.

'I'm having trouble with that man Peacock again.
He's the most pig-headed—— What are you in such
a hurry for, Margery?'

'George is here!'

'George? Well, I suppose he can wait till dinner.
I have a lot of things I want to tell you about. We had
a case of arson to-day. Old Quarryman was away, and

I was in the chair. It was that fellow Woodford that we convicted for poaching—a very gross case. And this is what he does when he comes out. They tried to prove insanity. It's the rankest case of revenge that ever came before me. We committed him, of course. He'll get a swingeing sentence. Of all dreadful crimes, arson is the most——'

Mr. Pendyce could find no word to characterize his opinion of this offence, and drawing his breath between his teeth, passed into his dressing-room. Mrs. Pendyce hastened quietly out, and went to her son's room. She found George in his shirt-sleeves, inserting the links of his cuffs.

'Let me do that for you, my dear boy! How dreadfully they starch your cuffs! It *is* so nice to do something for you sometimes!'

George answered her:

'Well, mother, and how have you been?'

Over Mrs. Pendyce's face came a look half sorrowful, half arch, but wholly pathetic. 'What! is it beginning already? Oh, don't put me away from you!' she seemed to say.

'Very well, thank you, dear. And you?'

George did not meet her eyes.

'So-so,' he said. 'I took rather a nasty knock over the "City" last week.'

'Is that a race?' asked Mrs. Pendyce.

And by some secret process she knew that he had hurried out that piece of bad news to divert her attention from another subject, for George had never been a 'cry-baby.'

She sat down on the edge of the sofa, and though the gong was about to sound, incited him to dawdle and stay with her.

'And have you any other news, dear? It seems such an age since we 've seen you. I think I 've told you all our budget in my letters. You know there 's going to be another event at the rectory?'

'Another? I passed Barter on the way up. I thought he looked a bit blue.'

A look of pain shot into Mrs. Pendyce's eyes.

'Oh, I 'm afraid that couldn't have been the reason, dear.' And she stopped, but to still her own fears hurried on again. 'If I 'd known you 'd been coming, I 'd have kept Cecil Tharp. Vic has had such dear little puppies. Would you like one? They 've all got that nice black smudge round the eye.'

She was watching him as only a mother can watch— stealthily, minutely, longingly, every little movement, every little change of his face, and more than all, that fixed something behind which showed the abiding temper and condition of his heart.

'Something is making him unhappy,' she thought. 'He is changed since I saw him last, and I can't get at it. I seem to be so far from him—so far!'

And somehow she knew he had come down this evening because he was lonely and unhappy, and instinct had made him turn to her.

But she knew that trying to get nearer would only make him put her further off, and she could not bear this, so she asked him nothing, and bent all her strength on hiding from him the pain she felt.

She went downstairs with her arm in his, and leaned very heavily on it, as though again trying to get close to him, and forget the feeling she had had all that winter—the feeling of being barred away, the feeling of secrecy and restraint.

Mr. Pendyce and the two girls were in the drawing-room.

'Well, George,' said the squire dryly, 'I'm glad you've come. How you can stick in London at this time of year! Now you're down you'd better stay a couple of days. I want to take you round the estate; you know nothing about anything. I might die at any moment, for all you can tell. Just make up your mind to stay.'

George gave him a moody look.

'Sorry,' he said; 'I've got an engagement in town.'

Mr. Pendyce rose and stood with his back to the fire.

'That's it,' he said: 'I ask you to do a simple thing for your own good—and—you've got an engagement. It's always like that, and your mother backs you up. Bee, go and play me something.'

The squire could not bear being played to, but it was the only command likely to be obeyed that came into his head.

The absence of guests made little difference to a ceremony esteemed at Worsted Skeynes the crowning blessing of the day. The courses, however, were limited to seven, and champagne was not drunk. The squire drank a glass or so of claret, for, as he said: 'My dear old father took his bottle of port every night of his life, and it never gave him a twinge. If I were to go on at that rate it would kill me in a year.'

His daughters drank water. Mrs. Pendyce, cherishing a secret preference for champagne, drank sparingly of a Spanish burgundy, procured for her by Mr. Pendyce at a very reasonable price, and corked between meals with a special cork. She offered it to George.

'Try some of my burgundy, dear; it's so nice.'

But George refused and asked for whisky-and-soda,

glancing at the butler, who brought it in a very yellow
state.

Under the influence of dinner the squire recovered
equanimity, though he still dwelt somewhat sadly on
the future.

'You young fellows,' he said, with a friendly look
at George, 'are such individualists. You make a
business of enjoying yourselves. With your piquet
and your racing and your billiards and what not, you 'll
be used up before you 're fifty. You don't let your
imaginations work. A green old age ought to be your
ideal, instead of which it seems to be a green youth.
Ha!' Mr. Pendyce looked at his daughters till they
said:

'Oh, father, how *can* you!'

Norah, who had the more character of the two, added:
'Isn't father rather dreadful, mother?'

But Mrs. Pendyce was looking at her son. She had
longed so many evenings to see him sitting there.

'We 'll have a game of piquet to-night, George.'

George looked up and nodded with a glum smile.

On the thick, soft carpet round the table the butler
and second footman moved. The light of the wax
candles fell lustrous and subdued on the silver and
fruit and flowers, on the girls' white necks, on George's
well-coloured face and glossy shirt-front, gleamed in
the jewels on his mother's long white fingers, showed
off the squire's erect and still spruce figure; the air
was languorously sweet with the perfume of azaleas
and narcissus bloom. Bee, with soft eyes, was thinking
of young Tharp, who to-day had told her that he loved
her, and wondering if father would object. Her mother
was thinking of George, stealing timid glances at his
moody face. There was no sound save the tinkle of

forks and the voices of Norah and the squire, talking
of little things. Outside, through the long, opened
windows, was the still, wide country; the full moon,
tinted apricot and figured like a coin, hung above the
cedar trees, and by her light the whispering stretches
of the silent fields lay half enchanted, half asleep, and
all beyond that little ring of moonshine, unfathomed
and unknown, was darkness—a great darkness wrapping
from their eyes the restless world.

CHAPTER III

THE SINISTER NIGHT

ON the day of the big race at Kempton Park, in which the Ambler, starting favourite, was left at the post, George Pendyce had just put his latchkey in the door of the room he had taken near Mrs. Bellew, when a man, stepping quickly from behind, said:

'Mr. George Pendyce, I believe.'

George turned.

'Yes; what do you want?'

The man put into George's hand a long envelope.

'From Messrs. Frost and Tuckett.'

George opened it, and read from the top of a slip of paper:

ADMIRALTY, PROBATE, AND DIVORCE
The humble petition of Jaspar Bellew——

He lifted his eyes, and his look, uncannily impassive, unresenting, unangered, dogged, caused the messenger to drop his gaze as though he had hit a man who was down.

'Thanks. Good night!'

He shut the door, and read the document through. It contained some precise details, and ended in a claim for damages, and George smiled.

Had he received this document three months ago, he would not have taken it thus. Three months ago he would have felt with rage that he was caught. His thoughts would have run thus: 'I have got her into a

mess; I have got myself into a mess. I never thought
this would happen. This is the devil! I must see
someone—I must stop it. There must be a way out.'
Having but little imagination, his thoughts would have
beaten their wings against this cage, and at once he
would have tried to act. But this was not three months
ago, and now——

He lit a cigarette and sat down on the sofa, and the
chief feeling in his heart was a strange hope, a sort of
funereal gladness. He would have to go and see her
at once, that very night; an excuse — no need to
wait in here — to wait — wait on the chance of her
coming.

He got up and drank some whisky, then went back
to the sofa and sat down again.

'If she is not here by eight,' he thought, 'I will go
round.'

Opposite was a full-length mirror, and he turned to
the wall to avoid it. There was fixed on his face a
look of gloomy determination, as though he were
thinking: 'I 'll show them all that I 'm not beaten
yet.'

At the click of a latchkey he scrambled off the sofa,
and his face resumed its mask. She came in as usual,
dropped her opera cloak, and stood before him with
bare shoulders. Looking in her face, he wondered if
she knew.

'I thought I 'd better come,' she said. 'I suppose
you 've had the same charming present?'

George nodded. There was a minute's silence.

'It 's really rather funny. I 'm sorry for you,
George.'

George laughed too, but his laugh was different.

'I will do all I can,' he said.

Mrs. Bellew came close to him.

'I've seen about the Kempton race. What shocking luck! I suppose you've lost a lot. Poor boy! It never rains but it pours.'

George looked down.

'That's all right; nothing matters when I have you.'

He felt her arms fasten behind his neck, but they were cool as marble; he met her eyes, and they were mocking and compassionate.

Their cab, wheeling into the main thoroughfare, joined in the race of cabs flying as for life toward the east—past the Park, where the trees, new-leafed, were swinging their skirts like ballet-dancers in the wind; past the Stoics' and the other clubs, rattling, jingling, jostling for the lead, shooting past omnibuses that looked cosy in the half-light with their lamps and rows of figures solemnly opposed.

At Blafard's the tall dark young waiter took her cloak with reverential fingers; the little wine-waiter smiled below the suffering in his eyes. The same red-shaded lights fell on her arms and shoulders, the same flowers of green and yellow grew bravely in the same blue vases. On the menu were written the same dishes. The same idle eye peered through the chink at the corner of the red blinds with its stare of apathetic wonder.

Often during that dinner George looked at her face by stealth, and its expression baffled him, so careless was it. And, unlike her mood of late, that had been glum and cold, she was in the wildest spirits.

People looked round from the other little tables, all full now that the season had begun, her laugh was so infectious; and George felt a sort of disgust. What was it in this woman that made her laugh, when his

own heart was heavy? But he said nothing; he dared
not even look at her, for fear his eyes should show
his feeling.

'We ought to be squaring our accounts,' he thought
—'looking things in the face. Something must be
done; and here she is laughing and making every one
stare!' Done! But what could be done, when it was
all like quicksand?

The other little tables emptied one by one.

'George,' she said, 'take me somewhere where we
can dance!'

George stared at her.

'My dear girl, how can I? There is no such place!'

'Take me to your Bohemians!'

'You can't possibly go to a place like that.'

'Why not? Who cares where we go, or what we do?'

'I care!'

'Ah, my dear George, you and your sort are only
half alive!'

Sullenly George answered:

'What do you take me for? A cad?'

But there was fear, not anger, in his heart.

'Well, then, let's drive into the East End. For
goodness' sake, let's do something not quite proper!'

They took a hansom and drove east. It was the
first time either had ever been in that unknown land.

'Close your cloak, dear; it looks odd down here.'

Mrs. Bellew laughed.

'You'll be just like your father when you're sixty,
George.'

And she opened her cloak the wider. Round a
barrel-organ at the corner of a street were girls in bright
colours dancing.

She called to the cabman to stop.

'Let 's watch those children!'

'You 'll only make a show of us.'

Mrs. Bellew put her hands on the cab door.

'I 've a good mind to get out and dance with them!'

'You 're mad to-night,' said George. 'Sit still!'

He stretched out his arm and barred her way. The passers-by looked curiously at the little scene. A crowd began to collect.

'Go on!' cried George.

There was a cheer from the crowd; the driver whipped his horse; they darted east again.

It was striking twelve when the cab put them down at last near the old church on Chelsea Embankment, and they had hardly spoken for an hour.

And all that hour George was feeling:

'This is the woman for whom I 've given it all up. This is the woman to whom I shall be tied. This is the woman I cannot tear myself away from. If I could, I would never see her again. But I can't live without her. I must go on suffering when she 's with me, suffering when she 's away from me. And God knows how it 's all to end!'

He took her hand in the darkness; it was cold and unresponsive as a stone. He tried to see her face, but could read nothing in those greenish eyes staring before them, like a cat's, into the darkness.

When the cab was gone they stood looking at each other by the light of a street lamp. And George thought:

'So I must leave her like this, and what then?'

She put her latchkey in the door, and turned round to him. In the silent, empty street, where the wind was rustling and scraping round the corners of tall houses, and the lamplight flickered, her face and figure were so strange, motionless, sphinx-like. Only her eyes seemed alive, fastened on his own.

'Good night!' he muttered.

She beckoned.

'Take what you can of me, George!' she said.

CHAPTER IV

MR. PENDYCE'S HEAD

MR. PENDYCE'S head, seen from behind at his library bureau, where it was his practice to spend most mornings from half-past nine to eleven or even twelve, was observed to be of a shape to throw no small light upon his class and character. Its contour was almost national. Bulging at the back, and sloping rapidly to a thin and wiry neck, narrow between the ears and across the brow, prominent in the jaw, the length of a line drawn from the back headland to the promontory at the chin would have been extreme. Upon the observer there was impressed the conviction that here was a skull denoting, by surplusage of length, great precision of character and disposition to action, and, by deficiency of breadth, a narrow tenacity which might at times amount to wrongheadedness. The thin cantankerous neck, on which little hairs grew low, and the intelligent ears, confirmed this impression; and when his face, with its clipped hair, dry rosiness, into which the east wind had driven a shade of yellow and the sun a shade of brown, and grey, rather discontented eyes, came into view, the observer had no longer any hesitation in saying that he was in the presence of an Englishman, a landed proprietor, and, but for Mr. Pendyce's rooted belief to the contrary, an individualist. His head, indeed, was like nothing so much as the Admiralty Pier at Dover—that strange long narrow thing, with a slight twist or bend at the end, which first disturbs the comfort of foreigners arriving on these shores, and strikes them with a sense of wonder and dismay.

He sat very motionless at his bureau, leaning a little over his papers like a man to whom things do not come too easily; and every now and then he stopped to refer to the calendar at his left hand, or to a paper in one of the many pigeon-holes. Open, and almost out of reach, was a back volume of *Punch*, of which periodical, as a landed proprietor, he had an almost professional knowledge. In leisure moments it was one of his chief recreations to peruse lovingly those aged pictures, and at the image of John Bull he never failed to think: 'Fancy making an Englishman out a fat fellow like that!'

It was as though the artist had offered an insult to himself, passing him over as the type, and conferring that distinction on someone fast going out of fashion. The rector, whenever he heard Mr. Pendyce say this, strenuously opposed him, for he was himself of a square, stout build, and getting stouter.

With all their aspirations to the character of typical Englishmen, Mr. Pendyce and Mr. Barter thought themselves far from the old beef and beer, port and pigskin types of the Georgian and early Victorian era. They were men of the world, abreast of the times, who by virtue of a public school and 'varsity training had acquired a manner, a knowledge of men and affairs, a standard of thought on which it had really never been needful to improve. Both of them, but especially Mr. Pendyce, kept up with all that was going forward by visiting the metropolis six or seven or even eight times a year. On these occasions they rarely took their wives, having almost always important business in hand

—old college, Church, or Conservative dinners, cricket-matches, Church Congress, the Gaiety Theatre, and for Mr. Barter, the Lyceum. Both, too, belonged to clubs—the rector to a comfortable, old-fashioned place where he could get a rubber without gambling, and Mr. Pendyce to the Temple of things as they had been, as became a man who, having turned all social problems over in his mind, had decided that there was no real safety but in the past.

They always went up to London grumbling, but this was necessary, and indeed salutary, because of their wives; and they always came back grumbling, because of their livers, which a good country rest always fortunately reduced in time for the next visit. In this way they kept themselves free from the taint of provincialism.

In the silence of his master's study the spaniel John, whose head, too, was long and narrow, had placed it over his paw, as though suffering from that silence, and when his master cleared his throat he fluttered his tail and turned up an eye with a little moon of white, without stirring his chin.

The clock ticked at the end of the long, narrow room; the sunlight through the long, narrow windows fell on the long, narrow backs of books in the glassed bookcase that took up the whole of one wall; and this room, with its slight leathery smell, seemed a fitting place for some long, narrow ideal to be worked out to its long and narrow ending.

But Mr. Pendyce would have scouted the notion of an ending to ideals having their basis in the hereditary principle.

'Let me do my duty and carry on the estate as my dear old father did, and hand it down to my son enlarged if possible,' was sometimes his saying, very,

very often his thought, not seldom his prayer. 'I want to do no more than that.'

The times were bad and dangerous. There was every chance of a Radical Government being returned, and the country going to the dogs. It was but natural and human that he should pray for the survival of the form of things which he believed in and knew, the form of things bequeathed to him, and embodied in the salutary words 'Horace Pendyce.' It was not his habit to welcome new ideas. A new idea invading the country of the squire's mind was at once met with a rising of the whole population, and either prevented from landing, or if already on shore instantly taken prisoner. In course of time the unhappy creature, causing its squeaks and groans to penetrate the prison walls, would be released from sheer humaneness and love of a quiet life, and even allowed certain privileges, remaining, however, 'that poor, queer devil of a foreigner.' One day, in an inattentive moment, the natives would suffer it to marry, or find that in some disgraceful way it had caused the birth of children unrecognized by law; and their respect for the accomplished fact, for something that already lay in the past, would then prevent their trying to unmarry it, or restoring the children to an unborn state, and very gradually they would tolerate this intrusive brood. Such was the process of Mr. Pendyce's mind. Indeed, like the spaniel John, a dog of conservative instincts, at the approach of any strange thing he placed himself in the way, barking and showing his teeth; and sometimes truly he suffered at the thought that one day Horace Pendyce would no longer be there to bark. But not often, for he had not much imagination.

All the morning he had been working at that old

vexed subject of Common Rights on Worsted Scotton, which his father had fenced in and taught him once for all to believe was part integral of Worsted Skeynes. The matter was almost beyond doubt, for the cottagers—in a poor way at the time of the fencing, owing to the price of bread—had looked on apathetically till the very last year required by law to give the old squire squatter's rights, when all of a sudden that man, Peacock's father, had made a gap in the fence and driven in beasts, which had reopened the whole unfortunate question. This had been in '65, and ever since there had been continual friction bordering on a lawsuit. Mr. Pendyce never for a moment allowed it to escape his mind that the man Peacock was at the bottom of it all; for it was his way to discredit all principles as ground of action, and to refer everything to facts and persons; except, indeed, when he acted himself, when he would somewhat proudly admit that it was on principle. He never thought or spoke on an abstract question; partly because his father had avoided them before him, partly because he had been discouraged from doing so at school, but mainly because he temperamentally took no interest in such unpractical things.

It was, therefore, a source of wonder to him that tenants of his own should be ungrateful. He did his duty by them, as the rector, in whose keeping were their souls, would have been the first to affirm; the books of his estate showed this, recording year by year an average gross profit of some sixteen hundred pounds, and (deducting raw material incidental to the upkeep of Worsted Skeynes) a net loss of three.

In less earthly matters, too, such as non-attendance at church, a predisposition to poaching, or any inclination to moral laxity, he could say with a clear conscience that the rector was sure of his support. A striking instance had occurred within the last month, when, discovering that his underkeeper, an excellent man at his work, had got into a scrape with the postman's wife, he had given the young fellow notice, and cancelled the lease of his cottage.

He rose and went to the plan of the estate fastened to the wall, which he unrolled by pulling a green silk cord, and stood there scrutinizing it carefully and placing his finger here and there. His spaniel rose too, and settled himself unobtrusively on his master's foot. Mr. Pendyce moved and trod on him. The spaniel yelped.

'D——n the dog! Oh, poor fellow, John!' said Mr. Pendyce. He went back to his seat, but since he had identified the wrong spot he was obliged in a minute to return again to the plan. The spaniel John, cherishing the hope that he had been justly treated, approached in a half-circle, fluttering his tail; he had scarcely reached Mr. Pendyce's foot when the door was opened, and the first footman brought in a letter on a silver salver.

Mr. Pendyce took the note, read it, turned to his bureau, and said: 'No answer.'

He sat staring at this document in the silent room, and over his face in turn passed anger, alarm, distrust, bewilderment. He had not the power of making very clear his thought, except by speaking aloud, and he muttered to himself. The spaniel John, who still nurtured a belief that he had sinned, came and lay down very close against his leg.

Mr. Pendyce, never having reflected profoundly on the working morality of his times, had the less difficulty in accepting it. Of violating it he had practically no opportunity, and this rendered his position stronger. It was from habit and tradition rather than from

principle and conviction that he was a man of good
moral character.

And as he sat reading this note over and over, he
suffered from a sense of nausea.

It was couched in these terms:

'THE FIRS,
'*20th May*.

'DEAR SIR,

'You may or may not have heard that I have made
your son, Mr. George Pendyce, co-respondent in a
divorce suit against my wife. Neither for your sake nor
your son's, but for the sake of Mrs. Pendyce, who is the
only woman in these parts that I respect, I will withdraw
the suit if your son will give his word not to see my
wife again.

'Please send me an early answer.

'I am,
'Your obedient servant,
'JASPAR BELLEW.'

The acceptance of tradition (and to accept it was
suitable to the squire's temperament) is occasionally
marred by the impingement of tradition on private
life and comfort. It was legendary in his class that
young men's peccadilloes must be accepted with a
certain indulgence. They would, he said, be young
men. They must, he would remark, sow their wild
oats. Such was his theory. The only difficulty he now
had was in applying it to his own particular case, a
difficulty felt by others in times past, and to be felt
again in times to come. But, since he was not a philo-
sopher, he did not perceive the inconsistency between
his theory and his dismay. He saw his universe reeling
before that note, and he was not a man to suffer tamely;

he felt that others ought to suffer too. It was monstrous
that a fellow like this Bellew, a loose fish, a drunkard,
a man who had nearly run over him, should have it
in his power to trouble the serenity of Worsted Skeynes.
It was like his impudence to bring such a charge against
his son. It was like his d——d impudence! And going
abruptly to the bell, he trod on his spaniel's ear.

'D——n the dog! Oh, poor fellow, John!' But
the spaniel John, convinced at last that he had sinned,
hid himself in a far corner whence he could see nothing,
and pressed his chin closely to the ground.

'Ask your mistress to come here.'

Standing by the hearth, waiting for his wife, the
squire displayed to greater advantage than ever the
shape of his long and narrow head; his neck had grown
conspicuously redder; his eyes, like those of an offended
swan, stabbed, as it were, at everything they saw.

It was not seldom that Mrs. Pendyce was summoned
to the study to hear him say: 'I want to ask your advice.
So-and-so has done such and such . . . I have made up
my mind.'

She came, therefore, in a few minutes. In compliance
with his 'Look at that, Margery,' she read the note,
and gazed at him with distress in her eyes, and he looked
back at her with wrath in his. For this was tragedy.

Not to every one is it given to take a wide view of
things—to look over the far, pale streams, the purple
heather, and moonlit pools of the wild marches, where
reeds stand black against the sundown, and from long
distance comes the cry of a curlew—nor to every one to
gaze from steep cliffs over the wine-dark, shadowy sea
—or from high mountain-sides to see crowned chaos,
smoking with mist, or gold-bright in the sun.

To most it is given to watch assiduously a row of

houses, a back-yard, or, like Mrs. and Mr. Pendyce, the
green fields, trim coverts, and Scotch garden of Worsted
Skeynes. And on that horizon the citation of their
eldest son to appear in the Divorce Court loomed like
a cloud, heavy with destruction.

So far as such an event could be realized—imagination
at Worsted Skeynes was not too vivid—it spelled ruin
to an harmonious edifice of ideas and prejudice and aspiration. It would be no use to say of that event: 'What
does it matter? Let people think what they like, talk as
they like.' At Worsted Skeynes (and Worsted Skeynes
was every country house) there was but one set of
people, one church, one pack of hounds, one everything.
The importance of a clear escutcheon was too great.
And they who had lived together for thirty-four years
looked at each other with a new expression in their
eyes; their feelings were for once the same. But since
it is always the man who has the nicer sense of honour,
their thoughts were not the same, for Mr. Pendyce was
thinking: 'I won't believe it—disgracing us all!' and
Mrs. Pendyce was thinking: 'My boy!'

It was she who spoke first.

'Oh, Horace!'

The sound of her voice restored the squire's fortitude.

'There you go, Margery! D' you mean to say you
believe what this fellow says? He ought to be horse-
whipped. He knows my opinion of him. It's a piece
of his confounded impudence! He nearly ran over me,
and now——'

Mrs. Pendyce broke in:

'But, Horace, I'm afraid it's true! Ellen Malden——'

'Ellen Malden?' said Mr. Pendyce. 'What business
has she——' He was silent, staring gloomily at the

plan of Worsted Skeynes, still unrolled, like an emblem of all there was at stake. 'If George has really,' he burst out, 'he's a greater fool than I took him for! A fool? He's a knave!'

Again he was silent.

Mrs. Pendyce flushed at that word, and bit her lips.

'George could never be a knave!' she said.

Mr. Pendyce answered heavily:

'Disgracing his name!'

Mrs. Pendyce bit deeper into her lips.

'Whatever he has done,' she said, 'George is sure to have behaved like a gentleman!'

An angry smile twisted the squire's mouth.

'Just like a woman!' he said.

But the smile died away, and on both their faces came a helpless look. Like people who have lived together without real sympathy—though, indeed, they had long ceased to be conscious of that—now that something had occurred in which their interests were actually at one, they were filled with a sort of surprise. It was no good to differ. Differing, even silent differing, would not help their son.

'I shall write to George,' said Mr. Pendyce at last. 'I shall believe nothing till I've heard from him. He'll tell us the truth, I suppose.'

There was a quaver in his voice.

Mrs. Pendyce answered quickly:

'Oh, Horace, be careful what you say! I'm sure he is suffering!'

Her gentle soul, disposed to pleasure, was suffering, too, and the tears stole up in her eyes. Mr. Pendyce's sight was too long to see them. The infirmity had been growing on him ever since his marriage.

'I shall say what I think right,' he said. 'I shall

take time to consider what I shall say; I won't be hurried by this ruffian.'

Mrs. Pendyce wiped her lips with her lace-edged handkerchief.

'I hope you will show me the letter,' she said.

The squire looked at her, and he realized that she was trembling and very white, and, though this irritated him, he answered almost kindly:

'It 's not a matter for you, my dear.'

Mrs. Pendyce took a step towards him; her gentle face expressed a strange determination.

'He is my son, Horace, as well as yours.'

Mr. Pendyce turned round uneasily.

'It 's no use your getting nervous, Margery. I shall do what 's best. You women lose your heads. That d——d fellow 's lying! If he isn't——'

At these words the spaniel John rose from his corner and advanced to the middle of the floor. He stood there curved in a half-circle, and looked darkly at his master.

'Confound it!' said Mr. Pendyce. 'It 's — it 's damnable!'

And as if answering for all that depended on Worsted Skeynes, the spaniel John deeply wagged that which had been left him of his tail.

Mrs. Pendyce came nearer still.

'If George refuses to give you that promise, what will you do, Horace?'

Mr. Pendyce stared.

'Promise? What promise?'

Mrs. Pendyce thrust forward the note.

'This promise not to see her again.'

Mr. Pendyce motioned it aside.

'I 'll not be dictated to by that fellow Bellew,' he

said. Then, by an afterthought: 'It won't do to give him a chance. George must promise me that in any case.'

Mrs. Pendyce pressed her lips together.

'But do you think he will?'

'Think—think who will? Think he will what? Why can't you express yourself, Margery? If George has really got us into this mess he must get us out again.'

Mrs. Pendyce flushed.

'He would never leave her in the lurch!'

The squire said angrily:

'Lurch! Who said anything about lurch? He owes it to *her*. Not that she deserves any consideration, if she's been—— You don't mean to say you think he'll refuse? He'd never be such a donkey!'

Mrs. Pendyce raised her hands and made what for her was a passionate gesture.

'Oh, Horace!' she said, 'you don't understand. *He's in love with her!*'

Mr. Pendyce's lower lip trembled, a sign with him of excitement or emotion. All the conservative strength of his nature, all the immense dumb force of belief in established things, all that stubborn hatred and dread of change, that incalculable power of imagining nothing, which, since the beginning of time, had made Horace Pendyce the arbiter of his land, rose up within his sorely tried soul.

'What on earth's that to do with it?' he cried in a rage. 'You women! You've no sense of anything! Romantic, idiotic, immoral—I don't know what you're at. For God's sake don't go putting ideas into his head!'

At this outburst Mrs. Pendyce's face became rigid; only the flicker of her eyelids betrayed how her nerves were quivering. Suddenly she threw her hands up to her ears.

'Horace!' she cried, 'do—— Oh, *poor* John!'

The squire had stepped hastily and heavily on to his dog's paw. The creature gave a grievous howl. Mr. Pendyce went down on his knees and raised the limb.

'D——n the dog!' he stuttered. 'Oh, poor fellow, John!'

And the two long and narrow heads for a moment were close together.

CHAPTER V

RECTOR AND SQUIRE

THE efforts of social man, directed from immemorial time towards the stability of things, have culminated in Worsted Skeynes. Beyond commercial competition —for the estate no longer paid for living on it—beyond the power of expansion, set with tradition and sentiment, it was an undoubted jewel, past need of warranty. Cradled within it were all those hereditary institutions of which the country was most proud, and Mr. Pendyce sometimes saw before him the time when, for services to his party, he should call himself Lord Worsted, and after his own death continue sitting in the House of Lords in the person of his son. But there was another feeling in the squire's heart—the air and the woods and the fields had passed into his blood a love for this, his home and the home of his fathers.

And so a terrible unrest pervaded the whole household after the receipt of Jaspar Bellew's note. Nobody was told anything, yet everybody knew there was something; and each after his fashion, down to the very dogs, betrayed their sympathy with the master and mistress of the house.

Day after day the girls wandered about the new golf course knocking the balls aimlessly; it was all they could do. Even Cecil Tharp, who had received from Bee the qualified affirmative natural under the circumstances, was infected. The off foreleg of her grey mare

was being treated by a process he had recently discovered, and in the stables he confided to Bee that the
dear old squire seemed 'off his feed'; he did not think
it was any good worrying him at present.   Bee, stroking
the mare's neck, looked at him shyly and slowly.

'It's about George,' she said; 'I know it's about
George!   Oh, Cecil, I do wish I had been a boy!'

Young Tharp assented in spite of himself:

'Yes; it must be beastly to be a girl.'

A faint flush coloured Bee's cheeks.   It hurt her a
little that he should agree; but her lover was passing
his hand down the mare's shin.

'Father *is* rather trying,' she said.   'I wish George
would marry.'

Cecil Tharp raised his bullet head; his blunt, honest
face was extremely red from stooping.

'Clean as a whistle,' he said; '*she's* all right, Bee.
I expect George has too good a time.'

Bee turned her face away and murmured:

'*I* should loathe living in London.'   And she, too,
stooped and felt the mare's shin.

To Mrs. Pendyce in these days the hours passed with
incredible slowness.   For thirty odd years she had
waited at once for everything and nothing; she had, so
to say, everything she could wish for, and—nothing,
so that even waiting had been robbed of poignancy;
but to wait like this, in direct suspense, for something
definite was terrible.   There was hardly a moment when
she did not conjure up George, lonely and torn by
conflicting emotions; for to her, long paralysed by
Worsted Skeynes, and ignorant of the facts, the proportions of the struggle in her son's soul appeared
titanic; her mother instinct was not deceived as to
the strength of his passion.   Strange and conflicting

were the sensations with which she awaited the result; at one moment thinking: 'It is madness; he *must* promise—it is too awful!' at another: 'Ah! but how can he, if he loves her so? It is impossible; and she, too—ah! how awful it is!'

Perhaps, as Mr. Pendyce had said, she was romantic; perhaps it was only the thought of the pain her boy must suffer. The tooth was too big, it seemed to her; and, as in old days, when she took him to Cornmarket to have an aching tooth out, she ever sat with his hand in hers while the little dentist pulled, and ever suffered the tug, too, in her own mouth, so now she longed to share this other tug, so terrible, so fierce.

Against Mrs. Bellew she felt only a sort of vague and jealous aching; and this seemed strange even to herself —but, again, perhaps she was romantic.

Now it was that she found the value of routine. Her days were so well and fully occupied that anxiety was forced below the surface. The nights were far more terrible; for then, not only had she to bear her own suspense, but, as was natural in a wife, the fears of Horace Pendyce as well. The poor squire found this the only time when he could get relief from worry; he came to bed much earlier on purpose. By dint of reiterating dreads and speculation he at length obtained some rest. Why had not George answered? What was the fellow about? And so on and so on, till, by sheer monotony, he caused in himself the need for slumber. But his wife's torments lasted till after the birds, starting with a sleepy cheeping, were at full morning chorus. Then only, turning softly for fear she should awaken him, the poor lady fell asleep.

For George had not answered.

In her morning visits to the village Mrs. Pendyce

found herself, for the first time since she had begun this practice, driven by her own trouble over that line of diffident distrust which had always divided her from the hearts of her poorer neighbours. She was astonished at her own indelicacy, asking questions, prying into their troubles, pushed on by a secret aching for distraction; and she was surprised how well they took it—how, indeed, they seemed to like it, as though they knew that they were doing her good. In one cottage, where she had long noticed with pitying wonder a white-faced, black-eyed girl, who seemed to crouch away from every one, she even received a request. It was delivered with terrified secrecy in a back-yard, out of Mrs. Barter's hearing.

'Oh, ma'am! Get me away from here! I'm in trouble—it's comin', and I don't know what I shall do.'

Mrs. Pendyce shivered, and all the way home she thought: 'Poor little soul—poor little thing!' racking her brains to whom she might confide this case and ask for a solution; and something of the white-faced, black-eyed girl's terror and secrecy fell on her, for she found no one—not even Mrs. Barter, whose heart, though soft, belonged to the rector. Then, by a sort of inspiration, she thought of Gregory.

'How can I write to him,' she mused, 'when my son——'

But she did write, for, deep down, the Totteridge instinct felt that others should do things for her; and she craved, too, to allude, however distantly, to what was on her mind. And, under the Pendyce eagle and the motto: *Strenuus aureâque pennâ*, thus her letter ran:

'DEAR GRIG,

'Can you do anything for a poor little girl in the village here who is "in trouble"?—you know what I mean. It is such a terrible crime in this part of the country, and she looks so wretched and frightened, poor little thing! She is twenty years old. She wants a hiding-place for her misfortune, and somewhere to go when it is over. Nobody, she says, will have anything to do with her where they know; and really, I have noticed for a long time how white and wretched she looks, with great black frightened eyes. I don't like to apply to our rector, for though he *is* a good fellow in many ways, he has such strong opinions; and, of course, Horace could do nothing. I *would* like to do something for her, and I could spare a little money, but I can't find a place for her to go, and that makes it difficult. She seems to be haunted, too, by the idea that wherever she goes it will come out. Isn't it dreadful? Do do something, if you can. I am rather anxious about George. I hope the dear boy is well. If you are passing his club some day you might look in and just ask after him. He is sometimes so naughty about writing. I wish we could see you here, dear Grig; the country is looking beautiful just now—the oak trees especially— and the apple blossom isn't over, but I suppose you are too busy. How is Helen Bellew? Is she in town?

'Your affectionate cousin,

'MARGERY PENDYCE.'

It was four o'clock this same afternoon when the second groom, very much out of breath, informed the butler that there was a fire at Peacock's farm. The butler repaired at once to the library. Mr. Pendyce, who had been on horseback all the morning, was standing in his riding-clothes, tired and depressed, before the plan of Worsted Skeynes.

'What do you want, Bester?'

'There is a fire at Peacock's farm, sir.'

Mr. Pendyce stared.

'What?' he said. 'A fire in broad daylight! Nonsense!'

'You can see the flames from the front, sir.'

The worn and querulous look left Mr. Pendyce's face.

'Ring the stable-bell!' he said. 'Tell them all to run with buckets and ladders. Send Higson off to Cornmarket on the mare. Go and tell Mr. Barter, and rouse the village. Don't stand there—God bless me! Ring the stable-bell!' And snatching up his riding-crop and hat, he ran past the butler, closely followed by the spaniel John.

Over the stile and along the footpath which cut diagonally across a field of barley he moved at a stiff trot, and his spaniel, who had not grasped the situation, frolicked ahead with a certain surprise. The squire was soon out of breath—it was twenty years or more since he had run a quarter of a mile. He did not, however, relax his speed. Ahead of him in the distance ran the second groom; behind him a labourer and a footman. The stable-bell at Worsted Skeynes began to ring. Mr. Pendyce crossed the stile and struck into the lane, colliding with the rector, who was running, too, his face flushed to the colour of tomatoes. They ran on side by side.

'You go on!' gasped Mr. Pendyce at last, 'and tell them I'm coming.'

The rector hesitated—he, too, was very out of breath—and started again, panting. The squire, with his hand to his side, walked painfully on; he had run himself to a standstill. At a gap in the corner of the lane he suddenly saw pale-red tongues of flame against the sunlight.

'God bless me!' he gasped, and in sheer horror started to run again. Those sinister tongues were licking at the air over a large barn, some ricks, and the roofs of stables and outbuildings. Half a dozen figures were dashing buckets of water on the flames. The true insignificance of their efforts did not penetrate the squire's mind. Trembling, and with a sickening pain in his lungs, he threw off his coat, wrenched a bucket from a huge agricultural labourer, who resigned it with awe, and joined the string of workers. Peacock, the farmer, ran past him; his face and round red beard were the colour of the flames he was trying to put out; tears dropped continually from his eyes and ran down that fiery face. His wife, a little dark woman with a twisted mouth, was working like a demon at the pump. Mr. Pendyce gasped to her:

'This is dreadful, Mrs. Peacock—this is dreadful!'

Conspicuous in black clothes and white shirt-sleeves, the rector was hewing with an axe at the boarding of a cow-house, the door end of which was already in flames, and his voice could be heard above the tumult shouting directions to which nobody paid any heed.

'What 's in that cow-house?' gasped Mr. Pendyce.

Mrs. Peacock, in a voice harsh with rage and grief, answered:

'It 's the old horse and two of the cows!'

'God bless me!' cried the squire, rushing forward with his bucket.

Some villagers came running up, and he shouted to these, but what he said neither he nor they could tell. The shrieks and snortings of the horse and cows, the steady whirr of the flames, drowned all lesser sounds. Of human cries, the rector's voice alone was heard, between the crashing blows of his axe upon the woodwork.

Mr. Pendyce tripped; his bucket rolled out of his hand; he lay where he had fallen, too exhausted to move. He could still hear the crash of the rector's axe, the sound of his shouts. Somebody helped him up, and trembling so that he could hardly stand, he caught an axe out of the hand of a strapping young fellow who had just arrived, and placing himself by the rector's side, swung it feebly against the boarding. The flames and smoke now filled the whole cow-house, and came rushing through the gap that they were making. The squire and the rector stood their ground. With a furious blow Mr. Barter cleared a way. A cheer rose behind them, but no beast came forth. All three were dead in the smoke and flames.

The squire, who could see in, flung down his axe, and covered his eyes with his hands. The rector uttered a sound like a deep oath, and he, too, flung down his axe.

Two hours later, with torn and blackened clothes, the squire stood by the ruins of the barn. The fire was out, but the ashes were still smouldering. The spaniel John, anxious, panting, was licking his master's boots, as though begging forgiveness that he had been so frightened, and kept so far away. Yet something in his eye seemed to be saying:

'Must you really have these fires, master?'

A black hand grasped the squire's arm, a hoarse voice said:

'I shan't forget, squire!'

'God bless me, Peacock!' returned Mr. Pendyce, 'that's nothing! You're insured, I hope?'

'Aye, I'm insured; but it's the beasts I'm thinking of!'

'Ah!' said the squire, with a gesture of horror.

The brougham took him and the rector back together. Under their feet crouched their respective dogs, faintly growling at each other. A cheer from the crowd greeted their departure.

They started in silence, deadly tired. Mr. Pendyce said suddenly:

'I can't get those poor beasts out of my head, Barter!'

The rector put his hand up to his eyes.

'I hope to God I shall never see such a sight again! Poor brutes, poor brutes!'

And feeling secretly for his dog's muzzle, he left his hand against the animal's warm, soft, rubbery mouth, to be licked again and again.

On his side of the brougham Mr. Pendyce, also unseen, was doing precisely the same thing.

The carriage went first to the rectory, where Mrs. Barter and her children stood in the doorway. The rector put his head back into the brougham to say:

'Good night, Pendyce. You 'll be stiff to-morrow. I shall get my wife to rub me with Elliman!'

Mr. Pendyce nodded, raised his hat, and the carriage went on. Leaning back, he closed his eyes; a pleasanter sensation was stealing over him. True, he would be stiff to-morrow, but he had done his duty. He had shown them all that blood told; done something to bolster up that system which was—himself. And he had a new and kindly feeling towards Peacock, too. There was nothing like a little danger for bringing the lower classes closer; then it was they felt the need for officers, for something!

The spaniel John's head rose between his knees, turning up eyes with a crimson touch beneath.

'Master,' he seemed to say, 'I am feeling old. I

know there are things beyond me in this life, but you, who know all things, will arrange that we shall be together even when we die.'

The carriage stopped at the entrance of the drive, and the squire's thoughts changed. Twenty years ago he would have beaten Barter running down that lane. Barter was only forty-five. To give him fourteen years and a beating was a bit too much to expect. He felt a strange irritation with Barter—the fellow had cut a very good figure! He had shirked nothing. Elliman was too strong! Homocea was the thing. Margery would have to rub him! And suddenly, as though springing naturally from the name of his wife, George came into Mr. Pendyce's mind, and the respite that he had enjoyed from care was over. But the spaniel John, who scented home, began singing feebly for the brougham to stop, and beating a careless tail against his master's boot.

It was very stiffly, with frowning brows and a shaking under-lip, that the squire descended from the brougham, and began sorely to mount the staircase to his wife's room.

CHAPTER VI

THE PARK

THERE comes a day each year in May when Hyde Park is possessed. A cool wind swings the leaves; a hot sun glistens on Long Water, on every bough, on every blade of grass. The birds sing their small hearts out, the band plays its gayest tunes, the white clouds race in the high blue heaven. Exactly why and how this day differs from those that came before and those that will come after, cannot be told; it is as though the Park said: 'To-day I live; the Past is past, I care not for the Future!'

And on this day they who chance in the Park cannot escape some measure of possession. Their steps quicken, their skirts swing, their sticks flourish, even their eyes brighten — those eyes so dulled with looking at the streets; and each one, if he has a Love, thinks of her, and here and there among the wandering throng he has her with him. To these the Park and all sweet-blooded mortals in it nod and smile.

There had been a meeting that afternoon at Lady Malden's in Prince's Gate to consider the position of the working-class woman. It had provided a somewhat heated discussion, for a person had got up and proved almost incontestably that the working-class woman had no position whatsoever.

Gregory Vigil and Mrs. Shortman had left this meeting together, and, crossing the Serpentine, struck a line over the grass.

'Mrs. Shortman,' said Gregory, 'don't you think we're all a little mad?'

He was carrying his hat in his hand, and his fine grizzled hair, rumpled in the excitement of the meeting, had not yet subsided on his head.

'Yes, Mr. Vigil. I don't exactly——'

'We *are* all a little mad! What did that woman, Lady Malden, mean by talking as she did? I detest her!'

'Oh, Mr. Vigil! She has the best intentions!'

'Intentions?' said Gregory. 'I loathe her! What did we go to her stuffy drawing-room for? Look at that sky!'

Mrs. Shortman looked at the sky.

'But, Mr. Vigil,' she said earnestly, 'things would never get done. Sometimes I think you look at everything too much in the light of the way it ought to be!'

'The Milky Way,' said Gregory.

Mrs. Shortman pursed her lips; she found it impossible to habituate herself to Gregory's habit of joking.

They had scant talk for the rest of their journey to the S.R.W.C., where Miss Mallow, at the typewriter, was reading a novel.

'There are several letters for you, Mr. Vigil.'

'Mrs. Shortman says I am unpractical,' answered Gregory. 'Is that true, Miss Mallow?'

The colour in Miss Mallow's cheeks spread to her sloping shoulders.

'Oh, no. You're most practical, only—perhaps—I don't know, perhaps you do try to do rather impossible things, Mr. Vigil.'

'Bilcock Buildings!'

There was a minute's silence. Then Mrs. Shortman

at her bureau beginning to dictate, the typewriter
started clicking.

Gregory, who had opened a letter, was seated with
his head in his hands. The voice ceased, the typewriter
ceased, but Gregory did not stir. Both women, turning
a little in their seats, glanced at him. Their eyes
caught each other's and they looked away at once.
A few seconds later they were looking at him again.
Still Gregory did not stir. An anxious appeal began
to creep into the women's eyes.

'Mr. Vigil,' said Mrs. Shortman at last, 'Mr. Vigil,
do you think——'

Gregory raised his face; it was flushed to the roots
of his hair.

'Read that, Mrs. Shortman.'

Handing her a pale grey letter stamped with an eagle
and the motto *Strenuus aureâque pennâ* he rose and
paced the room. And as with his long, light stride he
was passing to and fro, the woman at the bureau
conned steadily the writing, the girl at the typewriter
sat motionless with a red and jealous face.

Mrs. Shortman folded the letter, placed it on the
top of the bureau, and said without raising her eyes:

'Of course, it is very sad for the poor little girl;
but surely, Mr. Vigil, it must *always* be, so as to check,
to check——'

Gregory stopped, and his shining eyes disconcerted
her; they seemed to her unpractical. Sharply lifting
her voice, she went on:

'If there were no disgrace, there would be no way
of stopping it. I know the country better than you
do, Mr. Vigil.'

Gregory put his hands to his ears.

'We must find a place for her at once.'

The window was fully open, so that he could not open it any more, and he stood there as though looking for that place in the sky. And the sky he looked at was very blue, and large white birds of cloud were flying over it.

He turned from the window, and opened another letter.

'LINCOLN'S INN FIELDS,
'24th May 1892.

'MY DEAR VIGIL,

'I gathered from your ward when I saw her yesterday that she has not told you of what, I fear, will give you much pain. I asked her point-blank whether she wished the matter kept from you, and her answer was: "He had better know—only I'm sorry for him." In sum it is this: Bellew has either got wind of our watching him, or someone must have put him up to it; he has anticipated us and brought a suit against your ward, joining George Pendyce in the cause. George brought the citation to me. If necessary he's prepared to swear there's nothing in it. He takes, in fact, the usual standpoint of the "man of honour."

'I went at once to see your ward. She admitted that the charge is true. I asked her if she wished the suit defended, and a counter-suit brought against her husband. Her answer to that was: "I absolutely don't care." I got nothing from her but this, and, though it sounds odd, I believe it to be true. She appears to be in a reckless mood, and to have no particular ill-will against her husband.

'I want to see you, but only after you have turned this matter over carefully. It is my duty to put some considerations before you. The suit, if brought, will be a very unpleasant matter for George, a still more unpleasant, even disastrous one, for his people. The innocent in such cases are almost always the greatest sufferers. If the cross-suit is instituted, it will assume at once, considering their position in Society, the proportions of a *cause célèbre*, and probably occupy the Court and the daily press anything from three days to a week, perhaps more, and you know what that means. On the other hand, not to defend the suit, considering what we know, is, apart from ethics, revolting to my instincts as a fighter. My advice, therefore, is to make every effort to prevent matters being brought into court at all.

'I am an older man than you by thirteen years. I have a sincere regard for you, and I wish to save you pain. In the course of our interviews I have observed your ward very closely, and at the risk of giving you offence, I am going to speak out my mind. Mrs. Bellew is a rather remarkable woman. From two or three allusions that you have made in my presence, I believe that she is altogether different from what you think. She is, in my opinion, one of those very vital persons upon whom our judgments, censures, even our sympathies, are wasted. A woman of this sort, if she comes of a county family, and is thrown by circumstances with Society people, is always bound to be conspicuous. If you would realize something of this, it would, I believe, save you a great deal of pain. In short, I beg of you not to take her, or her circumstances, too seriously. There are quite a number of such men and women as her husband and herself, and they are always certain to be more or less before the public eye. Whoever else goes down, she will swim, simply because she can't help it. I want you to see things as they are.

'I ask you again, my dear Vigil, to forgive me for writing thus, and to believe that my sole desire is to try and save you unnecessary suffering.

'Come and see me as soon as you have reflected.

'I am,

'Your sincere friend,

'EDMUND PARAMOR.'

Gregory made a movement like that of a blind man. Both women were on their feet at once.

'What is it, Mr. Vigil? Can I get you anything?'

'Thanks; nothing, nothing. I 've had some rather bad news. I 'll go out and get some air. I shan't be back to-day.'

He found his hat and went.

He walked towards the Park, unconsciously attracted towards the biggest space, the freshest air; his hands were folded behind him, his head bowed. And since, of all things, Nature is ironical, it was fitting that he should seek the Park this day when it was gayest. And far in the Park, as near the centre as might be, he lay down on the grass. For a long time he lay without moving, his hands over his eyes, and in spite of Mr. Paramor's reminder that his suffering was unnecessary, he suffered.

And mostly he suffered from black loneliness, for he was a very lonely man, and now he had lost that which he had thought he had. It is difficult to divide suffering, difficult to say how much he suffered, because, being in love with her, he had secretly thought she must love him a little, and how much he suffered because his private portrait of her, the portrait that he, and he alone, had painted, was scored through with the knife. And he lay first on his face, and then on his back, with his hand always over his eyes. And around him were other men lying on the grass, and some were lonely, and some hungry, and some asleep, and some were lying there for the pleasure of doing nothing and for the sake of the hot sun on their cheeks; and by the side of some lay their girls, and it was these that Gregory could not bear to see, for his spirit and his senses were a-hungered. In the plantations close by were pigeons, and never for a moment did they stop cooing; never did the black-birds cease their courting songs; the sun its hot, sweet burning; the clouds above their love-chase in the sky. It was the day without a past, without a future, when it is not good for man to be alone. And no man looked at him, because it was no man's business, but a woman here and there cast a glance on that long, tweed-suited figure with the hand over the eyes, and wondered, perhaps, what was behind that hand. Had they but known, they would have smiled their woman's smile that he should so have mistaken one of their sex.

Gregory lay quite still, looking at the sky, and because he was a loyal man he did not blame her, but slowly, very slowly, his spirit, like a spring stretched to the point of breaking, came back upon itself, and since he could not bear to see things as they were, he began again to see them as they were not.

'She has been forced into this,' he thought. 'It is George Pendyce's fault. To me she is, she must be, the same!'

He turned again on to his face. And a small dog who had lost its master sniffed at his boots, and sat down a little way off, to wait till Gregory could do something for him, because he smelled that he was that sort of man.

CHAPTER VII

DOUBTFUL POSITION AT WORSTED SKEYNES

WHEN George's answer came at last, the flags were in full bloom round the Scotch garden at Worsted Skeynes. They grew in masses and of all shades, from deep purple to pale grey, and their scent, very penetrating, very delicate, floated on the wind.

While waiting for that answer, it had become Mr. Pendyce's habit to promenade between these beds, his hand to his back, for he was still a little stiff, followed at a distance of seven paces by the spaniel John, very black, and moving his rubbery nostrils uneasily from side to side.

In this way the two passed every day the hour from twelve to one. Neither could have said why they walked thus, for Mr. Pendyce had a horror of idleness, and the spaniel John disliked the scent of irises; both, in fact, obeyed that part of themselves which is superior to reason. During this hour, too, Mrs. Pendyce, though longing to walk between her flowers, also obeyed that part of her, superior to reason, which told her that it would be better not.

But George's answer came at last.

'STOICS' CLUB.

'DEAR FATHER,

'Yes, Bellew is bringing a suit. I am taking steps in the matter. As to the promise you ask for, I can give no promise of the sort. You may tell Bellew I will see him d——d first.

'Your affectionate son,
'GEORGE PENDYCE.'

Mr. Pendyce received this at the breakfast-table, and while he read it there was a hush, for all had seen the handwriting on the envelope.

Mr. Pendyce read it through twice, once with his glasses on and once without, and when he had finished the second reading he placed it in his breast pocket. No word escaped him; his eyes, which had sunk a little the last few days, rested angrily on his wife's white face. Bee and Norah looked down, and, as if they understood, the four dogs were still. Mr. Pendyce pushed his plate back, rose, and left the room.

Norah looked up.

'What 's the matter, mother?'

Mrs. Pendyce was swaying. She recovered herself in a moment.

'Nothing, dear. It 's very hot this morning, don't you think? I 'll just go to my room and take some sal volatile.'

She went out, followed by old Roy, the Skye; the spaniel John, who had been cut off at the door by his master's abrupt exit, preceded her. Norah and Bee pushed back their plates.

'I can't eat, Norah,' said Bee. 'It 's horrible not to know what 's going on.'

Norah answered:

'It 's perfectly brutal not being a man. You might just as well be a dog as a girl, for anything any one tells you!'

Mrs. Pendyce did not go to her room; she went to

the library. Her husband, seated at his table, had George's letter before him. A pen was in his hand, but he was not writing.

'Horace,' she said softly, 'here is poor John!'

Mr. Pendyce did not answer, but put down the hand that did not hold his pen. The spaniel John covered it with kisses.

'Let me see the letter, won't you?'

Mr. Pendyce handed it to her without a word. She touched his shoulder gratefully, for his unusual silence went to her heart. Mr. Pendyce took no notice, staring at his pen as though surprised that, of its own accord, it did not write his answer; but suddenly he flung it down and looked round, and his look seemed to say: 'You brought this fellow into the world; now see the result!'

He had had so many days to think and put his finger on the doubtful spots of his son's character. All that week he had become more and more certain of how, without his wife, George would have been exactly like himself. Words sprang to his lips, and kept on dying there. The doubt whether she would agree with him, the feeling that she sympathized with her son, the certainty that something even in himself responded to those words: 'You can tell Bellew I will see him d——d first!'—all this, and the thought, never out of his mind, 'The name—the estate!' kept him silent. He turned his head away, and took up his pen again.

Mrs. Pendyce had read the letter now three times, and instinctively had put it in her bosom. It was not hers, but Horace must know it by heart, and in his anger he might tear it up. That letter, for which they had waited so long, told her nothing; she had known all there was to tell. Her hand had fallen from Mr. Pen-

dyce's shoulder, and she did not put it back, but ran
her fingers through and through each other, while the
sunlight, traversing the narrow windows, caressed her
from her hair down to her knees. Here and there that
stream of sunlight formed little pools — in her eyes,
giving them a touching, anxious brightness; in a curious
heart-shaped locket of carved steel, worn by her mother
and her grandmother before her, containing now, not
locks of *their* son's hair, but a curl of George's; in her
diamond rings, and a bracelet of amethyst and pearl
which she wore for the love of pretty things. And the
warm sunlight disengaged from her a scent of lavender.
Through the library door a scratching noise told that
the dear dogs knew she was not in her bedroom. Mr.
Pendyce, too, caught that scent of lavender, and in
some vague way it augmented his discomfort. Her
silence, too, distressed him. It did not occur to him
that his silence was distressing her. He put down
his pen.

'I can't write with you standing there, Margery!'

Mrs. Pendyce moved out of the sunlight.

'George says he is taking steps. What does that
mean, Horace?'

This question, focusing his doubts, broke down the
squire's dumbness.

'I won't be treated like this!' he said. 'I 'll go up
and see him myself!'

He went by the 10.20, saying that he would be down
again by the 5.55.

Soon after seven the same evening a dog-cart, driven
by a young groom and drawn by a raking chestnut mare
with a blaze face, swung into the railway station at
Worsted Skeynes, and drew up before the booking-
office. Mr. Pendyce's brougham, behind a brown horse,

coming a little later, was obliged to range itself behind. A minute before the train's arrival a wagonette and a pair of bays, belonging to Lord Quarryman, wheeled in, and, filing past the other two, took up its place in front. Outside this little row of vehicles the station fly and two farmers' gigs presented their backs to the station buildings. And in this arrangement there was something harmonious and fitting, as though Providence itself had guided them all and assigned to each its place. And Providence had only made one error— that of placing Captain Bellew's dog-cart precisely opposite the booking-office, instead of Lord Quarryman's wagonette, with Mr. Pendyce's brougham next.

Mr. Pendyce came out first; he stared angrily at the dog-cart, and moved to his own carriage. Lord Quarryman came out second. His massive sun-burned head —the back of which, sparsely adorned by hairs, ran perfectly straight into his neck—was crowned by a grey top-hat. The skirts of his grey coat were square-shaped, and so were the toes of his boots.

'Hallo, Pendyce!' he called out heartily; 'didn't see you on the platform. How's your wife?'

Mr. Pendyce, turning to answer, met the little burning eyes of Captain Bellew, who came out third. They failed to salute each other, and Bellew, springing into his cart, wrenched his mare round, circled the farmers' gigs, and, sitting forward, drove off at a furious pace. His groom, running at full speed, clung to the cart and leaped on to the step behind. Lord Quarryman's wagonette backed itself into the place left vacant. And the mistake of Providence was rectified.

'Cracked chap, that fellow Bellew. D' you see anything of him?'

Mr. Pendyce answered:

'No; and I want to see less. I wish he'd take himself off!'

His lordship smiled.

'A huntin' country seems to breed fellows like that; there's always one of 'em to every pack of hounds. Where's his wife now? Good-lookin' woman; rather warm member, eh?'

It seemed to Mr. Pendyce that Lord Quarryman's eyes searched his own with a knowing look, and muttering 'God knows!' he vanished into his brougham.

Lord Quarryman looked kindly at his horses. He was not a man who reflected on the whys, the where-fores, the becauses, of this life. The good God had made him Lord Quarryman, had made his eldest son Lord Quantock; the good God had made the Gaddesdon hounds—it was enough!

When Mr. Pendyce reached home he went to his dressing-room. In a corner by the bath the spaniel John lay surrounded by an assortment of his master's slippers, for it was thus alone that he could soothe in measure the bitterness of separation. His dark brown eye was fixed upon the door, and round it gleamed a crescent moon of white. He came to the squire flutter-ing his tail, with a slipper in his mouth, and his eye said plainly: 'Oh, master, where have you been? Why have you been so long? I have been expecting you ever since half-past ten this morning!'

Mr. Pendyce's heart opened a moment and closed again. He said 'John!' and began to dress for dinner.

Mrs. Pendyce found him tying his white tie. She had plucked the first rosebud from her garden; she had plucked it because she felt sorry for him, and because of the excuse it would give her to go to his dressing-room at once.

'I've brought you a buttonhole, Horace. Did you see him?'

'No.'

Of all answers this was the one she dreaded most. She had not believed that anything would come of an interview; she had trembled all day long at the thought of their meeting; but now that they had not met she knew by the sinking in her heart that anything was better than uncertainty. She waited as long as she could, then burst out:

'Tell me something, Horace!'

Mr. Pendyce gave her an angry glance.

'How can I tell you, when there's nothing to tell? I went to his club. He's not living there now. He's got rooms, nobody knows where. I waited all the afternoon. Left a message at last for him to come down here to-morrow. I've sent for Paramor, and told him to come down too. I won't put up with this sort of thing.'

Mrs. Pendyce looked out of the window, but there was nothing to see save the ha-ha, the coverts, the village spire, the cottage roofs, which for so long had been her world.

'George won't come down here,' she said.

'George will do what I tell him.'

Again Mrs. Pendyce shook her head, knowing by instinct that she was right.

Mr. Pendyce stopped putting on his waistcoat.

'George had better take care,' he said; 'he's entirely dependent on me.'

And as if with those words he had summed up the situation, the philosophy of a system vital to his son, he no longer frowned. On Mrs. Pendyce those words had a strange effect. They stirred within her terror. It was like seeing her son's back bared to a lifted whip-lash; like seeing the door shut against him on a snowy night. But besides terror they stirred within her a more poignant feeling yet, as though someone had dared to show a whip to herself, had dared to defy that some-thing more precious than life in her soul, that something which was of her blood, so utterly and secretly passed by the centuries into her fibre that no one had ever thought of defying it before. And there flashed before her with ridiculous concreteness the thought: 'I 've got three hundred a year of my own!' Then the whole feeling left her, just as in dreams a mordant sensation grips and passes, leaving a dull ache, whose cause is forgotten, behind.

'There 's the gong, Horace,' she said. 'Cecil Tharp is here to dinner. I asked the Barters, but poor Rose didn't feel up to it. Of course they are expecting it very soon now. They talk of the 15th of June.'

Mr. Pendyce took from his wife his coat, passing his arms down the satin sleeves.

'If I could get the cottagers to have families like that,' he said, 'I shouldn't have much trouble about labour. They 're a pig-headed lot—do nothing that they 're told. Give me some eau-de-Cologne, Margery.'

Mrs. Pendyce dabbed the wicker flask on her husband's handkerchief.

'Your eyes look tired,' she said. 'Have you a headache, dear?'

CHAPTER VIII

COUNCIL AT WORSTED SKEYNES

It was on the following evening—the evening on which he was expecting his son and Mr. Paramor—that the squire leaned forward over the dining-table and asked:

'What do you say, Barter? I'm speaking to you as a man of the world.'

The rector bent over his glass of port and moistened his lower lip.

'There's no excuse for that woman,' he answered. 'I always thought she was a bad lot.'

Mr. Pendyce went on:

'We've never had a scandal in my family. I find the thought of it hard to bear, Barter—I find it hard to bear——'

The rector emitted a low sound. He had come from long usage to have a feeling like affection for his squire.

Mr. Pendyce pursued his thoughts.

'We've gone on,' he said, 'father and son for hundreds of years. It's a blow to me, Barter.'

Again the rector emitted that low sound.

'What will the village think?' said Mr. Pendyce; 'and the farmers?—I mind that more than anything. Most of them knew my dear old father—not that he was popular. It's a bitter thing.'

The rector said:

'Well, well, Pendyce, perhaps it won't come to that.'

He looked a little shamefaced, and his light eyes were full of something like contrition.

'How does Mrs. Pendyce take it?'

The squire looked at him for the first time.

'Ah,' he said, 'you never know anything about women. I 'd as soon trust a woman to be just as I 'd—I 'd finish that magnum; it 'd give me gout in no time.'

The rector emptied his glass.

'I 've sent for George and my solicitor,' pursued the squire; 'they 'll be here directly.'

Mr. Barter pushed his chair back, and raising his right ankle on to his left leg, clasped his hands round his right knee; then, leaning forward, he stared up under his jutting brows at Mr. Pendyce. It was the attitude in which he thought best.

Mr. Pendyce ran on:

'I 've nursed the estate ever since it came to me; I 've carried on the tradition as best I could; I 've not been as good a man, perhaps, as I should have wished, but I 've always tried to remember my old father's words: "I 'm done for, Horry; the estate 's in your hands now."' He cleared his throat.

For a full minute there was no sound save the ticking of the clock. Then the spaniel John, coming silently from under the sideboard, fell heavily down against his master's leg with a lengthy snore of satisfaction. Mr. Pendyce looked down.

'This fellow of mine,' he muttered, 'is getting fat.'

It was evident from the tone of his voice that he desired his emotion to be forgotten. Something very deep in Mr. Barter respected that desire.

'It 's a first-rate magnum,' he said.

Mr. Pendyce filled his rector's glass.

'I forget if you knew Paramor. He was before your time. He was at Harrow with me.'

The rector took a prolonged sip.

'I shall be in the way,' he said. 'I'll take myself off.'

The squire put out his hand affectionately.

'No, no, Barter, don't you go. It's all safe with you. I mean to act. I can't stand this uncertainty. My wife's cousin Vigil is coming too—he's her guardian. I wired for him. You know Vigil? He was about your time.'

The rector turned crimson, and set his under-lip. Having scented his enemy, nothing would now persuade him to withdraw; and the conviction that he had only done his duty, a little shaken by the squire's confidence, returned as though by magic.

'Yes, I know him.'

'We'll have it all out here,' muttered Mr. Pendyce, 'over this port. There's the carriage. Get up, John.'

The spaniel John rose heavily, looked sardonically at Mr. Barter, and again flopped down against his master's leg.

'Get up, John,' said Mr. Pendyce again. The spaniel John snored.

'If I move, you'll move too, and uncertainty will begin for me again,' he seemed to say.

Mr. Pendyce disengaged his leg, rose, and went to the door. Before reaching it he turned and came back to the table.

'Barter,' he said, 'I'm not thinking of myself—I'm not thinking of myself—we've been here for generations —it's the principle.' His face had the least twist to one side, as though conforming to a kink in his philosophy; his eyes looked sad and restless.

And the rector, watching the door for the sight of his enemy, also thought:

'I 'm not thinking of myself—I 'm satisfied that I did right—I 'm rector of this parish—it 's the principle.'

The spaniel John gave three short barks, one for each of the persons who entered the room. They were Mrs. Pendyce, Mr. Paramor, and Gregory Vigil.

'Where 's George?' asked the squire, but no one answered him.

The rector, who had resumed his seat, stared at a little gold cross which he had taken out of his waistcoat pocket. Mr. Paramor lifted a vase and sniffed at the rose it contained; Gregory walked to the window.

When Mr. Pendyce realized that his son had not come, he went to the door and held it open.

'Be good enough to take John out, Margery,' he said. 'John!'

The spaniel John, seeing what lay before him, rolled over on his back.

Mrs. Pendyce fixed her eyes on her husband, and in those eyes she put all the words which the nature of a lady did not suffer her to speak.

'I claim to be here. Let me stay; it is my right. *Don't* send me away.' So her eyes spoke, and so those of the spaniel John, lying on his back, in which attitude he knew that he was hard to move.

Mr. Pendyce turned him over with his foot.

'Get up, John! Be good enough to take John out, Margery.'

Mrs. Pendyce flushed, but did not move.

'John,' said Mr. Pendyce, 'go with your mistress.' The spaniel John fluttered a drooping tail. Mr. Pendyce pressed his foot to it. 'This is not a subject for women.'

Mrs. Pendyce bent down.

'Come, John,' she said. The spaniel John, showing the whites of his eyes, and trying to back through his collar, was assisted from the room. Mr. Pendyce closed the door behind them.

'Have a glass of port, Vigil; it's the '47. My father laid it down in '56, the year before he died. Can't drink it myself—I've had to put down two hogsheads of the Jubilee wine. Paramor, fill your glass. Take that chair next to Paramor, Vigil. You know Barter?'

Both Gregory's face and the rector's were very red.

'We're all Harrow men here,' went on Mr. Pendyce. And suddenly turning to Mr. Paramor, he said: 'Well?'

Just as round the hereditary principle are grouped the State, the Church, Law, and Philanthropy, so round the dining-table at Worsted Skeynes sat the squire, the rector, Mr. Paramor, and Gregory Vigil, and none of them wished to be the first to speak. At last Mr. Paramor, taking from his pocket Bellew's note and George's answer, which were pinned in strange alliance, returned them to the squire.

'I understand the position to be that George refuses to give her up; at the same time he is prepared to defend the suit and deny everything. Those are his instructions to me.' Taking up the vase again, he sniffed long and deep at the rose.

Mr. Pendyce broke the silence.

'As a gentleman,' he said in a voice sharpened by the bitterness of his feelings, 'I suppose he's obliged——'

Gregory, smiling painfully, added:

'To tell lies.'

Mr. Pendyce turned on him at once.

'I've nothing to say about that, Vigil. George has behaved abominably. I don't uphold him; but if the

woman wishes the suit defended he can't play the cur—
that's what I was brought up to believe.'

Gregory leaned his forehead on his hand.

'The whole system is odious——' he was beginning.

Mr. Paramor chimed in.

'Let us keep to the facts; they are enough without
the system.'

The rector spoke for the first time.

'I don't know what you mean about the system;
both this man and this woman are guilty——'

Gregory said in a voice that quivered with rage:

'Be so kind as not to use the expression, "this
woman."'

The rector glowered.

'What expression, then——'

Mr. Pendyce's voice, to which the intimate trouble of
his thoughts lent a certain dignity, broke in:

'Gentlemen, this is a question concerning the honour
of my house.'

There was another and a longer silence, during which
Mr. Paramor's eyes haunted from face to face, while
beyond the rose a smile writhed on his lips.

'I suppose you have brought me down here, Pendyce,
to give you my opinion,' he said at last. 'Well; don't
let these matters come into court. If there is anything
you can do to prevent it, do it. If your pride stands
in the way, put it in your pocket. If your sense of
truth stands in the way, forget it. Between personal
delicacy and our law of divorce there is no relation;
between absolute truth and our law of divorce there is
no relation. I repeat, don't let these matters come
into court. Innocent and guilty, you will all suffer;
the innocent will suffer more than the guilty, and
nobody will benefit. I have come to this conclusion

deliberately. There are cases in which I should give the opposite opinion. But in *this* case, I repeat, there's nothing to be gained by it. Once more, then, don't let these matters come into court. Don't give people's tongues a chance. Take my advice, appeal to George again to give you that promise. If he refuses, well, we must try and bluff Bellew out of it.'

Mr. Pendyce had listened, as he had formed the habit of listening to Edmund Paramor, in silence. He now looked up and said:

'It's all that red-haired ruffian's spite. I don't know what you were about to stir things up, Vigil. You must have put him on the scent.' He looked moodily at Gregory. Mr. Barter, too, looked at Gregory with a sort of half-ashamed defiance.

Gregory, who had been staring at his untouched wine-glass, turned his face, very flushed, and began speaking in a voice that emotion and anger caused to tremble. He avoided looking at the rector, and addressed himself to Mr. Paramor.

'George can't give up the woman who has trusted herself to him; *that* would be playing the cur, if you like. Let them go and live together honestly until they can be married. Why do you all speak as if it were the man who mattered? It is the woman that we should protect!'

The rector first recovered speech.

'You're talking rank immorality,' he said almost good-humouredly.

Mr. Pendyce rose.

'Marry her!' he cried. 'What on earth — that's worse than all — the very thing we're trying to prevent! We've been here, father and son—father and son—for generations!'

'All the more shame,' burst out Gregory, 'if you can't stand by a woman at the end of them!'

Mr. Paramor made a gesture of reproof.

'There's moderation in all things,' he said. 'Are you sure that Mrs. Bellew requires protection? If you are right, I agree; but are you right?'

'I will answer for it,' said Gregory.

Mr. Paramor paused a full minute with his head resting on his hand.

'I am sorry,' he said at last, 'I must trust to my own judgment.'

The squire looked up.

'If the worst comes to the worst, can I cut the entail, Paramor?'

'No.'

'What? But that's all wrong—that's——'

'You can't have it both ways,' said Mr. Paramor. The squire looked at him dubiously, then blurted out:

'If I choose to leave him nothing but the estate, he'll soon find himself a beggar. I beg your pardon, gentlemen; fill your glasses! I'm forgetting everything!'

The rector filled his glass.

'I've said nothing so far,' he began; 'I don't feel that it's my business. My conviction is that there's far too much divorce nowadays. Let this woman go back to her husband, and let him show her where she's to blame'—his voice and his eyes hardened—'then let them forgive each other like Christians. You talk,' he said to Gregory, 'about standing up for the woman. I've no patience with that; it's the way immorality's fostered in these days. I raise my voice against this sentimentalism. I always have, and I always shall!'

Gregory jumped to his feet.

'I 've told you once before,' he said, 'that you were indelicate; I tell you so again.'

Mr. Barter got up, and stood bending over the table, crimson in the face, staring at Gregory, and unable to speak.

'Either you or I,' he said at last, stammering with passion, 'must leave this room!'

Gregory tried to speak; then turning abruptly, he stepped out on to the terrace, and passed from the view of those within.

The rector said:

'Good night, Pendyce; I 'm going, too!'

The squire shook the hand held out to him with a face perplexed to sadness. There was silence when Mr. Barter had left the room.

The squire broke it with a sigh.

'I wish we were back at Oxenham's, Paramor! This serves me right for deserting the old house! What on earth made me send George to Eton?'

Mr. Paramor buried his nose in the vase. In this saying of his old schoolfellow was the whole of the squire's creed:

'I believe in my father, and his father, and his father's father, the makers and keepers of my estate; and I believe in myself and my son and my son's son. And I believe that we have made the country, and shall keep the country what it is. And I believe in the Public Schools, and especially the Public School that I was at. And I believe in my social equals and the country house and in things as they are, for ever and ever. Amen.'

Mr. Pendyce went on:

'I 'm not a Puritan, Paramor; I dare say there are allowances to be made for George. I don't even object to the woman herself; she may be too good for Bellew;

she must be too good for a fellow like that! But for George to marry her would be ruination. Look at Lady Rose's case! Any one but a star-gazing fellow like Vigil must see that! It's taboo! It's sheer taboo! And think—think of my—my grandson! No, no, Paramor; no, no, by God!'

The squire covered his eyes with his hand.

Mr. Paramor, who had no son himself, answered with feeling:

'Now, now, old fellow; it won't come to that!'

'God knows what it will come to, Paramor! My nerve's shaken! You know yourself that if there's a divorce he'll be bound to marry her!'

To this Mr. Paramor made no reply, but pressed his lips together.

'There's your poor dog whining,' he said.

And without waiting for permission he opened the door. Mrs. Pendyce and the spaniel John came in The squire looked up and frowned. The spaniel John, panting with delight, rubbed against him. 'I have been through torment, master,' he seemed to say. 'A second separation at present is not possible for me!'

Mrs. Pendyce stood waiting silently, and Mr. Paramor addressed himself to her.

'*You* can do more than any of us, Mrs. Pendyce, both with George and with this man Bellew—and, if I am not mistaken, with his wife.'

The squire broke in:

'Don't think that I'll have any humble pie eaten to that fellow Bellew!'

The look Mr. Paramor gave him at those words was like that of a doctor diagnosing a disease. Yet there was nothing in the expression of the squire's face with its thin grey whiskers and moustache, its twist to the left, its swan-like eyes, decided jaw, and sloping brow, different from what this idea might bring on the face of any country gentleman.

Mrs. Pendyce said eagerly:

'Oh, Mr. Paramor, if I could only see George!'

She longed so for a sight of her son that her thoughts carried her no further.

'See him!' cried the squire, 'You'll go on spoiling him till he's disgraced us all!'

Mrs. Pendyce turned from her husband to his solicitor. Excitement had fixed an unwonted colour in her cheeks; her lips twitched as if she wished to speak.

Mr. Paramor answered for her:

'No, Pendyce; if George is spoilt, the system is to blame.'

'System!' said the squire. 'I've never had a system for him. I'm no believer in systems! I don't know what you're talking of. I have another son, thank God!'

Mrs. Pendyce took a step forward.

'Horace,' she said, 'you would never——'

Mr. Pendyce turned from his wife, and said sharply:

'Paramor, are you sure I can't cut the entail?'

'As sure,' said Mr. Paramor, 'as I sit here!'

CHAPTER IX

DEFINITION OF 'PENDYCITIS'

GREGORY walked long in the Scotch garden with his
eyes on the stars. One, larger than all the rest, over the
larches, shone on him ironically, for it was the star of
love. And on his beat between the yew trees that,
living before Pendyces came to Worsted Skeynes,
would live when they were gone, he cooled his heart
in the silver light of that big star. The irises restrained
their perfume lest it should whip his senses; only the
young larch trees and the far fields sent him their
fugitive sweetness through the dark. And the same
brown owl that had hooted when Helen Bellew kissed
George Pendyce in the conservatory hooted again now
that Gregory walked grieving over the fruits of that kiss.

His thoughts were of Mr. Barter, and with the in-
justice natural to a man who took a warm and personal
view of things, he painted the rector in colours darker
than his cloth.

'Indelicate, meddlesome,' he thought. 'How dare
he speak of her like that!'

Mr. Paramor's voice broke in on his meditations.

'Still cooling your heels? Why did you play the
deuce with us in there?'

'I hate a sham,' said Gregory. 'This marriage of
my ward's is a sham. She had better live honestly with
the man she really loves!'

'So you said just now,' returned Mr. Paramor.
'Would you apply that to every one?'

'I would.'

'Well,' said Mr. Paramor with a laugh, 'there is nothing like an idealist for making hay! You once told me, if I remember, that marriage was sacred to you!'

'Those are my own private feelings, Paramor. But here the mischief's done already. It is a sham, a hateful sham, and it ought to come to an end!'

'That's all very well,' replied Mr. Paramor, 'but when you come to put it into practice in that wholesale way it leads to goodness knows what. It means reconstructing marriage on a basis entirely different from the present. It's marriage on the basis of the heart, and not on the basis of property. Are you prepared to go to that length?'

'I am.'

'You're as much of an extremist one way as Barter is the other. It's you extremists who do all the harm. There's a golden mean, my friend. I agree that something ought to be done. But what you don't see is that laws must suit those they are intended to govern. You're too much in the stars, Vigil. Medicine must be graduated to the patient. Come, man, where's your sense of humour? Imagine your conception of marriage applied to Pendyce and his sons, or his rector, or his tenants, and the labourers on his estate.'

'No, no,' said Gregory; 'I refuse to believe——'

'The country classes,' said Mr. Paramor quietly, 'are especially backward in such matters. They have strong, meat-fed instincts, and what with the county members, the bishops, the peers, all the hereditary force of the country, they still rule the roast. And there's a certain disease—to make a very poor joke, call it "Pendycitis"—with which most of these people are infected. They're "crass." They do things, but they do them the wrong way! They muddle through with the greatest possible amount of unnecessary labour and suffering! It's part of the hereditary principle. I haven't had to do with them thirty-five years for nothing!'

Gregory turned his face away.

'Your joke *is* very poor,' he said. 'I don't believe they are like that! I won't admit it. If there is such a disease, it's our business to find a remedy.'

'Nothing but an operation will cure it,' said Mr. Paramor; 'and before operating there's a preliminary process to be gone through. It was discovered by Lister.'

Gregory answered:

'Paramor, I hate your pessimism!'

Mr. Paramor's eyes haunted Gregory's back.

'But I am not a pessimist,' he said. 'Far from it.

> When daisies pied and violets blue,
> And lady-smocks all silver-white,
> And cuckoo-buds of yellow hue
> Do paint the meadows with delight,
> The cuckoo then, on every tree——'

Gregory turned on him.

'How can you quote poetry, and hold the views you do? We ought to construct——'

'You want to build before you've laid your foundations,' said Mr. Paramor. 'You let your feelings carry you away, Vigil. The state of the marriage laws is only a symptom. It's this disease, this grudging narrow spirit in men, that makes such laws necessary. Unlovely men, unlovely laws—what can you expect?'

'I will never believe that we shall be content to go on living in a slough of—of——'

'Provincialism!' said Mr. Paramor. 'You should

take to gardening; it makes one recognize what you idealists seem to pass over—that men, my dear friend, are, like plants, creatures of heredity and environment; their growth is slow. You can't get grapes from thorns, Vigil, or figs from thistles—at least, not in one generation—however busy and hungry you may be!'

'Your theory degrades us all to the level of thistles.'

'Social laws depend for their strength on the harm they have it in their power to inflict, and that harm depends for its strength on the ideals held by the man on whom the harm falls. If you dispense with the marriage tie, or give up your property and take to brotherhood, you'll have a very thistly time, but you won't mind that if you're a fig. And so on *ad lib*. It's odd, though, how soon the thistles that thought themselves figs get found out. There are many things I hate, Vigil. One is extravagance, and another humbug!'

But Gregory stood looking at the sky.

'We seem to have wandered from the point,' said Mr. Paramor, 'and I think we had better go in. It's nearly eleven.'

Throughout the length of the low white house there were but three windows lighted, three eyes looking at the moon, a fairy shallop sailing the night sky. The cedar trees stood black as pitch. The old brown owl had ceased his hooting. Mr. Paramor gripped Gregory by the arm.

'A nightingale! Did you hear him down in that spinney? It's a sweet place, this! I don't wonder Pendyce is fond of it. You're not a fisherman, I think? Did you ever watch a school of fishes coasting along a bank? How blind they are, and how they follow their leader! In our element we men know just about as much as the fishes do. A blind lot, Vigil! We take a mean view of things; we 're damnably provincial!'

Gregory pressed his hands to his forehead.

'I 'm trying to think,' he said, 'what will be the consequences to my ward of this divorce.'

'My friend, listen to some plain speaking. Your ward and her husband and George Pendyce are just the sort of people for whom our law of divorce is framed. They 've all three got courage, they 're all reckless and obstinate, and—forgive me—thick-skinned. Their case, if fought, will take a week of hard swearing, a week of the public's money and time. It will give admirable opportunities to eminent counsel, excellent reading to the general public, first-rate sport all round. The papers will have a regular carnival. I repeat, they are the very people for whom our law of divorce is framed. There 's a great deal to be said for publicity, but all the same it puts a premium on insensibility, and causes a vast amount of suffering to innocent people. I told you once before, to get a divorce, even if you deserve it, you mustn't be a sensitive person. Those three will go through it all splendidly, but every scrap of skin will be torn off you and our poor friends down here, and the result will be a drawn battle at the end! That 's if it 's fought, and if it comes on I don't see how we can let it go unfought; it 's contrary to my instincts. If we let it go undefended, mark my words, your ward and George Pendyce will be sick of each other before the law allows them to marry, and George, as his father says, for the sake of "morality," will have to marry a woman who is tired of him, or of whom he is tired. Now you 've got it straight from the shoulder, and I 'm going up to bed. It 's a heavy dew. Lock this door after you.'

Mr. Paramor made his way into the conservatory. He stopped and came back.

'Pendyce,' he said, 'perfectly understands all I've been telling you. He'd give his eyes for the case not to come on, but you'll see he'll rub everything up the wrong way, and it'll be a miracle if we succeed. That's "Pendycitis!" We've all got a touch of it. Good night!'

Gregory was left alone outside the country house with his big star. And as his thoughts were seldom of an impersonal kind he did not reflect on 'Pendycitis,' but on Helen Bellew. And the longer he thought the more he thought of her as he desired to think, for this was natural to him; and ever more ironical grew the twinkling of his star above the spinney where the nightingale was singing.

CHAPTER X

GEORGE GOES FOR THE GLOVES

ON the Thursday of the Epsom Summer Meeting, George Pendyce sat in the corner of a first-class railway carriage trying to make two and two into five. On a sheet of Stoics' Club note-paper his racing debts were stated to a penny—one thousand and forty-five pounds overdue, and below, seven hundred and fifty lost at the current meeting. Below these again his private debts were indicated by the round figure of one thousand pounds. It was round by courtesy, for he had only calculated those bills which had been sent in, and Providence, which knows all things, preferred the rounder figure of fifteen hundred. In sum, therefore, he had against him a total of three thousand two hundred and ninety-five pounds. And since at Tattersalls and the Stock Exchange, where men are engaged in perpetual motion, an almost absurd punctiliousness is required in the payment of those sums which have for the moment inadvertently been lost, seventeen hundred and ninety-five of this must infallibly be raised by Monday next. Indeed, only a certain liking for George, a good loser and a good winner, and the fear of dropping a good customer, had induced the firm of bookmakers to let that debt of one thousand and forty-five stand over the Epsom meeting.

To set against these sums (in which he had not counted his current trainer's bill, and the expenses,

183

which he could not calculate, of the divorce suit), he had, first, a bank balance which he might still overdraw another twenty pounds; secondly, the Ambler and two bad selling platers; and thirdly (more considerable item), X, or that which he might, or indeed must, win over the Ambler's race this afternoon.

Whatever else, it was not pluck that was lacking in the character of George Pendyce. This quality was in his fibre, in the consistency of his blood, and confronted with a situation which, to some men, and especially to men not brought up on the hereditary plan, might have seemed desperate, he exhibited no sign of anxiety or distress. Into the consideration of his difficulties he imported certain principles: (1) He did not intend to be posted at Tattersalls. Sooner than that he would go to the Jews; the entail was all he could look to borrow on; the Hebrews would force him to pay through the nose. (2) He did not intend to show the white feather, and in backing his horse meant to 'go for the gloves.' (3) He did not intend to think of the future; the thought of the present was quite bad enough.

The train bounded and swung as though rushing onwards to a tune, and George sat quietly in his corner.

Amongst his fellows in the carriage was the Hon. Geoffrey Winlow, who, though not a racing-man, took a kindly interest in our breed of horses, which by attendance at the principal meetings he hoped to improve.

'Your horse going to run, George?'

George nodded.

'I shall have a fiver on him for luck. I can't afford to bet. Saw your mother at the Foxholme garden-party last week. You seen them lately?'

George shook his head and felt an odd squeeze at his heart.

'You know they had a fire at old Peacock's farm; I hear the squire and Barter did wonders. He's as game as a pebble, the squire.'

Again George nodded, and again felt that squeeze at his heart.

'Aren't they coming to town this season?'

'Haven't heard,' answered George. 'Have a cigar?'

Winlow took the cigar, and cutting it with a small penknife, scrutinized George's square face with his leisurely eyes. It needed a physiognomist to penetrate its impassivity. Winlow thought to himself:

'I shouldn't be surprised if what they say about old George is true.' . . . 'Had a good meeting so far?'

'So-so.'

They parted on the racecourse. George went at once to see his trainer and thence into Tattersalls' ring. He took with him that equation with X, and sought the society of two gentlemen quietly dressed, one of whom was making a note in a little book with a gold pencil. They greeted him respectfully, for it was to them that he owed the bulk of that seventeen hundred and ninety-five pounds.

'What price will you lay against my horse?'

'Evens, Mr. Pendyce,' replied the gentleman with the gold pencil, 'to a monkey.'

George booked the bet. It was not his usual way of doing business, but to-day everything seemed different, and something stronger than custom was at work.

'I am going for the gloves,' he thought; 'if it doesn't come off, I'm done anyhow.'

He went to another quietly dressed gentleman with a diamond pin and a Jewish face. And as he went from one quietly dressed gentleman to another there preceded him some subtle messenger, who breathed the words: 'Mr. Pendyce is going for the gloves,' so that at each visit he found they had greater confidence than ever in his horse. Soon he had promised to pay two thousand pounds if the Ambler lost, and received the assurance of eminent gentlemen, quietly dressed, that they would pay him fifteen hundred if the Ambler won. The odds now stood at two to one on, and he had found it impossible to back the Ambler for 'a place,' in accordance with his custom.

'Made a fool of myself,' he thought; 'ought never to have gone into the ring at all; ought to have let Barney's work it quietly. It doesn't matter!'

He still required to win three hundred pounds to settle on the Monday, and laid a final bet of seven hundred to three hundred and fifty pounds upon his horse. Thus, without spending a penny, simply by making a few promises, he had solved the equation with X.

On leaving the ring, he entered the bar and drank some whisky. He then went to the paddock. The starting-bell for the second race had rung; there was hardly any one there, but in a far corner the Ambler was being led up and down by a boy. George glanced round to see that no acquaintances were near, and joined in this promenade. The Ambler turned his black, wild eye, crescented with white, threw up his head, and gazed far into the distance.

'If one could only make him understand!' thought George.

When his horse left the paddock for the starting-post George went back to the stand. At the bar he drank some more whisky, and heard someone say:

'I had to lay six to four. I want to find Pendyce; they say he's backed it heavily.'

George put down his glass, and instead of going to his usual place, mounted slowly to the top of the stand.

'I don't want them buzzing round me,' he thought.

At the top of the stand—that national monument, visible for twenty miles around—he knew himself to be safe. Only 'the many' came here, and amongst the many he thrust himself till at the very top he could rest his glasses on a rail and watch the colours. Besides his own peacock blue there was a straw, a blue with white stripes, a red with white stars.

They say that through the minds of drowning men troop ghosts of past experience. It was not so with George; his soul was fastened on that little daub of peacock blue. Below the glasses his lips were colourless from hard compression; he moistened them continually. The four little coloured daubs stole into line, the flag fell.

'They're off!' That roar, like the cry of a monster, sounded all around. George steadied his glasses on the rail. Blue with white stripes was leading, the Ambler lying last. Thus they came round the further bend. And Providence, as though determined that someone should benefit by his absorption, sent a hand sliding under George's elbows, to remove the pin from his tie and slide away. Round Tattenham Corner George saw his horse take the lead. So, with straw closing up, they came into the straight. The Ambler's jockey looked back and raised his whip; in that instant, as if by magic, straw drew level; down came the whip on the Ambler's flank; again as by magic straw was in

front. The saying of his old jockey darted through
George's mind: 'Mark my words, sir, that 'orse knows
what 's what, and when they 're like that they 're best
let alone.'

'Sit still, you fool!' he muttered.

The whip came down again; straw was two lengths
in front.

Someone behind said:

'The favourite 's beat! No, he 's not, by Jove!'

For as though George's groan had found its way to
the jockey's ears, he dropped his whip. The Ambler
sprang forward. George saw that he was gaining. All
his soul went out to his horse's struggle. In each of
those fifteen seconds he died and was born again; with
each stride all that was loyal and brave in his nature
leaped into flame, all that was base sank, for he
himself was racing with his horse, and the sweat
poured down his brow. And his lips babbled broken
sounds that no one heard, for all around were babbling
too.

Locked together, the Ambler and straw ran home.
Then followed a hush, for no one knew which of the
two had won. The numbers went up: 'Seven—Two
—Five.'

'The favourite 's second! Beaten by a nose!' said
a voice.

George bowed his head, and his whole spirit felt
numb. He closed his glasses and moved with the
crowd to the stairs. A voice behind him said:

'He 'd have won in another stride!'

Another answered:

'I hate that sort of horse. He curled up at the
whip.'

George ground his teeth.

'Curse you!' he muttered, 'you little Cockney; what do you know about a horse?'

The crowd surged; the speakers were lost to sight.

The long descent from the stand gave him time. No trace of emotion showed on his face when he appeared in the paddock. Blacksmith the trainer stood by the Ambler's stall.

'That idiot Tipping lost us the race, sir,' he began with quivering lips. 'If he 'd only left him alone, the horse would have won in a canter. What on earth made him use his whip? He deserves to lose his licence. He——'

The gall and bitterness of defeat surged into George's brain.

'It 's no good *your* talking, Blacksmith,' he said; 'you put him up. What the devil made you quarrel with Swells?'

The little man's chin dropped in sheer surprise.

George turned away, and went up to the jockey, but at the sick look on the poor youth's face the angry words died off his tongue.

'All right, Tipping; I 'm not going to rag you.' And with the ghost of a smile he passed into the Ambler's stall. The groom had just finished putting him to rights; the horse stood ready to be led from the field of his defeat. The groom moved out, and George went to the Ambler's head. There is no place, no corner, on a racecourse where a man may show his heart. George did but lay his forehead against the velvet of his horse's muzzle, and for one short second hold it there. The Ambler awaited the end of that brief caress, then with a snort threw up his head, and with his wild, soft eyes seemed saying: 'You fools! what do you know of me?'

George stepped to one side.

'Take him away,' he said, and his eyes followed the Ambler's receding form.

A racing-man of a different race, whom he knew and did not like, came up to him as he left the paddock.

'I suppothe you won't thell your horse, Pendythe?' he said. 'I 'll give you five thou. for him. He ought never to have lotht; the beating won't help him with the handicappers a little bit.'

'You carrion crow!' thought George.

'Thanks; he 's not for sale,' he answered.

He went back to the stand, but at every step and in each face, he seemed to see the equation which now he could only solve with $X2$. Thrice he went into the bar. It was on the last of these occasions that he said to himself: 'The horse must go. I shall never have a horse like him again.'

Over that green down which a hundred thousand feet had trodden brown, which a hundred thousand hands had strewn with bits of paper, cigar-ends, and the fragments of discarded food, over the great approaches to the battle-field, where all was pathway leading to and from the fight, those who make livelihood in such a fashion, least and littlest followers, were bawling, hawking, whining to the warriors flushed with victory or wearied by defeat. Over that green down, between one-legged men and ragged acrobats, women with babies at the breast, thimble-riggers, touts, walked George Pendyce, his mouth hard set and his head bent down.

'Good luck, captain, good luck to-morrow; good luck, good luck! . . . For the love of Gawd, your lordship! . . . Roll, bowl, or pitch!'

The sun, flaming out after long hiding, scorched the back of his neck; the free down wind, fouled by foetid odours, brought to his ears the monster's last cry: 'They 're off!'

A voice hailed him.

George turned and saw Winlow, and with a curse and a smile he answered:

'Hallo!'

The Hon. Geoffrey ranged alongside, examining George's face at leisure.

'Afraid you had a bad race, old chap! I hear you 've sold the Ambler to that fellow Guilderstein.'

In George's heart something snapped.

'Already?' he thought. 'The brute 's been crowing. And it 's *that* little bounder that my horse — my horse——'

He answered calmly:

'Wanted the money.'

Winlow, who was not lacking in cool discretion, changed the subject.

Late that evening George sat in the Stoics' window overlooking Piccadilly. Before his eyes, shaded by his hand, the hansoms passed, flying east and west, each with the single pale disk of face, or the twin disks of faces close together; and the gentle roar of the town came in, and the cool air refreshed by night. In the light of the lamps the trees of the Green Park stood burnished out of deep shadow where nothing moved; and high over all, the stars and purple sky seemed veiled with golden gauze. Figures without end filed by. Some glanced at the lighted windows and the man in the white shirt-front sitting there. And many thought: 'Wish I were that swell, with nothing to do but step into his father's shoes'; and to many no thought came.

But now and then some passer murmured to himself: 'Looks lonely sitting there.'

And to those faces gazing up, George's lips were grim, and over them came and went a little bitter smile; but on his forehead he felt still the touch of his horse's muzzle, and his eyes, which none could see, were dark with pain.

CHAPTER XI

MR. BARTER TAKES A WALK

THE event at the rectory was expected every moment. The rector, who practically never suffered, disliked the thought and sight of others' suffering. Up to this day, indeed, there had been none to dislike, for in answer to inquiries his wife had always said: 'No, dear, no; I'm all right — really, it's nothing.' And she had always said it smiling, even when her smiling lips were white. But this morning in trying to say it she had failed to smile. Her eyes had lost their hopelessly hopeful shining, and sharply between her teeth she said: 'Send for Dr. Wilson, Hussell.'

The rector kissed her, shutting his eyes, for he was afraid of her face with its lips drawn back, and its discoloured cheeks. In five minutes the groom was hastening to Cornmarket on the roan cob, and the rector stood in his study, looking from one to another of his household gods, as though calling them to his assistance. At last he took down a bat and began oiling it. Sixteen years ago, when Hussell was born, he had been overtaken by sounds that he had never to this day forgotten; they had clung to the nerves of his memory, and for no reward would he hear them again. They had never been uttered since, for like most wives, his wife was a heroine; but, used as he was to this event, the rector had ever since suffered from panic. It was as though Providence, storing all the anxiety which he

might have felt throughout, let him have it with a
rush at the last moment. He put the bat back into its
case, corked the oil-bottle, and again stood looking at
his household gods. None came to his aid. And his
thoughts were as they had nine times been before.
'I ought not to go out. I ought to wait for Wilson.
Suppose anything were to happen. Still, nurse is with
her, and I can do nothing. Poor Rose—poor darling!
It's my duty to—— What's that? I'm better out
of the way.'

Softly, without knowing that it was softly, he opened
the door; softly, without knowing it was softly, he
stepped to the hat-rack and took his black straw hat;
softly, without knowing it was softly, he went out,
and, unfaltering, hurried down the drive.

Three minutes later he appeared again, approaching
the house faster than he had set forth. He passed the
hall door, ran up the stairs, and entered his wife's room.

'Rose dear, Rose, can I do anything?'

Mrs. Barter put out her hand, a gleam of malice shot
into her eyes. Through her set lips came a vague
murmur, and the words:

'No, dear, nothing. Better go for your walk.'

Mr. Barter pressed his lips to her quivering hand, and
backed from the room. Outside the door he struck at
the air with his fist, and, running downstairs, was once
more lost to sight. Faster and faster he walked,
leaving the village behind, and among the country
sights and sounds and scents his nerves began to recover.
He was able to think again of other things: of Cecil's
school report—far from satisfactory; of old Hermon
in the village, whom he suspected of overdoing his
bronchitis with an eye to port; of the return match
with Coldingham, and his belief that their left-hand

bowler only wanted 'hitting'; of the new edition of
hymn-books, and the slackness of the upper village in
attending church — five households less honest and
ductile than the rest, a foreign look about them, dark
people, un-English. In thinking of these things he
forgot what he wanted to forget; but hearing the sound
of wheels, he entered a field as though to examine the
crops until the vehicle had passed. It was not Wilson,
but it might have been, and at the next turning he
unconsciously branched off the Cornmarket road.

It was noon when he came within sight of Coldingham,
six miles from Worsted Skeynes. He would have
enjoyed a glass of beer, but, unable to enter the public-
house, he went into the churchyard instead. He sat
down on a bench beneath a sycamore opposite the
Winlow graves, for Coldingham was Lord Montrossor's
seat, and it was here that all the Winlows lay. Bees
were busy above them in the branches, and Mr. Barter
thought:

'Beautiful site. We 've nothing like this at Worsted
Skeynes. . . .'

But suddenly he found that he could not sit there
and think. Suppose his wife were to die! It happened
sometimes; the wife of John Tharp of Bletchingham
had died in giving birth to her tenth child! His forehead was wet, and he wiped it. Casting an angry glance
at the Winlow graves, he left the seat.

He went down by the further path, and came out on
the green. A cricket-match was going on, and in spite
of himself the rector stopped. The Coldingham team
were in the field. Mr. Barter watched. As he had
thought, that left-hand bowler bowled a good pace,
and 'came in' from the off, but his length was poor,
very poor! A determined batsman would soon knock

him off! He moved into line with the wickets to see how much the fellow 'came in,' and he grew so absorbed that he did not at first notice the Hon. Geoffrey Winlow in pads and a blue and green blazer, smoking a cigarette astride of a camp-stool.

'Ah, Winlow, it's your team against the village. Afraid I can't stop to see you bat. I was just passing —matter I *had* to attend to—must get back!'

The real solemnity of his face excited Winlow's curiosity.

'Can't you stop and have lunch with us?'

'No, no; my wife—— Must get back!'

Winlow murmured:

'Ah, yes, of course.' His leisurely blue eyes, always in command of the situation, rested on the rector's heated face. 'By the way,' he said, 'I'm afraid George Pendyce is rather hard hit. Been obliged to sell his horse. I saw him at Epsom the week before last.'

The rector brightened.

'I made certain he'd come to grief over that betting,' he said. 'I'm very sorry—very sorry indeed.'

'They say,' went on Winlow, 'that he dropped four thousand over the Thursday race. He was pretty well dipped before, I know. Poor old George! such an awfully good chap!'

'Ah,' repeated Mr. Barter, 'I'm very sorry—very sorry indeed. Things were bad enough as it was.'

A ray of interest illumined the leisureliness of the Hon. Geoffrey's eyes.

'You mean about Mrs.—— H'm, yes?' he said. 'People are talking; you can't stop that. I'm so sorry for the poor squire, and Mrs. Pendyce. I hope something 'll be done.'

The rector frowned.

'I 've done *my* best,' he said. 'Well hit, sir! I 've always said that any one with a little pluck can knock off that left-hand man you think so much of. He "comes in" a bit, but he bowls a shocking bad length. Here I am dawdling. I must get back!'

And once more that real solemnity came over Mr. Barter's face.

'I suppose you 'll be playing for Coldingham against us on Thursday? Good-bye!'

Nodding in response to Winlow's salute, he walked away.

He avoided the churchyard, and took a path across the fields. He was hungry and thirsty. In one of his sermons there occurred this passage: 'We should habituate ourselves to hold our appetites in check. By constantly accustoming ourselves to abstinence— little abstinences in our daily life—we alone can attain to that true spirituality without which we cannot hope to know God.' And it was well known throughout his household and the village that the rector's temper was almost dangerously spiritual if anything detained him from his meals. For he was a man physiologically sane and healthy to the core, whose digestion and functions, strong, regular, and straightforward as the day, made calls upon him which would not be denied. After preaching that particular sermon, he frequently for a week or more denied himself a second glass of ale at lunch, or his after-dinner cigar, smoking a pipe instead. And he was perfectly honest in his belief that he attained a greater spirituality thereby, and perhaps indeed he did. But even if he did not, there was no one to notice this, for the majority of his flock accepted his spirituality as matter of course, and of the insignificant minority there were few who did not make allowance for the fact that he was their pastor by virtue of necessity, by virtue of a system which had placed him there almost mechanically, whether he would or no. Indeed, they respected him the more that he was their rector, and could not be removed, and were glad that theirs was no common vicar like that of Coldingham, dependent on the caprices of others. For, with the exception of two bad characters and one atheist, the whole village, Conservatives or Liberals (there were Liberals now that they were beginning to believe that the ballot was really secret), were believers in the hereditary system.

Insensibly the rector directed himself towards Bletch-ingham, where there was a temperance house. At heart he loathed lemonade and ginger-beer in the middle of the day, both of which made his economy cold and uneasy, but he felt he could go nowhere else. And his spirits rose at the sight of Bletchingham spire.

'Bread and cheese,' he thought. 'What's better than bread and cheese? And they shall make me a cup of coffee.'

In that cup of coffee there was something symbolic and fitting to his mental state. It was agitated and thick, and impregnated with the peculiar flavour of country coffee. He swallowed but little, and resumed his march. At the first turning he passed the village school, whence issued a rhythmic but discordant hum, suggestive of some dull machine that had served its time. The rector paused to listen. Leaning on the wall of the little play-yard, he tried to make out the words that, like a religious chant, were being intoned within. It sounded like: 'Twice two's four, twice four's six, twice six's eight,' and he passed on, thinking: 'A fine thing; but if we don't take care we shall go too far; we shall unfit them for their stations,' and he frowned. Crossing a stile, he took a footpath. The air was full of the singing of larks, and the bees were pulling down the clover-stalks. At the bottom of the field was a little pond overhung with willows. On a bare strip of pasture, within thirty yards, in the full sun, an old horse was tethered to a peg. It stood with its face towards the pond, baring its yellow teeth, and stretching out its head, all bone and hollows, to the water which it could not reach. The rector stopped. He did not know the horse personally, for it was three fields short of his parish, but he saw that the poor beast wanted water. He went up, and finding that the knot of the halter hurt his fingers, stooped down and wrenched at the peg. While he was thus straining and tugging, crimson in the face, the old horse stood still, gazing at him out of his bleary eyes. Mr. Barter sprang upright with a jerk, the peg in his hand, and the old horse started back.

'So ho, boy!' said the rector, and angrily he muttered: 'A shame to tie the poor beast up here in the sun. I should like to give his owner a bit of my mind!'

He led the animal towards the water. The old horse followed tranquilly enough, but as he had done nothing to deserve his misfortune, neither did he feel any gratitude towards his deliverer. He drank his fill, and fell to grazing. The rector experienced a sense of disillusionment, and drove the peg again into the softer earth under the willows; then raising himself, he looked hard at the old horse.

The animal continued to graze. The rector took out his handkerchief, wiped the perspiration from his brow, and frowned. He hated ingratitude in man or beast.

Suddenly he realized that he was very tired.

'It must be over by now,' he said to himself, and hastened on in the heat across the fields.

The rectory door was open. Passing into the study, he sat down a moment to collect his thoughts. People were moving above; he heard a long moaning sound that filled his heart with terror.

He got up and rushed to the bell, but did not ring it, and ran upstairs instead. Outside his wife's room he met his children's old nurse. She was standing on the mat, with her hands to her ears, and the tears were rolling down her face.

'Oh, sir!' she said—'oh, sir!'

The rector glared.

'Woman!' he cried—'woman!'

He covered his ears and rushed downstairs again. There was a lady in the hall. It was Mrs. Pendyce, and he ran to her, as a hurt child runs to its mother.

'My wife,' he said—'my poor wife! God knows what they're doing to her up there, Mrs. Pendyce!' and he hid his face in his hands.

She, who had been a Totteridge, stood motionless; then, very gently putting her gloved hand on his thick arm, where the muscles stood out from the clenching of his hands, she said:

'Dear Mr. Barter, Dr. Wilson is so clever! Come into the drawing-room!'

The rector, stumbling like a blind man, suffered himself to be led. He sat down on the sofa, and Mrs. Pendyce sat down beside him, her hand still on his arm; over her face passed little quivers, as though she were holding herself in. She repeated in her gentle voice:

'It will be all right—it will be all right. Come, come!'

In her concern and sympathy there was apparent,

not aloofness, but a faint surprise that she should be sitting there stroking the rector's arm.

Mr. Barter took his hands from before his face.

'If she dies,' he said in a voice unlike his own, 'I'll not bear it.'

In answer to those words, forced from him by that which is deeper than habit, Mrs. Pendyce's hand slipped from his arm and rested on the shiny chintz covering of the sofa, patterned with green and crimson. Her soul shrank from the violence in his voice.

'Wait here,' she said.   'I will go up and see.'

To command was foreign to her nature, but Mr. Barter, with a look such as a little rueful boy might give, obeyed.

When she was gone he stood listening at the door for some sound—for any sound, even the sound of her dress—but there was none, for her petticoat was of lawn, and the rector was alone with a silence that he could not bear. He began to pace the room in his thick boots, his hands clenched behind him, his forehead butting the air, his lips folded; thus a bull, penned for the first time, turns and turns, showing the whites of its full eyes.

His thoughts drove here and there, fearful, angered, without guidance; he did not pray. The words he had spoken so many times left him as though of malice. 'We are all in the hands of God!—we are all in the hands of God!' Instead of them he could think of nothing but the old saying Mr. Paramor had used in the squire's dining-room: 'There is moderation in all things,' and this with cruel irony kept humming in his ears. 'Moderation in all things—moderation in all things!' and his wife lying there—his doing, and——

There was a sound. The rector's face, so brown and

red, could not grow pale, but his great fists relaxed.
Mrs. Pendyce was standing in the doorway with a
peculiar half-pitiful, half-excited smile.

'It's all right—a boy. The poor dear has had a
dreadful time!'

The rector looked at her, but did not speak; then
abruptly he brushed past her in the doorway, hurried
into his study and locked the door. Then, and then
only, he kneeled down, and remained there many
minutes, thinking of nothing.

CHAPTER XII

THE SQUIRE MAKES UP HIS MIND

THAT same evening at nine o'clock, sitting over the
last glass of a pint of port, Mr. Barter felt an irresistible
longing for enjoyment, an impulse towards expansion
and his fellow-men.

Taking his hat and buttoning his coat—for though
the June evening was fine the easterly breeze was eager
—he walked towards the village.

Like an emblem of that path to God of which he
spoke on Sundays, the grey road between trim hedges
threaded the shadow of the elm trees where the rooks
had long since gone to bed. A scent of wood-smoke
clung in the air; the cottages appeared, the forge, the
little shops facing the village green. Lights in the
doors and windows deepened; a breeze, which hardly
stirred the chestnut leaves, fled with a gentle rustling
through the aspens. Houses and trees, houses and
trees! Shelter through the past and through the days
to come!

The rector stopped the first man he saw.

'Fine weather for the hay, Aiken. How's your wife
doing—a girl? Ah, ha! You want some boys! You
heard of our event at the rectory? I'm thankful
to say——'

From man to man and house to house he soothed
his thirst for fellowship, for the lost sense of dignity
that should efface again the scar of suffering. And

above him the chestnuts in their breathing stillness, the aspens with their tender rustling, seemed to watch and whisper: 'Oh, little men! oh, little men!'

The moon, at the end of her first quarter, sailed out of the shadow of the churchyard—the same young moon that had sailed in her silver irony when the first Barter preached, the first Pendyce was squire at Worsted Skeynes; the same young moon that, serene, ineffable, would come again when the last Barter slept, the last Pendyce was gone, and on their gravestones, through the amethystine air, let fall her gentle light.

The rector thought:

'I shall set Stedman to work on that corner. We must have more room; the stones there are a hundred and fifty years old if they 're a day. You can't read a single word. They 'd better be the first to go.'

He passed on along the paddock footway leading to the squire's.

Day was gone, and only the moonbeams lighted the tall grasses.

At the hall the long french windows of the dining-room were open; the squire was sitting there alone, brooding sadly above the remnants of the fruit he had been eating. Flanking him on either wall hung a silent company, the effigies of past Pendyces; and at the end, above the oak and silver of the sideboard, the portrait of his wife was looking at them under lifted brows, with her faint wonder.

He raised his head.

'Ah, Barter! How 's your wife?'

'Doing as well as can be expected.'

'Glad to hear that! A fine constitution—wonderful vitality. Port or claret?'

'Thanks; just a glass of port.'

'Very trying for your nerves. I know what it is.
We 're different from the last generation; they thought
nothing of it. When Charles was born my dear old
father was out hunting all day. When my wife had
George, it made *me* as nervous as a cat!'

The squire stopped, then hurriedly added:

'But you 're so used to it.'

Mr. Barter frowned.

'I was passing Coldingham to-day,' he said. 'I saw
Winlow. He asked after you.'

'Ah! Winlow! His wife 's a very nice woman.
They 've only the one child, I think?'

The rector winced.

'Winlow tells me,' he said abruptly, 'that George
has sold his horse.'

The squire's face changed. He glanced suspiciously
at Mr. Barter, but the rector was looking at his glass.

'Sold his horse! What 's the meaning of that? He
told you why, I suppose?'

The rector drank off his wine.

'I never ask for reasons,' he said, 'where racing-
men are concerned. It 's my belief they know no more
what they 're about than so many dumb animals.'

'Ah! racing-men!' said Mr. Pendyce. 'But George
doesn't bet.'

A gleam of humour shot into the rector's eyes. He
pressed his lips together.

The squire rose.

'Come now, Barter!' he said.

The rector blushed. He hated tale-bearing—that is,
of course, in the case of a man; the case of a woman
was different—and just as, when he went to Bellew he
had been careful not to give George away, so now he
was still more on his guard.

'No, no, Pendyce.'

The squire began to pace the room, and Mr. Barter
felt something stir against his foot; the spaniel John
emerging at the end, just where the moonlight shone,
a symbol of all that was subservient to the squire,
gazed up at his master with tragic eyes. 'Here,
again,' they seemed to say, 'is something to disturb
me!'

The squire broke the silence.

'I've always counted on you, Barter; I count on
you as I would on my own brother. Come, now,
what's this about George?'

'After all,' thought the rector, 'it's his father!' . . . 'I
know nothing but what they say,' he blurted forth;
'they talk of his having lost a lot of money. I dare say
it's all nonsense. I never set much store by rumour.
And if he's sold the horse, well, so much the better.
He won't be tempted to gamble again.'

But Horace Pendyce made no answer. A single
thought possessed his bewildered, angry mind:

'My son a gambler! Worsted Skeynes in the hands
of a gambler!'

The rector rose.

'It's all rumour. You shouldn't pay any attention.
I should hardly think he's been such a fool. I only
know that I must get back to my wife. Good
night.'

And, nodding but confused, Mr. Barter went away
through the french window by which he had come.

The squire stood motionless.

A gambler!

To him, whose existence was bound up in Worsted
Skeynes, whose every thought had some direct or
indirect connection with it, whose son was but the

occupier of that place he must at last vacate, whose
religion was ancestor-worship, whose dread was change,
no word could be so terrible. A gambler!

It did not occur to him that his system was in any
way responsible for George's conduct. He had said to
Mr. Paramor: 'I never had a system; I'm no believer
in systems.' He had brought him up simply as a
gentleman. He would have preferred that George
should go into the army, but George had failed; he
would have preferred that George should devote himself to the estate, marry, and have a son, instead of
idling away his time in town, but George had failed;
and so, beyond furthering his desire to join the Yeomanry, and getting him proposed for the Stoics' Club,
what was there he could have done to keep him out of
mischief? And now he was a gambler!

Once a gambler always a gambler!

To his wife's face, looking down from the wall, he
said:

'He gets it from you!'

But for all answer the face stared gently.

Turning abruptly, he left the room, and the spaniel
John, for whom he had been too quick, stood with his
nose to the shut door, scenting for someone to come
and open it.

Mr. Pendyce went to his study, took some papers
from a locked drawer, and sat a long time looking at
them. One was the draft of his will, another a list of
the holdings at Worsted Skeynes, their acreage and
rents, a third a fair copy of the settlement, resettling
the estate when he had married. It was at this piece
of supreme irony that Mr. Pendyce looked longest.
He did not read it, but he thought:

'And I can't cut it! Paramor says so! A gambler!'

That 'crassness' common to all men in this strange
world, and in the squire intensified, was rather a process
than a quality—obedience to an instinctive dread of
what was foreign to himself, an instinctive fear of seeing
another's point of view, an instinctive belief in prece-
dent. And it was closely allied to his most deep and
moral quality—the power of making a decision. Those
decisions might be 'crass' and stupid, conduce to unnecessary suffering, have no relation to morality or
reason; but he could make them, and he could stick
to them. By virtue of this power he was where he was,
had been for centuries, and hoped to be for centuries
to come. It was in his blood. By this alone he kept
at bay the destroying forces that Time brought against
him, his order, his inheritance; by this alone he could
continue to hand down that inheritance to his son.
And at the document which did hand it down he
looked with angry and resentful eyes.

Men who conceive great resolutions do not always
bring them forth with the ease and silence which they
themselves desire. Mr. Pendyce went to his bedroom
determined to say no word of what he had resolved
to do. His wife was asleep. The squire's entrance
wakened her, but she remained motionless, with her
eyes closed, and it was the sight of that immobility,
when he himself was so disturbed, which drew from
him the words:

'Did you know that George was a gambler?'

By the light of the candle in his silver candlestick
her dark eyes seemed suddenly alive.

'He's been betting; he's sold his horse. He'd never
have sold that horse unless he were pushed. For all I
know, he may be posted at Tattersalls!'

The sheets shivered as though she who lay within

them were struggling. Then came her voice, cool and gentle:

'All young men bet, Horace; you must know that!'

The squire at the foot of the bed held up the candle; the movement had a sinister significance.

'Do you defend him?' it seemed to say. 'Do you defy me?'

Gripping the bed-rail, he cried:

'I'll have no gambler and profligate for my son! I'll not risk the estate!'

Mrs. Pendyce raised herself, and for many seconds stared at her husband. Her heart beat furiously. It had come! What she had been expecting all these days had come! Her pale lips answered:

'What do you mean? I don't understand you, Horace.'

Mr. Pendyce's eyes searched here and there—for what, he did not know.

'This has decided me,' he said. 'I'll have no half-measures. Until he can show me he's done with that woman, until he can prove he's given up this betting, until—until the heaven's fallen, I'll have no more to do with him!'

To Margery Pendyce, with all her senses quivering, that saying, 'Until the heaven's fallen,' was frightening beyond the rest. On the lips of her husband, those lips which had never spoken in metaphors, never swerved from the direct and commonplace, nor deserted the shibboleth of his order, such words had an evil and malignant sound.

He went on:

'I've brought him up as I was brought up myself. I never thought to have had a scamp for my son!'

Mrs. Pendyce's heart stopped fluttering.

'How dare you, Horace!' she cried.

The squire, letting go the bed-rail, paced to and fro. There was something savage in the sound of his footsteps through the utter silence.

'I 've made up my mind,' he said. 'The estate——'

There broke from Mrs. Pendyce a torrent of words: 'You talk of the way you brought George up! You—you never understood him! You—you never did anything for him! He just grew up like you all grow up in this——' But no word followed, for she did not know herself what was that against which her soul had blindly fluttered its wings. 'You never loved him as I do! What do I care about the estate? I wish it were sold! D' you think I like living here? D' you think I 've ever liked it? D' you think I 've ever——' But she did not finish that saying: D' you think I 've ever loved you? 'My boy a scamp! I 've heard you laugh and shake your head and say a hundred times: "Young men will be young men!" You think I don't know how you 'd all go on if you dared! You think I don't know how you talk among yourselves! As for gambling, you 'd gamble too, if you weren't afraid! And now George is in trouble——'

As suddenly as it had broken forth the torrent of her words dried up.

Mr. Pendyce had come back to the foot of the bed, and once more gripped the rail whereon the candle, still and bright, showed them each other's faces, very changed from the faces that they knew. In the squire's lean, brown throat, between the parted points of his stiff collar, a string seemed working. He stammered:

'You—you 're talking like a madwoman! My father would have cut me off, his father would have cut him off! By God! do you think I 'll stand quietly by and

see it all played ducks and drakes with, and see that
woman here, and see her son, a—a bastard, or as bad
as a bastard, in my place?   You don't know me!'

The last words came through his teeth like the growl
of a dog. Mrs. Pendyce made the crouching movement of one who gathers herself to spring.

'If you give him up, I shall go to him; I will never
come back!'

The squire's grip on the rail relaxed; in the light
of the candle, still and steady and bright, his jaw could
be seen to fall. He snapped his teeth together, and
turning abruptly, said:

'Don't talk such rubbish!'

Then, taking the candle, he went into his dressing-
room.

And at first his feelings were simple enough; he had
merely that sore sensation, that sense of raw offence,
as at some gross and violent breach of taste.

'What madness,' he thought, 'gets into women!
It would serve her right if I slept here!'

He looked around him.   There was no place where he
could sleep, not even a sofa, and taking up the candle,
he moved towards the door.   But a feeling of hesitation
and forlornness rising, he knew not whence, made him
pause irresolute before the window.

The young moon, riding low, shot her light upon his
still, lean figure, and in that light it was strange to see
how grey he looked—grey from head to foot, grey,
and sad, and old, as though in summary of all the squires
who in turn had looked upon that prospect frosted with
young moonlight to the boundary of their lands.   Out
in the paddock he saw his old hunter Bob, with his
head turned towards the house; and from the very
bottom of his heart he sighed.

In answer to that sigh came a sound of something falling outside against the door. He opened it to see what might be there. The spaniel John, lying on a cushion of blue linen, with his head propped up against the wall, darkly turned his eyes.

'I am here, master,' he seemed to say; 'it is late— I was about to go to sleep; it has done me good, however, to see you'; and hiding his eyes from the light under a long black ear, he drew a stertorous breath. Mr. Pendyce shut-to the door. He had forgotten the existence of his dog. But, as though with the sight of that faithful creature he had regained belief in all that he was used to, in all that he was master of, in all that was—himself, he opened the bedroom door and took his place beside his wife.

And soon he was asleep.

PART III

CHAPTER I

BUT Mrs. Pendyce did not sleep. That blessed anodyne of the long day spent in his farmyards and fields was on her husband's eyes—no anodyne on hers; and through them, all that was deep, most hidden, sacred, was laid open to the darkness. If only those eyes could have seen that night! But if the darkness had been light, nothing of all this so deep and sacred would have been there to see, for more deep, more sacred still, in Margery Pendyce, was the instinct of a lady. So elastic and so subtle, so interwoven of consideration for others and consideration for herself, so old, so very old, this instinct wrapped her from all eyes, like a suit of armour of the finest chain. The night must have been black indeed when she took that off and lay without it in the darkness.

With the first light she put it on again, and stealing from bed, bathed long and stealthily those eyes which felt as though they had been burned all night; thence went to the open window and leaned out. Dawn had passed, the birds were at morning music. Down there in the garden her flowers were meshed with the grey dew, and the trees were grey, spun with haze; dim and spectre-like, the old hunter, with his nose on the paddock rail, dozed in the summer mist.

And all that had been to her like prison out there, and all that she had loved, stole up on the breath of the unaired morning, and kept beating in her face, fluttering

215

at the white linen above her heart like the wings of birds flying.

The first morning song ceased, and at the silence the sun smiled out in golden irony, and everything was shot with colour. A wan glow fell on Mrs. Pendyce's spirit, that for so many hours had been heavy and grey in lonely resolution. For to her gentle soul, unused to action, shrinking from violence, whose strength was the gift of the ages, passed into it against her very nature, the resolution she had formed was full of pain. Yet painful, even terrible in its demand for action, it did not waver, but shone like a star behind the dark and heavy clouds. In Margery Pendyce (who had been a Totteridge) there was no irascible and acrid 'people's blood,' no fierce misgivings, no ill-digested beer and cider—it was pure claret in her veins—she had nothing thick and angry in her soul to help her; that which she had resolved she must carry out, by virtue of a thin, fine flame, breathing far down in her—so far that nothing could extinguish it, so far that it had little warmth. It was not 'I will not be overridden' that her spirit felt, but 'I must not be overridden, for if I am overridden, I, and in me something beyond me, more important than myself, is all undone.' And though she was far from knowing this, that *something* was her country's civilization, its very soul, the meaning of it all—gentleness, balance. Her spirit, of that quality so little gross that it would never set up a mean or petty quarrel, make mountains out of mole-hills, distort proportion, or get images awry, had taken its stand unconsciously, no sooner than it must, no later than it ought, and from that stand would not recede. The issue had passed beyond mother-love to that self-love, deepest of all which says: 'Do this, or forfeit the essence of your soul.'

And now that she stole to her bed again, she looked at her sleeping husband whom she had resolved to leave, with no anger, no reproach, but rather with a long, incurious look which told nothing even to herself.

So, when the morning came of age and it was time to rise, by no action, look, or sign did she betray the presence of the unusual in her soul. If this which was before her must be done, it would be carried out as though it were of no import, as though it were a daily action; nor did she force herself to quietude, or pride herself thereon, but acted thus from instinct, the instinct for avoiding fuss and unnecessary suffering that was bred in her.

Mr. Pendyce went out at half-past ten accompanied by his bailiff and the spaniel John. He had not the least notion that his wife still meant the words she had spoken overnight. He had told her again while dressing that he would have no more to do with George, that he would cut him out of his will, that he would force him by sheer rigour to come to heel, that, in short, he meant to keep his word, and it would have been unreasonable in him to believe that a woman, still less his wife, meant to keep hers.

Mrs. Pendyce spent the early part of the morning in the usual way. Half an hour after the squire went out she ordered the carriage round, had two small trunks, which she had packed herself, brought down, and leisurely, with her little green bag, got in. To her maid, to the butler Bester, to the coachman Benson, she said that she was going up to stay with Mr. George. Norah and Bee were at the Tharps', so that there was no one to take leave of but old Roy, the Skye; and lest that leave-taking should prove too much for her, she took him with her to the station.

For her husband she left a little note, placing it where she knew he must see it at once, and no one else see it at all.

'DEAR HORACE,

'I have gone up to London to be with George. My address will be Green's Hotel, Bond Street. You will remember what I said last night. Perhaps you did not quite realize that I meant it. Take care of poor old Roy, and don't let them give him too much meat this hot weather. Jackman knows better than Ellis how to manage the roses this year. I should like to be told how poor Rose Barter gets on. Please do not worry about me. I shall write to dear Gerald when necessary, but I don't feel like writing to him or the girls at present.

'Good-bye, dear Horace; I am sorry if I grieve you.

'Your wife,

'MARGERY PENDYCE.'

Just as there was nothing violent in her manner of taking this step, so there was nothing violent in her conception of it. To her it was not running away, a setting of her husband at defiance; there was no concealment of address, no melodramatic 'I cannot come back to you.' Such methods, such pistol-holdings, would have seemed to her ridiculous. It is true that practical details, such as the financial consequences, escaped the grasp of her mind, but even in this, her view, or rather lack of view, was really the wide, the even one. Horace would not let her starve: the idea was inconceivable. There was, too, her own three hundred a year. She had, indeed, no idea how much this meant, or what it represented, neither was she concerned, for she said to herself, 'I should be quite happy in a cottage with Roy and my flowers'; and though, of course, she had not the smallest experience to go by, it was quite possible that she was right. Things which to others came only by money, to a Totteridge came without, and even if they came not, could well be dispensed with—for to this quality of soul, this gentle self-sufficiency, had the ages worked to bring her.

Yet it was hastily and with her head bent that she stepped from the carriage at the station, and the old Skye, who from the brougham seat could just see out of the window, from the tears on his nose that were not his own, from something in his heart that was, knew this was no common parting and whined behind the glass.

Mrs. Pendyce told her cabman to drive to Green's Hotel, and it was only after she had arrived, arranged her things, washed, and had lunch, that the beginnings of confusion and homesickness stirred within her. Up to then a simmering excitement had kept her from thinking of how she was to act, or of what she had hoped, expected, dreamed, would come of her proceedings. Taking her sunshade, she walked out into Bond Street.

A passing man took off his hat.

'Dear me,' she thought, 'who was that? I ought to know!'

She had a rather vague memory for faces, and though she could not recall his name, felt more at home at once, not so lonely and adrift. Soon a quaint brightness showed in her eyes, looking at the toilets of the passers-by, and at each shop-front, more engrossing than the last. Pleasure, like that which touches the soul of a young girl at her first dance, the souls of men landing on strange shores, touched Margery Pendyce. A delicious sense of entering the unknown, of braving

the unexpected, and of the power to go on doing this
delightfully for ever, enveloped her with the gay London
air of this bright June day. She passed a perfume shop,
and thought she had never smelt anything so nice.
And next door she lingered long looking at some lace;
and though she said to herself, 'I must not buy anything;
I shall want all my money for poor George,' it made
no difference to that sensation of having all things to
her hand.

A list of theatres, concerts, operas, confronted her in
the next window, together with the effigies of prominent
artists. She looked at them with an eagerness that
might have seemed absurd to any one who saw her
standing there. Was there, indeed, all this going on all
day and every day, to be seen and heard for so few
shillings? Every year, religiously, she had visited the
opera once, the theatre twice, and no concerts; her
husband did not care for music that was 'classical.'
While she was standing there a woman begged of her,
looking very tired and hot, with a baby in her arms so
shrivelled and so small that it could hardly be seen.
Mrs. Pendyce took out her purse and gave her half a
crown, and as she did so felt a gush of feeling which
was almost rage.

'Poor little baby!' she thought. 'There must be
thousands like that, and I know nothing of them!'

She smiled to the woman, who smiled back at her;
and a fat Jewish youth in a shop doorway, seeing them
smile, smiled too, as though he found them charming.
Mrs. Pendyce had a feeling that the town was saying
pretty things to her, and this was so strange and pleasant
that she could hardly believe it, for Worsted Skeynes
had omitted to say that sort of thing to her for over
thirty years. She looked in the window of a hat shop,

and found pleasure in the sight of herself. The window was kind to her grey linen with black velvet knots and guipure, though it was two years old; but, then, she had only been able to wear it once last summer, owing to poor Hubert's death. The window was kind, too, to her cheeks, and eyes, which had that touching brightness, and to the silver-powdered darkness of her hair. And she thought: 'I don't look so very old!' But her own hat reflected in the hat-shop window displeased her now; it turned down all round, and though she loved that shape, she was afraid it was not fashionable this year. And she looked long in the window of that shop, trying to persuade herself that the hats in there would suit her, and that she liked what she did not like. In other shop windows she looked, too. It was a year since she had seen any, and for thirty-four years past she had only seen them in company with the squire or with her daughters, none of whom cared much for shops.

The people, too, were different from the people that she saw when she went about with Horace or her girls. Almost all seemed charming, having a new, strange life, in which she—Margery Pendyce—had unaccountably a little part; as though really she might come to know them, as though they might tell her something of themselves, of what they felt and thought, and even might stand listening, taking a kindly interest in what she said. This, too, was strange, and a friendly smile became fixed upon her face, and of those who saw it—shopgirls, women of fashion, coachmen, clubmen, policemen—most felt a little warmth about their hearts; it was pleasant to see on the lips of that faded lady with the silvered arching hair under a hat whose brim turned down all round.

So Mrs. Pendyce came to Piccadilly and turned west-ward towards George's club. She knew it well, for she never failed to look at the windows when she passed, and once—on the occasion of Queen Victoria's Jubilee —had spent a whole day there to see that royal show.

She began to tremble as she neared it, for though she did not, like the squire, torture her mind with what might or might not come to pass, care had nested in her heart.

George was not in his club, and the porter could not tell her where he was. Mrs. Pendyce stood motionless. He was her son; how could she ask for his address? The porter waited, knowing a lady when he saw one. Mrs. Pendyce said gently:

'Is there a room where I could write a note, or would it be——'

'Certainly not, ma'am. I can show you to a room at once.'

And though it was only a mother to a son, the porter preceded her with the quiet discretion of one who aids a mistress to her lover; and perhaps he was right in his view of the relative values of love, for he had great experience, having lived long in the best society.

On paper headed with the fat white 'Stoics' Club,' so well known on George's letters, Mrs. Pendyce wrote what she had to say. The little dark room where she sat was without sound, save for the buzzing of a largish fly in a streak of sunlight below the blind. It was dingy in colour; its furniture was old. At the Stoics' was found neither the new art nor the resplendent drapings of those larger clubs sacred to the middle classes. The little writing-room had an air of mourn-ing: 'I am so seldom used; but be at home in me;

you might find me tucked away in almost any country
house!'

Yet many a solitary Stoic had sat there and written
many a note to many a woman. George, perhaps, had
written to Helen Bellew at that very table with that very
pen, and Mrs. Pendyce's heart ached jealously.

'DEAREST GEORGE' (she wrote),

'I have something very particular to tell you. Do
come to me at Green's Hotel. Come soon, my dear.
I shall be lonely and unhappy till I see you.

'Your loving
'MARGERY PENDYCE.'

And this note, which was just what she would have
sent to a lover, took that form, perhaps unconsciously,
because she had never had a lover thus to write to.

She slipped the note and half a crown diffidently into
the porter's hand; refused his offer of some tea, and
walked vaguely towards the Park.

It was five o'clock; the sun was brighter than ever.
People in carriages and people on foot in one leisurely,
unending stream were filing in at Hyde Park Corner.
Mrs. Pendyce went, too, and timidly—she was unused
to traffic—crossed to the further side and took a chair.
Perhaps George was in the Park and she might see him;
perhaps Helen Bellew was there, and she might see
her; and the thought of this made her heart beat and
her eyes under their uplifted brows stare gently at each
figure—old men and young men, women of the world,
fresh young girls. How charming they looked, how
sweetly they were dressed! A feeling of envy mingled
with the joy she ever felt at seeing pretty things; she
was quite unconscious that she herself was pretty under

that hat whose brim turned down all round. But as she sat a leaden feeling slowly closed her heart, varied by nervous flutterings, when she saw someone whom she ought to know. And whenever, in response to a salute, she was forced to bow her head, a blush rose in her cheeks, a wan smile seemed to make confession:

'I know I look a guy; I know it's odd for me to be sitting here alone!'

She felt old—older than she had ever felt before. In the midst of this gay crowd, of all this life and sunshine, a feeling of loneliness which was almost fear—a feeling of being utterly adrift, cut off from all the world—came over her; and she felt like one of her own plants, plucked up from its native earth, with all its poor roots hanging bare, as though groping for the earth to cling to. She knew now that she had lived too long in the soil that she had hated; and was too old to be transplanted. The custom of the country—that weighty, wingless creature born of time and of the earth—had its limbs fast twined around her. It had made of her its mistress, and was not going to let her go.

CHAPTER II

THE SON AND THE MOTHER

HARDER than for a camel to pass through the eye of a needle is it for a man to become a member of the Stoics' Club, except by virtue of the hereditary principle; for unless he be nourished he cannot be elected, and since by the club's first rule he may have no occupation whatsoever, he must be nourished by the efforts of those who have gone before. And the longer they have gone before the more likely he is to receive no blackballs.

Yet without entering into the Stoics' Club it is difficult for a man to attain that supreme outward control which is necessary to conceal his lack of control within; and, indeed, the club is an admirable instance of how Nature places the remedy to hand for the disease. For, perceiving how George Pendyce and hundreds of other young men 'to the manner born' had lived from their birth up in no connection whatever with the struggles and sufferings of life, and fearing lest, when Life in her careless and ironical fashion brought them into abrupt contact with ill-bred events they should make themselves a nuisance by their cries of dismay and wonder, Nature had devised a mask and shaped it to its highest form within the portals of the Stoics' Club. With this mask she clothed the faces of these young men whose souls she doubted, and called them—gentlemen. And when she, and she alone, heard their poor squeaks behind that mask, as Life placed clumsy feet on them, she pitied them, knowing that it was not they who were in fault, but the unpruned system which had made them what they were. And in her pity she endowed many of them with thick skins, steady feet, and complacent souls, so that, treading in well-worn paths their lives long, they might slumber to their deaths in those halls where their fathers had slumbered to their deaths before them. But sometimes Nature (who was not yet a Socialist) rustled her wings and heaved a sigh, lest the excesses and excrescences of their system should bring about excesses and excrescences of the opposite sort. For extravagance of all kinds was what she hated, and of that particular form of extravagance which Mr. Paramor so vulgarly called 'Pendycitis' she had a horror.

It may happen that for long years the likeness between father and son will lie dormant, and only when disintegrating forces threaten the links of the chain binding them together will that likeness leap forth, and by a piece of Nature's irony become the main factor in destroying the hereditary principle for which it is the silent, the most worthy, excuse.

It is certain that neither George nor his father knew the depth to which this 'Pendycitis' was rooted in the other; neither suspected, not even in themselves, the amount of essential bulldog at the bottom of their souls, the strength of their determination to hold their own in the way that would cause the greatest amount of unnecessary suffering. They did not deliberately desire to cause unnecessary suffering; they simply could not help an instinct passed by time into their fibre, through atrophy of the reasoning powers and the constant mating, generation after generation, of those whose motto had been: 'Kings of our own dunghills.' And now

George came forward, defying his mother's belief that he was a Totteridge, as champion of the principle in tail male; for in the Totteridges, from whom in this stress he diverged more and more towards his father's line, there was some freer strain, something non-provincial, and this had been so ever since Hubert de Toterydge had led his private crusade, from which he had neglected to return. With the Pendyces it had been otherwise; from immemorial time 'a county family,' they had construed the phrase literally, had taken no poetical licences. Like innumerable other county families, they were perforce what their tradition decreed —provincial in their souls.

George, a man-about-town, would have stared at being called provincial, but a man cannot stare away his nature. He was provincial enough to keep Mrs. Bellew bound when she herself was tired of him, and consideration for her, and for his own self-respect, asked him to give her up. He had been keeping her bound for two months or more. But there was much excuse for him. His heart was sore to breaking-point; he was sick with longing, and deep, angry wonder that he, of all men, should be cast aside like a worn-out glove. Men tired of women daily—that was the law. But what was this? His dogged instinct had fought against the knowledge as long as he could, and now that it was certain he fought against it still. George was a true Pendyce!

To the world, however, he behaved as usual. He came to the club about ten o'clock to eat his breakfast and read the sporting papers. Towards noon a hansom took him to the railway station appropriate to whatever race-meeting was in progress, or, failing that, to the cricket ground at Lord's, or Prince's Tennis Club. Half-past six saw him mounting the staircase at the

Stoics' to that card-room where his effigy still hung, with its look of 'hard work, hard work; but I must keep it going!' At eight he dined, a bottle of champagne screwed deep down into ice, his face flushed with the day's sun, his shirt-front and his hair shining with gloss. What happier man in all great London!

But with the dark the club's swing-doors opened for his passage into the lighted streets, and till next morning the world knew him no more. It was then that he took revenge for all the hours he wore a mask. He would walk the pavements for miles trying to wear himself out, or in the Park fling himself down on a chair in the deep shadow of the trees, and sit there with his arms folded and his head bowed down. On other nights he would go into some music-hall, and amongst the glaring lights, the vulgar laughter, the scent of painted women, try for a moment to forget the face, the laugh, the scent of that woman for whom he craved. And all the time he was jealous, with a dumb, vague jealousy of he knew not whom; it was not his nature to think impersonally, and he could not believe that a woman would drop him except for another man. Often he went to her mansions, and walked round and round casting a stealthy stare at her windows. Twice he went up to her door, but came away without ringing the bell. One evening, seeing a light in her sitting-room, he rang, but there came no answer. Then an evil spirit leaped up in him, and he rang again and again. At last he went away to his room—a studio he had taken near—and began to write to her. He was long composing that letter, and many times tore it up; he despised the expression of feelings in writing. He only tried because his heart wanted relief so badly. And this, in the end, was all that he produced:

'I know you were in to-night. It 's the only time I 've come. Why couldn't you have let me in? You 've no right to treat me like this. You are leading me the life of a dog.

'GEORGE.'

The first light was silvering the gloom above the river, the lamps were paling to the day, when George went out and dropped this missive in the letter-box. He came back to the river and lay down on an empty bench under the plane trees of the Embankment, and while he lay there one of those without refuge or home, who lie there night after night, came up unseen and looked at him.

But morning comes, and with it that sense of the ridiculous, so merciful to suffering men. George got up lest any one should see a Stoic lying there in his evening clothes; and when it became time he put on his mask and sallied forth. At the club he found his mother's note, and set out for her hotel.

Mrs. Pendyce was not yet down, but sent to ask him to come up. George found her standing in her dressing-gown in the middle of the room, as though she knew not where to place herself for this, their meeting. Only when he was quite close did she move and throw her arms round his neck. George could not see her face, and his own was hidden from her, but through the thin dressing-gown he felt her straining to him, and her arms that had pulled his head down quivering; and for a moment it seemed to him as if he were dropping a burden. But only for a moment, for at the clinging of those arms his instinct took fright. And though she was smiling, the tears were in her eyes, and this offended him.

'Don't, mother!'

Mrs. Pendyce's answer was a long look. George could not bear it, and turned away.

'Well,' he said gruffly, 'when you can tell me what's brought you up——'

Mrs. Pendyce sat down on the sofa. She had been brushing her hair; though silvered, it was still thick and soft, and the sight of it about her shoulders struck George. He had never thought of her having hair that would hang down.

Sitting on the sofa beside her, he felt her fingers stroking his, begging him not to take offence and leave her. He felt her eyes trying to see his eyes, and saw her lips trembling; but a stubborn, almost evil smile was fixed upon his face.

'And so, dear—and so,' she stammered, 'I told your father that I couldn't see that done, and so I came up to you.'

Many sons have found no hardship in accepting all that their mothers do for them as a matter of right, no difficulty in assuming their devotion a matter of course, no trouble in leaving their own affections to be understood; but most sons have found great difficulty in permitting their mothers to diverge one inch from the conventional, to swerve one hair's breadth from the standard of propriety appropriate to mothers of men of their importance.

It is decreed of mothers that their birth pangs shall not cease until they die.

And George was shocked to hear his mother say that she had left his father to come to him. It affected his self-esteem in a strange and subtle way. The thought that tongues might wag about her revolted his manhood and his sense of form. It seemed strange, incom-

prehensible, and wholly wrong; the thought, too, flashed
through his mind: 'She is trying to put pressure
on me!'

'If you think I 'll give her up, mother——' he said.

Mrs. Pendyce's fingers tightened.

'No, dear,' she answered painfully; 'of course, if
she loves you so much, I couldn't ask you. That 's
why I——'

George gave a grim little laugh.

'What on earth can you do, then? What 's the good
of your coming up like this? How are you to get on
here all alone? I can fight my own battles. You 'd
much better go back.'

Mrs. Pendyce broke in:

'Oh, George, I can't see you cast off from us! I
must be with you!'

George felt her trembling all over. He got up
and walked to the window. Mrs. Pendyce's voice
followed:

'I won't try to separate you, George; I promise,
dear. I couldn't, if she loves you, and you love her
so!'

Again George laughed that grim little laugh. And
the fact that he was deceiving her, meant to go on
deceiving her, made him as hard as iron.

'Go back, mother!' he said. 'You 'll only make
things worse. This isn't a woman's business. Let
father do what he likes; I can hold on!'

Mrs. Pendyce did not answer, and he was obliged to
look round. She was sitting perfectly still with her
hands in her lap, and his man's hatred of anything
conspicuous happening to a woman, to his own mother
of all people, took fiercer fire.

'Go back!' he repeated, 'before there 's any fuss!

What good can you possibly do? You can't leave father; that's absurd! You *must* go!'

Mrs. Pendyce answered:

'I can't do that, dear.'

George made an angry sound, but she was so motionless and pale that he dimly perceived how she was suffering, and how little he knew of her who had borne him.

Mrs. Pendyce broke the silence:

'But you, George dear? What is going to happen? How are you going to manage?' And suddenly clasping her hands: 'Oh! what is coming?'

Those words, embodying all that had been in his heart so long, were too much for George. He went abruptly to the door.

'I can't stop now,' he said; 'I'll come again this evening.'

Mrs. Pendyce looked up.

'Oh, George——'

But as she had the habit of subordinating her feelings to the feelings of others, she said no more, but tried to smile.

That smile smote George to the heart.

'Don't worry, mother; try and cheer up. We'll go to the theatre. You get the tickets!'

And trying to smile too, but turning lest he should lose his self-control, he went away.

In the hall he came on his uncle, General Pendyce. He came on him from behind, but knew him at once by that look of feeble activity about the back of his knees, by his sloping yet upright shoulders, and the sound of his voice, with its dry and querulous precision, as of a man whose occupation has been taken from him.

The general turned round.

'Ah, George,' he said, 'your mother 's here, isn't she? Look at this that your father 's sent me!'

He held out a telegram in a shaky hand:

'Margery up at Green's Hotel. Go and see her at once.—HORACE.'

And while George read the general looked at his nephew with eyes that were ringed by little circles of darker pigment, and had crow's-footed purses of skin beneath, earned by serving his country in tropical climes.

'What 's the meaning of it?' he said. 'Go and see her? Of course I 'll go and see her! Always glad to see your mother. But where 's all the hurry?'

George perceived well enough that his father's pride would not let him write to her, and though it was for himself that his mother had taken this step, he sympathized with his father. The general fortunately gave him little time to answer.

'She 's up to get herself some dresses, I suppose? I 've seen nothing of you for a long time. When are you coming to dine with me? I heard at Epsom that you 'd sold your horse. What made you do that? What 's your father telegraphing to me like this for? It 's not like him. Your mother 's not ill, is she?'

George shook his head, and muttering something about 'Sorry, an engagement—awful hurry,' was gone.

Left thus abruptly to himself, General Pendyce summoned a page, slowly pencilled something on his card, and with his back to the only persons in the hall, waited, his hands folded on the handle of his cane. And while he waited he tried as far as possible to think of nothing. Having served his country, his time now was nearly all devoted to waiting, and to think fatigued and made him feel discontented, for he had had sunstroke

once, and fever several times. In the perfect precision
of his collar, his boots, his dress, his figure; in the
way from time to time he cleared his throat, in the
strange yellow driedness of his face between his carefully brushed whiskers, in the immobility of his white
hands on his cane, he gave the impression of a man
sucked dry by a system. Only his eyes, restless and
opinionated, betrayed the essential Pendyce that was
behind.

He went up to the ladies' drawing-room, clutching
that telegram. It worried him. There was something
odd about it, and he was not accustomed to pay calls
in the morning. He found his sister-in-law seated at an
open window, her face unusually pink, her eyes rather
defiantly bright. She greeted him gently, and General
Pendyce was not the man to discern what was not put
under his nose. Fortunately for him, that had never
been his practice.

'How are you, Margery?' he said. 'Glad to see you
in town. How's Horace? Look here what he's sent
me!' He offered her the telegram, with the air of
slightly avenging an offence; then added in surprise,
as though he had just thought of it: 'Is there anything
I can do for you?'

Mrs. Pendyce read the telegram, and she, too, like
George, felt sorry for the sender.

'Nothing, thanks, dear Charles,' she said slowly.
'I'm all right. Horace gets so nervous!'

General Pendyce looked at her; for a moment his
eyes flickered, then, since the truth was so improbable
and so utterly in any case beyond his philosophy, he
accepted her statement.

'He shouldn't go sending telegrams like this,' he
said. 'You might have been ill for all I could tell. It

spoiled my breakfast!' For though, as a fact, it had
not prevented his completing a hearty meal, he fancied
that he felt hungry. 'When I was quartered at Halifax
there was a fellow who never sent anything but telegrams. Telegraph Jo they called him. He commanded
the old Bluebottles. You know the old Bluebottles?
If Horace is going to take to this sort of thing he'd
better see a specialist; it's almost certain to mean a
breakdown. You're up about dresses, I see. When do
you come to town? The season's getting on.'

Mrs. Pendyce was not afraid of her husband's brother,
for though punctilious and accustomed to his own way
with inferiors, he was hardly a man to inspire awe in
his social equals. It was, therefore, not through fear
that she did not tell him the truth, but through an
instinct for avoiding all unnecessary suffering too strong
for her, and because the truth was really untellable.
Even to herself it seemed slightly ridiculous, and she
knew the poor general would take it so dreadfully
to heart.

'I don't know about coming up this season. The
garden is looking so beautiful, and there's Bee's engagement. The dear child is so happy!'

The general caressed a whisker with his white
hand.

'Ah, yes,' he said, 'young Tharp! Let's see, he's
not the eldest. His brother's in my old corps. What
does this young fellow do with himself?'

Mrs. Pendyce answered:

'He's only farming. I'm afraid he'll have nothing
to speak of, but he's a dear good boy. It'll be a long
engagement. Of course, there's nothing in farming,
and Horace insists on their having a thousand a year.
It depends so much on Mr. Tharp. I think they could

do perfectly well on seven hundred to start with, don't you, Charles?'

General Pendyce's answer was not more conspicuously to the point than usual, for he was a man who loved to pursue his own trains of thought.

'What about George?' he said. 'I met him in the hall as I was coming in, but he ran off in the very deuce of a hurry. They told me at Epsom that he was hard hit.'

His eyes, distracted by a fly for which he had taken a dislike, failed to observe his sister-in-law's face.

'Hard hit?' she repeated.

'Lost a lot of money. That won't do, you know, Margery—that won't do. A little mild gambling's one thing.'

Mrs. Pendyce said nothing; her face was rigid. It was the face of a woman on the point of saying: 'Do not compel me to hint that you are boring me!'

The general went on:

'A lot of new men have taken to racing that no one knows anything about. That fellow who bought George's horse, for instance; you'd never have seen *his* nose in Tattersalls when I was a young men. I find when I go racing I don't know half the colours. It spoils the pleasure. It's no longer the close borough that it was. George had better take care what he's about. I can't imagine what we're coming to!'

On Margery Pendyce's hearing, those words, 'I can't imagine what we're coming to,' had fallen for four-and-thirty years, in every sort of connection, from many persons. It had become part of her life, indeed, to take it for granted that people could imagine nothing; just as the solid food and solid comfort of Worsted

Skeynes and the misty mornings and the rain had become part of her life. And it was only the fact that her nerves were on edge and her heart bursting that made those words seem intolerable that morning; but habit was even now too strong, and she kept silence.

The general, to whom an answer was of no great moment, pursued his thoughts.

'And you mark my words, Margery; the elections will go against us. The country's in a dangerous state.'

Mrs. Pendyce said:

'Oh, do you think the Liberals will really get in?'

From custom there was a shade of anxiety in her voice which she did not feel.

'Think?' repeated General Pendyce. 'I pray every night to God they won't!'

Folding both hands on the silver knob of his Malacca cane, he stared over them at the opposing wall; and there was something universal in that fixed stare, a sort of blank and not quite selfish apprehension. Behind his personal interests his ancestors had drilled into him the impossibility of imagining that he did not stand for the welfare of his country. Mrs. Pendyce, who had so often seen her husband look like that, leaned out of the window above the noisy street.

The general rose.

'Well,' he said, 'if I can't do anything for you, Margery, I'll take myself off; you're busy with your dressmakers. Give my love to Horace, and tell him not to send me another telegram like that.'

And bending stiffly, he pressed her hand with a touch of real courtesy and kindness, took up his hat, and went away. Mrs. Pendyce, watching him descend the stairs, watching his stiff sloping shoulders, his head with its grey hair brushed carefully away from the centre parting, the backs of his feeble, active knees, put her hand to her breast and sighed, for with him she seemed to see descending all her past life, and that one cannot see unmoved.

CHAPTER III

MRS. BELLEW sat on her bed smoothing out the halves of a letter; by her side was her jewel-case. Taking from it an amethyst necklet, an emerald pendant, and a diamond ring, she wrapped them in cotton-wool, and put them in an envelope. The other jewels she dropped one by one into her lap, and sat looking at them. At last, putting two necklets and two rings back into the jewel-case, she placed the rest in a little green box, and taking that and the envelope, went out. She called a hansom, drove to a post office, and sent a telegram:

'PENDYCE, STOICS' CLUB.
    'Be at studio six to seven.—H.'

From the post office she drove to her jeweller's, and many a man who saw her pass with the flush on her cheeks and the smouldering look in her eyes, as though a fire were alight within her, turned in his tracks and bitterly regretted that he knew not who she was, or whither going. The jeweller took the jewels from the green box, weighed them one by one, and slowly examined each through his lens. He was a little man with a yellow wrinkled face and a weak little beard, and having fixed in his mind the sum that he would give, he looked at his client prepared to mention less. She was sitting with her elbows on the counter, her chin resting in her hands, and her eyes were fixed on him. He decided somehow to mention the exact sum.

'Is that all?'

'Yes, madam; that is the utmost.'

'Very well, but I must have it now in cash!'

The jeweller's eyes flickered.

'It's a large sum,' he said—'most unusual. I haven't got such a sum in the place.'

'Then please send out and get it, or I must go elsewhere.'

The jeweller brought his hands together, and washed them nervously.

'Excuse me a moment; I'll consult my partner.'

He went away, and from afar he and his partner spied her nervously. He came back with a forced smile. Mrs. Bellew was sitting as he had left her.

'It's a fortunate chance; I think we can just do it, madam.'

'Give me notes, please, and a sheet of paper.'

The jeweller brought them.

Mrs. Bellew wrote a letter, enclosed it with the bank notes in the bulky envelope she had brought, addressed it, and sealed the whole.

'Call a cab, please!'

The jeweller called a cab.

'Chelsea Embankment!'

The cab bore her away.

Again in the crowded streets so full of traffic, people turned to look after her. The cabman, who put her down at the Albert Bridge, gazed alternately at the coins in his hands and the figure of his fare, and wheeling his cab towards the stand, jerked his thumb in her direction.

Mrs. Bellew walked fast down a street till, turning a corner, she came suddenly on a small garden with three poplar trees in a row. She opened its green gate without pausing, went down a path, and stopped at the first of three green doors. A young man with a beard, resembling an artist, who was standing behind the last of the three doors, watched her with a knowing smile on his face. She took out a latchkey, put it in the lock, opened the door, and passed in.

The sight of her face seemed to have given the artist an idea. Propping his door open, he brought an easel and canvas, and setting them so that he could see the corner where she had gone in, began to sketch.

An old stone fountain with three stone frogs stood in the garden near that corner, and beyond it was a flowering currant bush, and beyond this again the green door on which a slanting gleam of sunlight fell. He worked for an hour, then put his easel back and went out to get his tea.

Mrs. Bellew came out soon after he was gone. She closed the door behind her, and stood still. Taking from her pocket the bulky envelope, she slipped it into the letter-box; then bending down, picked up a twig, and placed it in the slit to prevent the lid falling with a rattle. Having done this, she swept her hands down her face and breast as though to brush something from her, and walked away. Beyond the outer gate she turned to the left, and took the same street back to the river. She walked slowly, luxuriously, looking about her. Once or twice she stopped, and drew a deep breath, as though she could not have enough of the air. She went as far as the Embankment, and stood leaning her elbows on the parapet. Between the finger and thumb of one hand she held a small object on which the sun was shining. It was a key. Slowly, luxuriously, she stretched her hand out over the water, parted her thumb and finger, and let it fall.

CHAPTER IV

MRS. PENDYCE'S INSPIRATION

BUT George did not come to take his mother to the theatre, and she whose day had been passed in looking forward to the evening, passed that evening in a drawing-room full of furniture whose history she did not know, and a dining-room full of people eating in twos and threes and fours, at whom she might look, but to whom she must not speak, to whom she did not even want to speak, so soon had the wheel of life rolled over her wonder and her expectation, leaving it lifeless in her breast. And all that night, with one short interval of sleep, she ate of bitter isolation and futility, and of the still more bitter knowledge: 'George does not want me; I'm no good to him!'

Her heart, seeking consolation, went back again and again to the time when he *had* wanted her; but it was far to go, to the days of holland suits, when all those things that he desired—slices of pineapple, Benson's old carriage - whip, the daily reading out of *Tom Brown's Schooldays*, the rub with Elliman when he sprained his little ankle, the tuck-up in bed—were in her power alone to give.

This night she saw with fatal clearness that since he went to school he had never wanted her at all. She had tried so many years to believe that he did, till it had become part of her life, as it was part of her life to say her prayers night and morning; and now she found it was all pretence. But, lying awake, she still tried to believe it, because to that she had been bound when she brought him, first-born, into the world. Her other son, her daughters, she loved them too, but it was not the same thing, quite; she had never wanted them to want her, because that part of her had been given once for all to George.

The street noises died down at last; she had slept two hours when they began again. She lay listening. And the noises and her thoughts became tangled in her exhausted brain—one great web of weariness, a feeling that it was all senseless and unnecessary, the emanation of cross-purposes and cross-grainedness, the negation of that gentle moderation, her own most sacred instinct. And an early wasp, attracted by the sweet perfumes of her dressing-table, roused himself from the corner where he had spent the night, and began to hum and hover over the bed. Mrs. Pendyce was a little afraid of wasps, so, taking a moment when he was otherwise engaged, she stole out, and fanned him with her night-dress-case, till, perceiving her to be a lady, he went away. Lying down again, she thought: 'People *will* worry them until they sting, and then kill them; it 's so unreasonable,' not knowing that she was putting all her thoughts on suffering in a single nutshell.

She breakfasted upstairs, unsolaced by any news from George. Then with no definite hope, but a sort of inner certainty, she formed the resolution to call on Mrs. Bellew. She determined, however, first to visit Mr. Paramor, and, having but a hazy notion of the hour when men begin to work, she did not dare to start till past eleven, and told her cabman to drive her slowly. He drove her, therefore, faster than his wont. In Leicester Square the passage of a Personage between two stations blocked the traffic, and on the footways were gathered a crowd of simple folk with much in their hearts and little in their stomachs, who raised a cheer as the Personage passed. Mrs. Pendyce looked eagerly from her cab, for she too loved a show.

The crowd dispersed, and the cab went on.

It was the first time she had ever found herself in the business apartment of any professional man less important than a dentist. From the little waiting-room, where they handed her *The Times*, which she could not read from excitement, she caught sight of rooms lined to the ceilings with leather books and black tin boxes, initialed in white to indicate the brand, and of young men seated behind lumps of paper that had been written on. She heard a perpetual clicking noise which roused her interest, and smelled a peculiar odour of leather and disinfectant which impressed her disagreeably. A youth with reddish hair and a pen in his hand passed through and looked at her with a curious stare immediately averted. She suddenly felt sorry for him and all those other young men behind the lumps of paper, and the thought went flashing through her mind: 'I suppose it's all because people can't agree.'

She was shown in to Mr. Paramor at last. In his large empty room, with its air of past grandeur, she sat gazing at three La France roses in a tumbler of water with the feeling that she would never be able to begin.

Mr. Paramor's eyebrows, which jutted from his clean, brown face like little clumps of pot-hooks, were iron-grey, and iron-grey his hair brushed back from his high forehead. Mrs. Pendyce wondered why he looked five years younger than Horace, who was his junior, and ten years younger than Charles, who, of course, was younger still. His eyes, which from iron-grey some

inner process of spiritual manufacture had made into
steel colour, looked young too, although they were
grave, and the smile which twisted up the corners of
his mouth looked very young.

'Well,' he said, 'it's a great pleasure to see you.'

Mrs. Pendyce could only answer with a smile.

Mr. Paramor put the roses to his nose.

'Not so good as yours,' he said, 'are they? but the
best I can do.'

Mrs. Pendyce blushed with pleasure.

'My garden is looking so beautiful——' Then,
remembering that she no longer had a garden, she
stopped; but remembering also that, though she had
lost her garden, Mr. Paramor still had his, she added
quickly: 'And yours, Mr. Paramor—I'm sure it must
be looking lovely.'

Mr. Paramor drew out a kind of dagger with which
he had stabbed some papers to his desk, and took a
letter from the bundle.

'Yes,' he said, 'it's looking very nice. You'd like
to see this, I expect.'

'Bellew v. Bellew and Pendyce' was written at the
top. Mrs. Pendyce stared at those words as though
fascinated by their beauty; it was long before she got
beyond them. For the first time the full horror of these
matters pierced the kindly armour that lies between
mortals and what they do not like to think of. Two men
and a woman wrangling, fighting, tearing each other
before the eyes of all the world. A woman and two men
stripped of charity and gentleness, of moderation and
sympathy—stripped of all that made life decent and
lovable, squabbling like savages before the eyes of all
the world. Two men, and one of them her son, and
between them a woman whom both of them had *loved*!

'Bellew v. Bellew and Pendyce!' And this would go down to fame in company with the pitiful stories she had read from time to time with a sort of offended interest; in company with 'Snooks v. Snooks and Stiles,' 'Horaday v. Horaday,' 'Bethany v. Bethany and Sweetenham.' In company with all those cases where everybody seemed so dreadful, yet where she had often and often felt so sorry, as if these poor creatures had been fastened in the stocks by some malignant, loutish spirit, for all that would to come and jeer at. And horror filled her heart. It was all so mean, and gross, and common.

The letter contained but a few words from a firm of solicitors confirming an appointment. She looked up at Mr. Paramor. He stopped pencilling on his blotting-paper, and said at once:

'I shall be seeing these people myself to-morrow afternoon. I shall do my best to make them see reason.'

She felt from his eyes that he knew what she was suffering, and was even suffering with her.

'And if—if they won't?'

'Then I shall go on a different tack altogether, and they must look out for themselves.'

Mrs. Pendyce sank back in her chair; she seemed to smell again that smell of leather and disinfectant, and hear a sound of incessant clicking. She felt faint, and to disguise that faintness asked at random: 'What does "without prejudice" in this letter mean?'

Mr. Paramor smiled.

'That's an expression we always use,' he said. 'It means that when we give a thing away, we reserve to ourselves the right of taking it back again.'

Mrs. Pendyce, who did not understand, murmured:

'I see. But what have they given away?'

Mr. Paramor put his elbows on the desk, and lightly pressed his finger-tips together.

'Well,' he said, 'properly speaking, in a matter like this, the other side and I are cat and dog. We are supposed to know nothing about each other and to want to know less, so that when we do each other a courtesy we are obliged to save our faces by saying: "We don't really do you one." D' you understand?'

Again Mrs. Pendyce murmured:

'I see.'

'It sounds a little provincial, but we lawyers exist by reason of provincialism. If people were once to begin making allowances for each other, I don't know where we should be.'

Mrs. Pendyce's eyes fell again on those words, 'Bellew v. Bellew and Pendyce,' and again, as though fascinated by their beauty, rested there.

'But you wanted to see me about something else too, perhaps?' said Mr. Paramor.

A sudden panic came over her.

'Oh, no, thank you. I just wanted to know what had been done. I've come up on purpose to see George. You told me that I——'

Mr. Paramor hastened to her aid.

'Yes, yes; quite right—quite right.'

'Horace hasn't come with me.'

'Good!'

'He and George sometimes don't quite——'

'Hit it off? They're too much alike.'

'Do you think so? I never saw——'

'Not in face, not in face; but they've both got——'

Mr. Paramor's meaning was lost in a smile; and Mrs. Pendyce, who did not know that the word 'Pendycitis' was on the tip of his tongue, smiled vaguely too.

'George is very determined,' she said. 'Do you think—oh, do you think, Mr. Paramor, that you will be able to persuade Captain Bellew's solicitors——'

Mr. Paramor threw himself back in his chair, and his hand covered what he had written on his blotting-paper.

'Yes,' he said slowly—'oh, yes, yes!'

But Mrs. Pendyce had had her answer. She had meant to speak of her visit to Helen Bellew, but now her thought was:

'He won't persuade them; I feel it. Let me get away!'

Again she seemed to hear the incessant clicking, to smell leather and disinfectant, to see those words, 'Bellew *v.* Bellew and Pendyce.'

She held out her hand.

Mr. Paramor took it in his own and looked at the floor.

'Good-bye,' he said—'good-bye. What's your address—Green's Hotel? I'll come and tell you what I do. I know—I know!'

Mrs. Pendyce, on whom those words 'I know—I know!' had a strange, emotionalizing effect, as though no one had ever known before, went away with quivering lips. In her life no one *had* ever 'known'—not indeed that she could or would complain of such a trifle, but the fact remained. And at this moment, oddly, she thought of her husband, and wondered what he was doing, and felt sorry for him.

But Mr. Paramor went back to his seat and stared at what he had written on his blotting-paper. It ran thus:

> We stand on our petty rights here,
> And our potty dignity there;
> We make no allowance for others,
> They make no allowance for us;

> We catch hold of them by the ear,
> They grab hold of us by the hair—
> The result is a bit of a muddle
> That ends in a bit of a fuss.

He saw that it neither rhymed nor scanned, and with a grave face he tore it up.

Again Mrs. Pendyce told her cabman to drive slowly, and again he drove her faster than usual; yet that drive to Chelsea seemed to last for ever, and interminable were the turnings which the cabman took, each one shorter than the last, as if he had resolved to see how much his horse's mouth could bear.

'Poor thing!' thought Mrs. Pendyce; 'its mouth must be so sore, and it's quite unnecessary.' She put her hand up through the trap. 'Please take me in a straight line. I don't like corners.'

The cabman obeyed. It worried him terribly to take one corner instead of the six he had purposed on his way; and when she asked him his fare, he charged her a shilling extra for the distance he had saved by going straight. Mrs. Pendyce paid it, knowing no better, and gave him sixpence over, thinking it might benefit the horse; and the cabman, touching his hat, said:

'Thank you, my lady,' for to say 'my lady' was his principle when he received eighteenpence above his fare.

Mrs. Pendyce stood quite a minute on the pavement, stroking the horse's nose and thinking:

'I *must* go in; it's silly to come all this way and not go in!'

But her heart beat so that she could hardly swallow.

At last she rang.

Mrs. Bellew was seated on the sofa in her little drawing-room whistling to a canary in the open window.

In the affairs of men there is an irony constant and deep, mingled with the very springs of life. The expectations of Mrs. Pendyce, those timid apprehensions of this meeting which had racked her all the way, were lamentably unfulfilled. She had rehearsed the scene ever since it came into her head; the reality seemed unfamiliar. She felt no nervousness and no hostility, only a sort of painful interest and admiration. And how could this or any other woman help falling in love with George?

The first uncertain minute over, Mrs. Bellew's eyes were as friendly as if she had been quite within her rights in all she had done; and Mrs. Pendyce could not help meeting friendliness half-way.

'Don't be angry with me for coming. George doesn't know. I felt I must come to see you. Do you think that you two quite know all you're doing? It seems so dreadful, and it's not only yourselves, is it?'

Mrs. Bellew's smile vanished.

'Please don't say "you two,"' she said.

Mrs. Pendyce stammered:

'I don't understand.'

Mrs. Bellew looked her in the face and smiled; and as she smiled she seemed to become a little coarser.

'Well, I think it's quite time you did! I don't love your son. I did once, but I don't now. I told him so yesterday, once for all.'

Mrs. Pendyce heard those words, which made so vast, so wonderful a difference—words which should have been like water in a wilderness—with a sort of horror, and all her spirit flamed up into her eyes.

'You don't love him?' she cried.

She felt only a blind sense of insult and affront.

This woman tire of George? Tire of her son? She looked at Mrs. Bellew, on whose face was a kind of

inquisitive compassion, with eyes that had never before
held hatred.

'You have tired of him? You have given him up?
Then the sooner I go to him the better! Give me the
address of his rooms, please.'

Helen Bellew knelt down at the bureau and wrote on
an envelope, and the grace of the woman pierced Mrs.
Pendyce to the heart.

She took the paper. She had never learned the art
of abuse, and no words could express what was in her
heart, so she turned and went out.

Mrs. Bellew's voice sounded quick and fierce behind
her:

'How could I help getting tired? I am not you.
Now go!'

Mrs. Pendyce wrenched open the outer door. Descending the stairs, she felt for the banister. She had
that awful sense of physical soreness and shrinking
which violence, whether their own or others', brings
to gentle souls.

CHAPTER V

THE MOTHER AND THE SON

To Mrs. Pendyce, Chelsea was an unknown land, and
to find her way to George's rooms would have taken
her long had she been by nature what she was by
name, for Pendyces never asked their way to anything,
or believed what they were told, but found out for
themselves with much unnecessary trouble, of which
they afterwards complained.

A policeman first, and then a young man with a
beard, resembling an artist, guided her footsteps. The
latter, who was leaning by a gate, opened it.

'In here,' he said; 'the door in the corner on the
right.'

Mrs. Pendyce walked down the little path, past the
ruined fountain with its three stone frogs, and stood
by the first green door and waited. And while she
waited she struggled between fear and joy; for now
that she was away from Mrs. Bellew she no longer felt
a sense of insult. It was the actual sight of her that
had aroused it, so personal is even the most gentle
heart.

She found the rusty handle of a bell amongst the
creeper-leaves, and pulled it. A cracked metallic tinkle
answered her, but no one came; only a faint sound as
of someone pacing to and fro. Then in the street
beyond the outer gate a coster began calling to the
sky, and in the music of his prayers the sound was lost.

The young man with a beard, resembling an artist, came down the path.

'Perhaps you could tell me, sir, if my son is out?'

'I 've not seen him go out, and I 've been painting here all the morning.'

Mrs. Pendyce looked with wonder at an easel which stood outside another door a little further on. It seemed to her strange that her son should live in such a place.

'Shall I knock for you?' said the artist. 'All these knockers are stiff.'

'If you would be so kind!'

The artist knocked.

'He must be in,' he said. 'I haven't taken my eyes off his door, because I 've been painting it.'

Mrs. Pendyce gazed at the door.

'I can't get it,' said the artist. 'It 's worrying me to death.'

Mrs. Pendyce looked at him doubtfully.

'Has he no servant?' she said.

'Oh, no,' said the artist; 'it 's a studio. The light 's all wrong. I wonder if you would mind standing just as you are for one second; it would help me a lot!'

He moved back and curved his hand over his eyes, and through Mrs. Pendyce there passed a shiver.

'Why doesn't George open the door?' she thought. 'What—what is this man doing?'

The artist dropped his hand.

'Thanks so much!' he said. 'I 'll knock again. There! that would raise the dead!'

And he laughed.

An unreasoning terror seized on Mrs. Pendyce.

'Oh,' she stammered, 'I *must* get in—I *must* get in!'

She took the knocker herself, and fluttered it against the door.

'You see,' said the artist, 'they're all alike; these knockers are as stiff as pokers.'

He again curved his hand over his eyes. Mrs. Pendyce leaned against the door; her knees were trembling violently.

'What is happening?' she thought. 'Perhaps he's only asleep, perhaps—— O God!'

She beat the knocker with all her force. The door yielded, and in the space stood George. Choking back a sob, Mrs. Pendyce went in. He banged the door behind her.

For a full minute she did not speak, possessed still by that strange terror and by a sort of shame. She did not even look at her son, but cast timid glances round his room. She saw a gallery at the far end, and a conical roof half made of glass. She saw curtains hanging all the gallery length, a table with tea-things and decanters, a round iron stove, rugs on the floor, and a large full-length mirror in the centre of the wall. A silver cup of flowers was reflected in that mirror. Mrs. Pendyce saw that they were dead, and the sense of their vague and nauseating odour was her first definite sensation.

'Your flowers are dead, my darling,' she said. 'I must get you some fresh!'

Not till then did she look at George. There were circles under his eyes; his face was yellow; it seemed to her that it had shrunk. This terrified her, and she thought:

'I must show nothing; I must keep my head!'

She was afraid—afraid of something desperate in his face, of something desperate and headlong, and she was afraid of his stubbornness, the dumb, unthinking stubbornness that holds to what has been because it

has been, that holds to its own when its own is dead.
She had so little of this quality herself that she could
not divine where it might lead him; but she had lived
in the midst of it all her married life, and it seemed
natural that her son should be in danger from it now.

Her terror called up her self-possession. She drew
George down on the sofa by her side, and the thought
flashed through her: 'How many times has he not sat
here with that woman in his arms!'

'You didn't come for me last night, dear! I got the
tickets, such good ones!'

George smiled.

'No,' he said; 'I had something else to see to!'

At sight of that smile Margery Pendyce's heart beat
till she felt sick, but she, too, smiled.

'What a nice place you have here, darling!'

'There's room to walk about.'

Mrs. Pendyce remembered the sound she had heard
of pacing to and fro. From his not asking her how she
had found out where he lived she knew that he must
have guessed where she had been, that there was
nothing for either of them to tell the other. And
though this was a relief, it added to her terror—the
terror of that which is desperate. All sorts of images
passed through her mind. She saw George back in
her bedroom after his first run with the hounds, his
chubby cheek scratched from forehead to jaw, and the
blood-stained pad of a cub fox in his little gloved hand.
She saw him sauntering into her room the last day of
the 1880 match at Lord's, with a battered top-hat, a
blackened eye, and a cane with a light-blue tassel. She
saw him deadly pale with tightened lips that afternoon
after he had escaped from her, half cured of laryngitis,
and stolen out shooting by himself, and she remembered

his words: 'Well, mother, I couldn't stand it any longer; it was too beastly slow!'

Suppose he could not stand it now! Suppose he should do something rash! She took out her handkerchief.

'It's very hot in here, dear; your forehead is quite wet!'

She saw his eyes turn on her suspiciously, and all her woman's wit stole into her own eyes, so that they did not flicker, but looked at him with matter-of-fact concern.

'That skylight is what does it,' he said. 'The sun gets full on there.'

Mrs. Pendyce looked at the skylight.

'It seems odd to see you here, dear, but it's very nice—so unconventional. You must let me put away those poor flowers!' She went to the silver cup and bent over them. 'My dear boy, they're quite nasty! Do throw them outside somewhere; it's so dreadful, the smell of old flowers!'

She held the cup out, covering her nose with her handkerchief.

George took the cup, and like a cat spying a mouse, Mrs. Pendyce watched him take it out into the garden. As the door closed, quicker, more noiseless than a cat, she slipped behind the curtains.

'I know he has a pistol,' she thought.

She was back in an instant, gliding round the room, hunting with her eyes and hands, but she saw nothing, and her heart lightened, for she was terrified of all such things.

'It's only these terrible first hours,' she thought.

When George came back she was standing where he had left her. They sat down in silence, and in that

silence, the longest of her life, she seemed to feel all
that was in his heart, all the blackness and bitter aching,
the rage of defeat and starved possession, the lost
delight, the sensation of ashes and disgust; and yet her
heart was full enough already of relief and shame,
compassion, jealousy, love, and deep longing. Only
twice was the silence broken. Once when he asked
her whether she had lunched, and she who had eaten
nothing all day answered:

'Yes, dear; yes.'

Once when he said:

'You shouldn't have come here, mother; I'm a bit
out of sorts!'

She watched his face, dearest to her in all the world,
bent towards the floor, and she so yearned to hold it
to her breast that, since she dared not, the tears stole
up, and silently rolled down her cheeks. The stillness
in that room, chosen for remoteness, was like the stillness of a tomb, and, as in a tomb, there was no outlook
on the world, for the glass of the skylight was opaque.

That deathly stillness settled round her heart; her
eyes fixed themselves on the skylight, as though be-
seeching it to break and let in sound. A cat, making
a pilgrimage from roof to roof, the four dark moving
spots of its paws, the faint blur of its body, was all
she saw. And suddenly, unable to bear it any longer,
she cried:

'Oh, George, speak to me! Don't put me away
from you like this!'

George answered:

'What do you want me to say, mother?'

'Nothing—only——'

And falling on her knees beside her son, she pulled
his head down against her breast, and stayed rocking

herself to and fro, silently shifting closer till she could
feel his head lie comfortably; so, she had his face
against her heart, and she could not bear to let it go.
Her knees hurt her on the boarded floor, her back and
all her body ached; but not for worlds would she relax
an inch, believing that she could comfort him with her
pain, and her tears fell on his neck. When at last he
drew his face away she sank down on the floor, and
could not rise, but her fingers felt that the bosom of
her dress was wet. He said hoarsely:

'It's all right, mother; you needn't worry!'

For no reward would she have looked at him just
then, but with a deeper certainty than reason she knew
that he was safe.

Stealthily on the sloping skylight the cat retraced
her steps, its four paws dark moving spots, its body a
faint blur.

Mrs. Pendyce rose.

'I won't stay now, darling. May I use your glass?'

Standing before that mirror, smoothing back her
hair, passing her handkerchief over her cheeks and eyes
and lips, she thought:

'That woman has stood here! That woman has
smoothed her hair, looking in this glass, and wiped his
kisses from her cheeks! May God give to her the pain
that she has given to my son!'

But when she had wished that wish she shivered.

She turned to George at the door with a smile that
seemed to say:

'It's no good to weep, or try and tell you what is
in my heart, and so, you see, I'm smiling. Please
smile, too, so as to comfort me a little.'

George put a small paper parcel in her hand and
tried to smile.

Mrs. Pendyce went quickly out. Bewildered by the sunlight, she did not look at this parcel till she was beyond the outer gate. It contained an amethyst necklace, an emerald pendant, and a diamond ring. In the little grey street that led to this garden with its poplars, old fountain, and green gate, the jewels glowed and sparkled as though all light and life had settled there. Mrs. Pendyce, who loved colour and glowing things, saw that they were beautiful.

That woman had taken them, used their light and colour, and then flung them back! She wrapped them again in the paper, tied the string, and went towards the river. She did not hurry, but walked with her eyes steadily before her. She crossed the Embankment, and stood leaning on the parapet with her hands over the grey water. Her thumb and fingers unclosed; the white parcel dropped, floated a second, and then disappeared.

Mrs. Pendyce looked round her with a start. A young man with a beard, whose face was familiar, was raising his hat.

'So your son *was* in,' he said. 'I 'm very glad. I must thank you again for standing to me just that minute; it made all the difference. It was the relation between the figure and the door that I wanted to get. Good morning!'

Mrs. Pendyce murmured 'Good morning,' following him with startled eyes, as though he had caught her in the commission of a crime. She had a vision of those jewels, buried, poor things! in the grey slime, a prey to gloom, and robbed for ever of their light and colour. And, as though she had sinned, wronged the gentle essence of her nature, she hurried away.

CHAPTER VI

GREGORY LOOKS AT THE SKY

WHEN Gregory Vigil called Mr. Paramor a pessimist it
was because, like other people, he did not know the
meaning of the term; for with a confusion common to
the minds of many persons who have been conceived
in misty moments, he thought that, to see things as
they were, meant, to try and make them worse.   Gregory
had his own way of seeing things that was very dear to
him—so dear that he would shut his eyes sooner than
see them any other way.   And since things to him were
not the same as things to Mr. Paramor, it cannot, after
all, be said that he did not see things as they were.   But
dirt upon a face that he wished to be clean he could not
see—a fluid in his blue eyes dissolved that dirt while
the image of the face was passing on to their retinae.
The process was unconscious, and has been called
idealism.   This was why the longer he reflected the more
agonizedly certain he became that his ward was right
to be faithful to the man she loved, right to join her
life to his.   And he went about pressing the blade of
this thought into his soul.

About four o'clock on the day of Mrs. Pendyce's
visit to the studio a letter was brought him by a
page-boy.

'GREEN'S HOTEL,
'*Thursday*.
'DEAR GRIG,

'I have seen Helen Bellew, and have just come from
George.   We have all been living in a bad dream.   She
260

does not love him—perhaps has never loved him. I do not know; I do not wish to judge. *She has given him up*. I will not trust myself to say anything about that. From beginning to end it all seems so unnecessary, such a needless, cross-grained muddle. I write this line to tell you how things really are, and to beg you, if you have a moment to spare, to look in at George's club this evening and let me know if he is there and how he seems. There is no one else that I could possibly ask to do this for me. Forgive me if this letter pains you.

'Your affectionate cousin,

'MARGERY PENDYCE.'

To those with the single eye, the narrow personal view of all things human, by whom the irony underlying the affairs of men is unseen and unenjoyed, whose simple hearts afford that irony its most precious smiles, who, vanquished by that irony, remain invincible—to these no blow of Fate, no reversal of their ideas, can long retain importance. The darts stick, quiver, and fall off, like arrows from chain-armour, and the last dart, slipping upwards under the harness, quivers into the heart to the cry of 'What—you! No, no; I don't believe you 're here!'

Such as these have done much of what has had to be done in this old world, and perhaps still more of what has had to be undone.

When Gregory received this letter he was working on the case of a woman with the morphia habit. He put it into his pocket and went on working. It was all he was capable of doing.

'Here is the memorandum, Mrs. Shortman. Let them take her for six weeks. She will come out a different woman.'

Mrs. Shortman, supporting her thin face in her thin hand, rested her glowing eyes on Gregory.

'I'm afraid she has lost all moral sense,' she said. 'Do you know, Mr. Vigil, I'm almost afraid she never had any!'

'What do you mean?'

Mrs. Shortman turned her eyes away.

'I'm sometimes tempted to think,' she said, 'that there are such people. I wonder whether we allow enough for that. When I was a girl in the country I remember the daughter of our vicar, a very pretty creature. There were dreadful stories about her, even before she was married, and then we heard she was divorced. She came up to London and earned her own living by playing the piano until she married again. I won't tell you her name, but she is very well known, and nobody has ever seen her show the slightest signs of being ashamed. If there is one woman like that there may be dozens, and I sometimes think we waste——'

Gregory said dryly:

'I have heard you say that before.'

Mrs. Shortman bit her lips.

'I don't think,' she said, 'that I grudge my efforts or my time.'

Gregory went quickly up, and took her hand.

'I know that — oh, I know that,' he said with feeling.

The sound of Miss Mallow furiously typing rose suddenly from the corner. Gregory removed his hat from the peg on which it hung.

'I must go now,' he said. 'Good night.'

Without warning, as is the way with hearts, his heart had begun to bleed, and he felt that he must be in the open air. He took no omnibus or cab, but strode along with all his might, trying to think, trying to understand. But he could only feel—confused and battered feelings, with now and then odd throbs of pleasure of which he was ashamed. Whether he knew it or not, he was making his way to Chelsea, for though a man's eyes may be fixed on the stars, his feet cannot take him there, and Chelsea seemed to them the best alternative. He was not alone upon this journey, for many another man was going there, and many a man had been and was coming now away, and the streets were the one long streaming crowd of the summer afternoon. And the men he met looked at Gregory, and Gregory looked at them, and neither saw the other, for so it is written of men, lest they pay attention to cares that are not their own. The sun that scorched his face fell on their backs, the breeze that cooled his back blew on their cheeks. For the careless world, too, was on its way, along the pavement of the universe, one of millions going to Chelsea, meeting millions coming away. . . .

'Mrs. Bellew at home?'

He went into a room fifteen feet square and perhaps ten high, with a sulky canary in a small gilt cage, an upright piano with an open operatic score, a sofa with piled-up cushions, and on it a woman with a flushed and sullen face, whose elbows were resting on her knees, whose chin was resting on her hand, whose gaze was fixed on nothing. It was a room of that size, with all these things, but Gregory took into it with him something that made it all seem different to Gregory. He sat down by the window with his eyes carefully averted, and spoke in soft tones broken by something that sounded like emotion. He began by telling her of his woman with the morphia habit, and then he told her that he knew everything. When he had said this

he looked out of the window, where builders had left
by inadvertence a narrow strip of sky. And thus he
avoided seeing the look on her face, contemptuous,
impatient, as though she were thinking: 'You are a
good fellow, Gregory, but for Heaven's sake do see
things for once as they are! I have had enough of it.'
And he avoided seeing her stretch her arms out and
spread the fingers, as an angry cat will stretch and
spread its toes. He told her that he did not want to
worry her, but that when she wanted him for anything
she must send for him—he was always there; and he
looked at her feet, so that he did not see her lip curl.
He told her that she would always be the same to him,
and he asked her to believe that. He did not see the
smile which never left her lips again while he was there
—the smile he could not read, because it was the smile
of life, and of a woman that he did not understand.
But he did see on that sofa a beautiful creature for whom
he had longed for years, and so he went away, and left
her standing at the door with her teeth fastened on her
lip. And since with him Gregory took his eyes, he did
not see her reseated on the sofa, just as she had been
before he came in, her elbows on her knees, her chin in
her hand, her moody eyes like those of a gambler
staring into the distance. . . .

In the streets of tall houses leading away from Chelsea
were many men, some, like Gregory, hungry for love,
and some hungry for bread—men in twos and threes,
in crowds, or by themselves, some with their eyes on
the ground, some with their eyes level, some with their
eyes on the sky, but all with courage and loyalty of one
poor kind or another in their hearts. For by courage
and loyalty alone it is written that man shall live,
whether he goes to Chelsea or whether he comes away.

Of all these men, not one but would have smiled to hear Gregory saying to himself: 'She will always be the same to me! She will always be the same to me!' And not one that would have grinned. . . .

It was getting on for the Stoics' dinner hour when Gregory found himself in Piccadilly, and, Stoic after Stoic, they were getting out of cabs and passing the club doors. The poor fellows had been working hard all day on the racecourse, the cricket ground, at Hurlingham, or in the Park; some had been to the Royal Academy, and on their faces was a pleasant look: 'Ah, God is good—we can rest at last!' And many of them had had no lunch, hoping to keep their weights down, and many who had lunched had not done themselves as well as might be hoped, and some had done themselves too well; but in all their hearts the trust burned bright that they might do themselves better at dinner, for their God *was* good, and dwelt between the kitchen and the cellar of the Stoics' Club. And all—for all had poetry in their souls—looked forward to those hours in paradise when, with cigars between their lips, good wine below, they might dream the daily dream that comes to all true Stoics for about fifteen shillings or even less, all told.

From a little back slum, within two stones'-throw of the god of the Stoics' Club, there had come out two seamstresses to take the air; one was in consumption, having neglected to earn enough to feed herself properly for some years past, and the other looked as if she would be in consumption shortly, for the same reason. They stood on the pavement, watching the cabs drive up. Some of the Stoics saw them and thought: 'Poor girls! they look awfully bad.' Three or four said to themselves: 'It oughtn't to be allowed. I mean, it's so

painful to see; and it 's not as if one could do anything.
They 're not beggars, don't you know, and so what
can one do?'

But most of the Stoics did not look at them at all,
feeling that their soft hearts could not stand these
painful sights, and anxious not to spoil their dinners.
Gregory did not see them either, for it so happened that
he was looking at the sky, and just then the two girls
crossed the road and were lost among the passers-by,
for they were not dogs, who could smell out the kind
of man he was.

'Mr. Pendyce *is* in the club; I will send your name
up, sir.' And rolling a little, as though Gregory's name
were heavy, the porter gave it to the boy, who went
away with it.

Gregory stood by the empty hearth and waited, and
while he waited, nothing struck him at all, for the
Stoics seemed very natural, just mere men like himself,
except that their clothes were better, which made him
think: 'I shouldn't care to belong here and have to
dress for dinner every night.'

'Mr. Pendyce is very sorry, sir, but he 's engaged.'

Gregory bit his lips, said 'Thank you,' and went
away.

'That 's all Margery wants,' he thought; 'the rest is
nothing to me,' and, getting on a bus, he fixed his eyes
once more on the sky.

But George was not engaged. Like a wounded
animal taking its hurt for refuge to its lair, he sat in his
favourite window overlooking Piccadilly. He sat there
as though youth had left him, unmoving, never lifting
his eyes. In his stubborn mind a wheel seemed turning,
grinding out his memories to the last grain. And
Stoics, who could not bear to see a man sit thus

throughout that sacred hour, came up from time to time.

'Aren't you going to dine, Pendyce?'

Dumb brutes tell no one of their pains; the law is silence. So with George. And as each Stoic came up, he only set his teeth and said:

'Presently, old chap.'

CHAPTER VII

TOUR WITH THE SPANIEL JOHN

Now the spaniel John—whose habit it was to smell of heather and baked biscuits when he rose from a night's sleep—was in disgrace that Thursday. Into his long and narrow head it took time for any new idea to enter, and not till forty hours after Mrs. Pendyce had gone did he recognize fully that something definite had happened to his master. During the agitated minutes that this conviction took in forming, he worked hard. Taking two and a half brace of his master's shoes and slippers, and placing them in unaccustomed spots, he lay on them one by one till they were warm, then left them for some bird or other to hatch out, and returned to Mr. Pendyce's door. It was for all this that the squire said 'John!' several times, and threatened him with a razor-strop. And partly because he could not bear to leave his master for a single second—the scolding had made him love him so—and partly because of that new idea, which let him have no peace, he lay in the hall waiting.

Having once in his hot youth inadvertently followed the squire's horse, he could never be induced to follow it again. He both personally disliked this needlessly large and swift form of animal, and suspected it of designs upon his master; for when the creature had taken his master up, there was not a smell of him left anywhere—not a whiff of that pleasant scent that so endeared him to the heart. As soon, therefore, as the

268

horse appeared, the spaniel John would lie down on his stomach with his forepaws close to his nose, and his nose close to the ground; nor until the animal vanished could he be induced to abandon an attitude in which he resembled a couching Sphinx.

But this afternoon, with his tail down, his lips pouting, his shoulders making heavy work of it, his nose lifted in deprecation of that ridiculous and unnecessary plane on which his master sat, he followed at a measured distance. In such-wise, aforetime, the village had followed the squire and Mr. Barter when they introduced into it its one and only drain.

Mr. Pendyce rode slowly; his feet, in their well-blacked boots, his nervous legs in Bedford cord and mahogany-coloured leggings, moved in rhyme to the horse's trot. A long-tailed coat fell clean and full over his thighs; his back and shoulders were a wee bit bent to lessen motion, and above his neat white stock under a grey bowler hat his lean, grey-whiskered and moustachioed face, with harassed eyes, was preoccupied and sad. His horse, a brown blood mare, ambled lazily, head raking forward, and bang tail floating outward from her hocks. And so, in the June sunshine, they went, all three, along the leafy lane to Worsted Scotton. . . .

On Tuesday, the day that Mrs. Pendyce had left, the squire had come in later than usual, for he felt that after their difference of the night before, a little coolness would do her no harm. The first hour of discovery had been as one confused and angry minute, ending in a burst of nerves and the telegram to General Pendyce. He took the telegram himself, returning from the village with his head down, a sudden prey to a feeling of shame—an odd and terrible feeling that he never

remembered to have felt before, a sort of fear of his
fellow-creatures. He would have chosen a secret way,
but there was none, only the high road, or the path
across the village green, and through the churchyard to
his paddocks. An old cottager was standing at the
turnstile, and the squire made for him with his head
down, as a bull makes for a fence. He had meant to
pass in silence, but between him and this old broken
husbandman there was a bond forged by the ages.
Had it meant death, Mr. Pendyce could not have passed
one whose fathers had toiled for his fathers, eaten his
fathers' bread, died with his fathers, without a word
and a movement of his hand.

'Evenin', squire; naice evenin'. Faine weather fur
th' hay!'

The voice was warped and wavery.

'This is my squire,' it seemed to say, 'whatever ther'
be agin him!'

Mr. Pendyce's hand went up to his hat.

'Evenin', Hermon. Aye, fine weather for the hay!
Mrs. Pendyce has gone up to London. We young
bachelors, ha!'

He passed on.

Not until he had gone some way did he perceive
why he had made that announcement. It was simply
because he must tell every one, every one; then no one
could be astonished.

He hurried on to the house to dress in time for dinner,
and show all that nothing was amiss. Seven courses
would have been served him had the sky fallen; but
he ate little, and drank more claret than was his wont.
After dinner he sat in his study with the windows open,
and in the mingled day and lamp light read his wife's
letter over again. As it was with the spaniel John, so

with his master—a new idea penetrated but slowly into his long and narrow head.

She was cracked about George; she did not know what she was doing; would soon come to her senses. It was not for him to take any steps. What steps, indeed, could he take without confessing that Horace Pendyce had gone too far, that Horace Pendyce was in the wrong? That had never been his habit, and he could not alter now. If she and George chose to be stubborn, they must take the consequences, and fend for themselves.

In the silence and the lamplight, growing mellower each minute under the green silk shade, he sat confusedly thinking of the past. And in that dumb reverie, as though of fixed malice, there came to him no memories that were not pleasant, no images that were not fair. He tried to think of her unkindly, he tried to paint her black; but with the perversity born into the world when he was born, to die when he was dead, she came to him softly, like the ghost of gentleness, to haunt his fancy. She came to him smelling of sweet scents, with a slight rustling of silk, and the sound of her expectant voice, saying, 'Yes, dear?' as though she were not bored. He remembered when he brought her first to Worsted Skeynes thirty-four years ago, 'That timid, and like a rose, but a lady every hinch, the love!' as his old nurse had said.

He remembered her when George was born, like wax for whiteness and transparency, with eyes that were all pupils, and a hovering smile. So many other times he remembered her throughout those years, but never as a woman faded, old; never as a woman of the past. Now that he had not got her, for the first time Mr. Pendyce realized that she had not grown old, that she was still to him 'timid, and like a rose, but a lady every hinch, the love!' And he could not bear this thought; it made him feel so miserable and lonely in the lamplight, with the grey moths hovering round, and the spaniel John asleep upon his foot.

So, taking his candle, he went up to bed. The doors that barred away the servants' wing were closed. In all that great remaining space of house his was the only candle, the only sounding footstep. Slowly he mounted as he had mounted many thousand times, but never once like this, and behind him, like a shadow, mounted the spaniel John.

And She that knows the hearts of men and dogs, the Mother from whom all things come, to whom they all go home, was watching, and presently, when they were laid, the one in his deserted bed, the other on blue linen, propped against the door, She gathered them to sleep.

But Wednesday came, and with it Wednesday duties. They who have passed the windows of the Stoics' Club and seen the Stoics sitting there have haunting visions of the idle landed classes. These visions will not let them sleep, will not let their tongues to cease from bitterness, for they so long to lead that 'idle' life themselves. But though in a misty land illusions be our cherished lot, that we may all think falsely of our neighbours and enjoy ourselves, the word 'idle' is not at all the word.

Many and heavy tasks weighed on the squire at Worsted Skeynes. There was the visit to the stables to decide as to firing Beldame's hock, or selling the new bay horse because he did not draw men fast enough, and the vexed question of Bruggan's oats or Beal's, talked out with Benson, in a leather belt and flannel shirt-sleeves, like a corpulent, white-whiskered boy.

Then the long sitting in the study with memorandums and accounts, all needing care, lest So-and-so should give too little for too little, or too little for too much; and the smart walk across to Jarvis, the head-keeper, to ask after the health of the new Hungarian bird, or discuss a scheme whereby in the last drive so many of those creatures he had nurtured from their youth up might be deterred from flying over to his friend Lord Quarryman. And this took long, for Jarvis's feelings forced him to say six times: 'Well, Mr. Pendyce, sir, what I say is we didn't oughter lose s'many birds in that last drive'; and Mr. Pendyce to answer: 'No, Jarvis, certainly not. Well, what do you suggest?' And that other grievous question—how to get plenty of pheasants and plenty of foxes to dwell together in perfect harmony—discussed with endless sympathy, for, as the squire would say: 'Jarvis is quite safe with foxes.' He could not bear his coverts to be drawn blank.

Then back to a sparing lunch, or perhaps no lunch at all, that he might keep fit and hard; and out again at once on horseback or on foot to the home farm or further, as need might take him, and a long afternoon, with eyes fixed on the ribs of bullocks, the colour of swedes, the surfaces of walls or gates or fences.

Then home again to tea and to *The Times*, which had as yet received but fleeting glances, with close attention to all those Parliamentary measures threatening, remotely, the existing state of things, except, of course, that future tax on wheat so needful to the betterment of Worsted Skeynes. There were occasions, too, when they brought him tramps to deal with, to whom his one remark would be: 'Hold out your hands, my man,' which, being found unwarped by honest toil, were promptly sent to gaol. When found so warped,

Mr. Pendyce was at a loss, and would walk up and down, earnestly trying to discover what his duty was to them. There were days, too, almost entirely occupied by Sessions, when many classes of offenders came before him, to whom he meted justice according to the heinousness of the offence, from poaching at the top down and down to wife-beating at the bottom; for, though a humane man, tradition did not suffer him to look on this form of sport as really criminal—at any rate, not in the country.

It was true that all these matters could have been settled in a fraction of the time by a young and trained intelligence, but this would have wronged tradition, disturbed the squire's settled conviction that he was doing his duty, and given cause for slanderous tongues to hint at idleness. And though, further, it was true that all this daily labour was devoted directly or indirectly to interests of his own, what was that but doing his duty to the country and asserting the prerogative of every Englishman at all costs to be provincial?

But on this Wednesday the flavour of the dish was gone. To be alone amongst his acres, quite alone—to have no one to care whether he did anything at all, no one to whom he might confide that Beldame's hock was to be fired, that Peacock was asking for more gates, was almost more than he could bear. He would have wired to the girls to come home, but he could not bring himself to face their questions. Gerald was at Gib! George—George was no son of his—and his pride forbade him to write to her who had left him thus to solitude and shame. For deep down below his stubborn anger it was shame that the squire felt—shame that he should have to shun his neighbours, lest they

should ask him questions which, for his own good name
and his own pride, he must answer with a lie; shame
that he should not be master in his own house—still
more, shame that any one should see that he was not.
To be sure, he did not know that he felt shame, being
unused to introspection, having always kept it at arm's
length. For he always meditated concretely, as, for
instance, when he looked up and did not see his wife at
breakfast, but saw Bester making coffee, he thought:
'That fellow knows all about it, I shouldn't wonder!'
and he felt angry for thinking that. When he saw Mr.
Barter coming down the drive he thought: 'Confound
it! I can't meet him,' and slipped out, and felt angry
that he had thus avoided him. When in the Scotch
garden he came on Jackman syringeing the rose trees,
he said to him: 'Your mistress has gone to London,'
and abruptly turned away, angry that he had been
obliged by a mysterious impulse to tell him that.

So it was, all through that long, sad day, and the only
thing that gave him comfort was to score through, in
the draft of his will, bequests to his eldest son, and
busy himself over drafting a clause to take their place:

'Forasmuch as my eldest son, George Hubert, has
by conduct unbecoming to a gentleman and a Pendyce,
proved himself unworthy of my confidence, and forasmuch as to my regret I am unable to cut the entail of
my estate, I hereby declare that he shall in no way
participate in any division of my other property or of
my personal effects, conscientiously believing that it
is my duty so to do in the interests of my family and of
the country, and I make this declaration without anger.'

For, all the anger that he was balked of feeling against

his wife, because he missed her so, was added to that already felt against his son.

By the last post came a letter from General Pendyce. He opened it with fingers as shaky as his brother's writing.

'ARMY AND NAVY CLUB.

'DEAR HORACE,

'What the deuce and all made you send that telegram? It spoiled my breakfast, and sent me off in a tearing hurry, to find Margery perfectly well. If she'd been seedy or anything I should have been delighted, but there she was, busy about her dresses and what not, and I dare say she thought me a lunatic for coming at that time in the morning. You shouldn't get into the habit of sending telegrams. A telegram is a thing that means something—at least, I've always thought so. I met George coming away from her in a deuce of a hurry. I can't write any more now. I'm just going to have my lunch.

'Your affectionate brother,
'CHARLES PENDYCE.'

She was well: she had been seeing George. With a hardened heart the squire went up to bed.

And Wednesday came to an end. . . .

And so on the Thursday afternoon the brown blood mare carried Mr. Pendyce along the lane, followed by the spaniel John. They passed the Firs, where Bellew lived, and, bending sharply to the right, began to mount towards the common; and with them mounted the image of that fellow who was at the bottom of it all— an image that ever haunted the squire's mind nowadays: a ghost, high-shouldered, with little burning eyes, clipped red moustaches, thin bowed legs. A plague

spot on that system which he loved, a whipping-post
to heredity, a scourge like Attila the Hun; a sort of
damnable caricature of all that a country gentleman
should be—of his love of sport and open air, of his
'hardness' and his pluck; of his powers of knowing
his own mind, and taking his liquor like a man; of his
creed, now out of date, of gallantry. Yes—a kind of
cursed bogy of a man, a spectral follower of the hounds,
a desperate character—a man that in old days someone
would have shot; a drinking, white-faced devil who
despised Horace Pendyce, whom Horace Pendyce hated,
yet could not quite despise. 'Always one like that in a
hunting country!' A black dog on the shoulders of
his order. *Post equitem sedet Jaspar Bellew!*

The squire came out on the top of the rise, and all
Worsted Scotton was in sight. It was a sandy stretch
of broom and gorse and heather, with a few Scotch firs;
it had no value at all, and he longed for it, as a boy
might long for the bite someone else had snatched out
of his apple. It distressed him lying there, his and
yet not his, like a wife who was no wife—as though
Fortune were enjoying her at his expense. Thus was
he deprived of the fullness of his mental image; for as
with all men, so with the squire, that which he loved
and owned took definite form—a something that he
saw. Whenever the words 'Worsted Skeynes' were in
his mind —and that was almost always — there rose
before him an image defined and concrete, however
indescribable; and whatever this image was, he knew
that Worsted Scotton spoiled it. It was true that he
could not think of any use to which to put the common,
but he felt deeply that it was pure dog-in-the-mangerism
of the cottagers, and this he could not stand. Not one
beast in two years had fattened on its barrenness. Three

old donkeys alone eked out the remnants of their days.
A bundle of firewood or old bracken, a few peat sods
from one especial corner, were all the selfish peasants
gathered. But the cottagers were no great matter—
he could soon have settled them; it was that fellow
Peacock whom he could not settle, just because he
happened to abut on the common, and his fathers had
been nasty before him. Mr. Pendyce rode round looking at the fence his father had put up, until he came to
the portion that Peacock's father had pulled down;
and here, by a strange fatality—such as will happen
even in printed records—he came on Peacock himself
standing in the gap, as though he had foreseen this
visit of the squire's. The mare stopped of her own
accord, the spaniel John at a measured distance lay
down to think, and all those yards away he could be
heard doing it, and now and then swallowing his tongue.

Peacock stood with his hands in his breeches pockets.
An old straw hat was on his head, his little eyes were
turned towards the ground; and his cob, which he had
tied to what his father had left standing of the fence,
had his eyes, too, turned towards the ground, for he
was eating grass. Mr. Pendyce's fight with his burning
stable had stuck in the farmer's 'gizzard' ever since.
He felt that he was forgetting it day by day—would
soon forget it altogether. He felt the old sacred doubts
inherited from his fathers rising every hour within him.
And so he had come up to see what looking at the gap
would do for his sense of gratitude. At sight of the
squire his little eyes turned here and there, as a pig's
eyes turn when it receives a blow behind. That Mr.
Pendyce should have chosen this moment to come up
was as though Providence, that knoweth all things,
knew the natural thing for Mr. Pendyce to do.

'Afternoon, squire. Dry weather; rain's badly wanted. I'll get no feed if this goes on.'

Mr. Pendyce answered:

'Afternoon, Peacock. Why, your fields are first-rate for grass.'

They hastily turned their eyes away, for at that moment they could not bear to see each other.

There was a silence; then Peacock said:

'What about those gates of mine, squire?' and his voice quavered, as though gratitude might yet get the better of him.

The squire's irritable glance swept over the unfenced space to right and left, and the thought flashed through his mind:

'Suppose I were to give the beggar those gates, would he—would he let me enclose the Scotton again?'

He looked at that square, bearded man, and the infallible instinct, christened so wickedly by Mr. Paramor, guided him.

'What's wrong with *your* gates, man, I should like to know?'

Peacock looked at him full this time; there was no longer any quaver in his voice, but a sort of rough good humour.

'Wy, the 'arf o' them's as rotten as matchwood!' he said; and he took a breath of relief, for he knew that gratitude was dead within his soul.

'Well, I wish mine at the home farm were half as good. Come, John!' and, touching the mare with his heel, Mr. Pendyce turned; but before he had gone a dozen paces he was back.

'Mrs. Peacock well, I hope? Mrs. Pendyce has gone up to London.'

And touching his hat, without waiting for Peacock's

answer, he rode away. He took the lane past Peacock's farm across the home paddocks, emerging on the cricket ground, a field of his own which he had caused to be converted.

The return match with Coldingham was going on, and, motionless on his horse, the squire stopped to watch. A tall figure in the 'long field' came leisurely towards him. It was the Hon. Geoffrey Winlow. Mr. Pendyce subdued an impulse to turn the mare and ride away.

'We 're going to give you a licking, squire! How 's Mrs. Pendyce? My wife sent her love.'

On the squire's face in the full sun was more than the sun's flush.

'Thanks,' he said, 'she 's very well. She 's gone up to London.'

'And aren't you going up yourself this season?'

The squire crossed those leisurely eyes with his own.

'I don't think so,' he said slowly.

The Hon. Geoffrey returned to his duties.

'We got poor old Barter for a "blob"!' he said over his shoulder.

The squire became aware that Mr. Barter was approaching from behind.

'You see that left-hand fellow?' he said, pouting. 'Just watch his foot. D' you mean to say that wasn't a no-ball? He bowled *me* with a no-ball. He 's a rank no-baller. That fellow Locke 's no more an umpire than——'

He stopped and looked earnestly at the bowler.

The squire did not answer, sitting on his mare as though carved in stone. Suddenly his throat clicked.

'How 's your wife?' he said. 'Margery would have come to see her, but—but she 's gone up to London.'

The rector did not turn his head.

'My wife? Oh, going on first-rate. There's another! I say, Winlow, this is too bad!'

The Hon. Geoffrey's pleasant voice was heard:

'Please not to speak to the man at the wheel!'

The squire turned the mare and rode away; and the spaniel John, who had been watching from a measured distance, followed after, his tongue lolling from his mouth.

The squire turned through a gate down the main aisle of the home covert, and the nose and the tail of the spaniel John, who scented creatures to the left and right, were in perpetual motion. It was cool in there. The June foliage made one long colonnade, broken by a winding river of sky. Among the oaks and hazels, the beeches and the elms, the ghostly body of a birch tree shone here and there, captured by those grosser trees which seemed to cluster round her, proud of their prisoner, loath to let her go, that subtle spirit of their wood. They knew that, were she gone, their forest lady, wilder and yet gentler than themselves — they would lose credit, lose the grace and essence of their corporate being.

The squire dismounted, tethered his horse, and sat under one of those birch trees, on the fallen body of an elm. The spaniel John also sat and loved him with his eyes. And sitting there they thought their thoughts, but their thoughts were different.

For under this birch tree Horace Pendyce had stood and kissed his wife the very day he brought her home to Worsted Skeynes, and though he did not see the parallel between her and the birch tree that some poor imaginative creature might have drawn, yet was he thinking of that long past afternoon. But the spaniel John was not thinking of it; his recollection was too dim, for he had been at that time twenty-eight years short of being born.

Mr. Pendyce sat there long with his horse and with his dog, and from out the blackness of the spaniel John, who was more than less asleep, there shone at times an eye turned on his master like some devoted star. The sun, shining too, gilded the stem of the birch tree. The birds and beasts began their evening stir all through the undergrowth, and rabbits, popping out into the ride, looked with surprise at the spaniel John, and popped in back again. They knew that men with horses had no guns, but could not bring themselves to trust that black and hairy thing whose nose so twitched whenever they appeared. The gnats came out to dance, and at their dancing, every sound and scent and shape became the sounds and scents and shapes of evening; and there was evening in the squire's heart.

Slowly and stiffly he got up from the log and mounted to ride home. It would be just as lonely when he got there, but a house is better than a wood, where the gnats dance, the birds and creatures stir and stir, and shadows lengthen; where the sun steals upwards on the tree-stems, and all is careless of its owner, Man.

It was past seven o'clock when he went to his study. There was a lady standing at the window, and Mr. Pendyce said:

'I beg your pardon?'

The lady turned; it was his wife. The squire stopped with a hoarse sound, and stood silent, covering his eyes with his hand.

CHAPTER VIII

ACUTE ATTACK OF—'PENDYCITIS'

MRS. PENDYCE felt very faint when she hurried away from Chelsea. She had passed through hours of great emotion, and eaten nothing.

Like sunset clouds or the colours in mother-o'-pearl, so, it is written, shall be the moods of men—interwoven as the threads of an embroidery, less certain than an April day, yet with a rhythm of their own that never fails, and no one can quite scan.

A single cup of tea on her way home, and her spirit revived. It seemed suddenly as if there had been a great ado about nothing! As if someone had known how stupid men could be, and been playing a fantasia on that stupidity. But this gaiety of spirit soon died away, confronted by the problem of what she should do next.

She reached her hotel without making a decision. She sat down in the reading-room to write to Gregory, and while she sat there with her pen in her hand a dreadful temptation came over her to say bitter things to him, because by not seeing people as they were he had brought all this upon them. But she had so little practice in saying bitter things that she could not think of any that were nice enough, and in the end she was obliged to leave them out. After finishing and sending off the note she felt better. And it came to her suddenly that, if she packed at once, there was just time to catch the 5.55 to Worsted Skeynes.

As in leaving her home, so in returning, she followed her instinct, and her instinct told her to avoid unnecessary fuss and suffering.

The decrepit station fly, mouldy and smelling of stables, bore her almost lovingly towards the hall. Its old driver, clean-faced, cheery, somewhat like a bird, drove her almost furiously, for, though he knew nothing, he felt that two whole days and half a day were quite long enough for her to be away. At the lodge gate old Roy, the Skye, was seated on his haunches, and the sight of him set Mrs. Pendyce trembling as though till then she had not realized that she was coming home.

Home! The long narrow lane without a turning, the mists and stillness, the driving rain and hot bright afternoons; the scents of wood-smoke and hay and the scent of her flowers; the squire's voice, the dry rattle of grass-cutters, the barking of dogs, and distant hum of thrashing; and Sunday sounds—church bells and rooks, and Mr. Barter's preaching; the tastes, too, of the very dishes! And all these scents and sounds and tastes, and the feel of the air to her cheeks, seemed to have been for ever in the past, and to be going on for ever in the time to come.

She turned red and white by turns, and felt neither joy nor sadness, for in a wave the old life came over her. She went at once to the study to wait for her husband to come in. At the hoarse sound he made, her heart beat fast, while old Roy and the spaniel John growled gently at each other.

'John,' she murmured, 'aren't you glad to see me, dear?'

The spaniel John, without moving, beat his tail against his master's foot.

The squire raised his head at last.

'Well, Margery?' was all he said.

It shot through her mind that he looked older, and very tired!

The dinner-gong began to sound, and as though attracted by its long monotonous beating, a swallow flew in at one of the narrow windows and fluttered round the room.   Mrs. Pendyce's eyes followed its flight.

The squire stepped forward suddenly and took her hand.

'Don't run away from me again, Margery!' he said; and stooping down, he kissed it.

At this action, so unlike her husband, Mrs. Pendyce blushed like a girl.   Her eyes above his grey and close-cropped head seemed grateful that he did not reproach her, glad of that caress.

'I have some news to tell you, Horace.   Helen Bellew has given George up!'

The squire dropped her hand.

'And quite time too,' he said.   'I dare say George has refused to take his dismissal.   He's as obstinate as a mule.'

'I found him in a dreadful state.'

Mr. Pendyce asked uneasily:

'What?   What's that?'

'He looked so desperate.'

'Desperate?' said the squire, with a sort of startled anger.

Mrs. Pendyce went on:

'It was dreadful to see his face.   I was with him this afternoon——'

The squire said suddenly:

'He's not ill, is he?'

'No, not ill.   Oh, Horace, don't you understand? I was afraid he might do something rash.   He was so— miserable.'

The squire began to walk up and down.

'Is he—is he safe now?' he burst out.

Mrs. Pendyce sat down rather suddenly in the nearest chair.

'Yes,' she said with difficulty, 'I—I think so.'

'Think! What's the good of that? What——— Are you feeling faint, Margery?'

Mrs. Pendyce, who had closed her eyes, said:

'No, dear, it's all right.'

Mr. Pendyce came close, and since air and quiet were essential to her at that moment, he bent over and tried by every means in his power to rouse her; and she, who longed to be let alone, sympathized with him, for she knew that it was natural that he should do this. In spite of his efforts the feeling of faintness passed, and, taking his hand, she stroked it gratefully.

'What is to be done now, Horace?'

'Done!' cried the squire. 'Good God! how should I know? Here you are in this state, all because of that d——d fellow Bellew and his d——d wife! What you want is some dinner.'

So saying, he put his arm around her, and half leading, half carrying, took her to her room.

They did not talk much at dinner, and of indifferent things, of Mrs. Barter, Peacock, the roses, and Beldame's hock. Only once they came too near to that which instinct told them to avoid, for the squire said suddenly:

'I suppose you saw that woman?'

And Mrs. Pendyce murmured:

'Yes.'

She soon went to her room, and had barely got into bed when he appeared, saying as though ashamed:

'I'm very early.'

She lay awake, and every now and then the squire

would ask her, 'Are you asleep, Margery?' hoping that she might have dropped off, for he himself could not sleep. And she knew that he meant to be nice to her, and she knew, too, that as he lay awake, turning from side to side, he was thinking like herself: 'What's to be done next?' And that his fancy, too, was haunted by a ghost, high-shouldered, with little burning eyes, red hair, and white freckled face. For, save that George was miserable, nothing was altered, and the cloud of vengeance still hung over Worsted Skeynes. Like some weary lesson she rehearsed her thoughts: 'Now Horace can answer that letter of Captain Bellew's, can tell him that George will not—indeed, cannot—see her again. He *must* answer it. But will he?'

She groped after the secret springs of her husband's character, turning and turning and trying to understand, that she might know the best way of approaching him. And she could not feel sure, for behind all the little outside points of his nature, that she thought so 'funny,' yet could comprehend, there was something which seemed to her as unknown, as impenetrable as the dark, a sort of thickness of soul, a sort of hardness, a sort of barbaric—what? And as when in working at her embroidery the point of her needle would often come to a stop against stiff buckram, so now was the point of her soul brought to a stop against the soul of her husband. 'Perhaps,' she thought, 'Horace feels like that with me.' She need not so have thought, for the squire never worked embroideries, nor did the needle of his soul make voyages of discovery.

By lunch-time the next day she had not dared to say a word. 'If I say nothing,' she thought, 'he may write it of his own accord.'

Without attracting his attention, therefore, she

watched every movement of his morning. She saw
him sitting at his bureau with a creased and crumpled
letter, and knew it was Bellew's; and she hovered about,
coming softly in and out, doing little things here and
there and in the hall, outside. But the squire gave
no sign, motionless as the spaniel John couched along
the ground with his nose between his paws.

After lunch she could bear it no longer.

'What do you think ought to be done now, Horace?'

The squire looked at her fixedly.

'If you imagine,' he said at last, 'that I'll have
anything to do with that fellow Bellew, you're very
much mistaken.'

Mrs. Pendyce was arranging a vase of flowers, and
her hand shook so that some of the water was spilled
over the cloth. She took out her handkerchief and
dabbed it up.

'You never answered his letter, dear,' she said.

The squire put his back against the sideboard; his
stiff figure, with lean neck and angry eyes, whose pupils
were mere pin-points, had a certain dignity.

'Nothing shall induce me!' he said, and his voice
was harsh and strong, as though he spoke for something
bigger than himself. 'I've thought it over all the
morning, and I'm d——d if I do! The man is a
ruffian. I won't knuckle under to him!'

Mrs. Pendyce clasped her hands.

'Oh, Horace,' she said; 'but for the sake of us all!
Only just give him that assurance.'

'And let him crow over me!' cried the squire. 'By
Jove, no!'

'But, Horace, I thought that was what you wanted
George to do. You wrote to him and asked him to
promise.'

The squire answered:

'You know nothing about it, Margery; you know nothing about me. D'you think I'm going to tell him that his wife has thrown my son over—let him keep me gasping like a fish all this time, and then get the best of it in the end? Not if I have to leave the country—not if I——'

But, as though he had imagined the most bitter fate of all, he stopped.

Mrs. Pendyce, putting her hands on the lapels of his coat, stood with her head bent. The colour had flushed into her cheeks, her eyes were bright with tears. And there came from her in her emotion a warmth and fragrance, a charm, as though she were again young, like the portrait under which they stood.

'Not if *I* ask you, Horace?'

The squire's face was suffused with dusky colour; he clenched his hands and seemed to sway and hesitate.

'No, Margery,' he said hoarsely; 'it's—it's—I can't!'

And, breaking away from her, he left the room

Mrs. Pendyce looked after him; her fingers, from which he had torn his coat, began twining the one with the other.

CHAPTER IX

BELLEW BOWS TO A LADY

THERE was silence at the Firs, and in that silent house, where only five rooms were used, an old manservant sat in his pantry on a wooden chair, reading from an article out of *Rural Life*. There was no one to disturb him, for the master was asleep, and the housekeeper had not yet come to cook the dinner. He read slowly, through spectacles, engraving the words for ever on the tablets of his mind. He read about the construction and habits of the owl: 'In the tawny, or brown, owl there is a manubrial process; the furcula, far from being joined to the keel of the sternum, consists of two stylets, which do not even meet; while the posterior margin of the sternum presents two pairs of projections, with corresponding fissures between.' The old manservant paused, resting his blinking eyes on the pale sunlight through the bars of his narrow window, so that a little bird on the window-sill looked at him and instantly flew away.

The old manservant read on again: 'The pterological characters of Photodilus seem not to have been investigated, but it has been found to want the tarsal loop, as well as the manubrial process, while its clavicles are not joined in a furcula, nor do they meet the keel, and the posterior margin of the sternum has processes and fissures like the tawny section.' Again he paused, and his gaze was satisfied and bland.

Up in the little smoking-room in a leather chair his master sat asleep. In front of him were stretched his legs in dusty riding-boots. His lips were closed, but through a little hole at one corner came a tiny puffing sound. On the floor by his side was an empty glass, between his feet a Spanish bulldog. On a shelf above his head reposed some frayed and yellow novels with sporting titles, written by persons in their inattentive moments. Over the chimney-piece presided the portrait of Mr. Jorrocks persuading his horse to cross a stream.

And the face of Jaspar Bellew asleep was the face of a man who has ridden far, to get away from himself, and to-morrow will have to ride far again. His sandy eyebrows twitched with his dreams against the dead-white, freckled skin above high cheekbones, and two hard ridges were fixed between his brows; now and then over the sleeping face came the look of one riding at a gate.

In the stables behind the house she who had carried him on his ride, having rummaged out her last grains of corn, lifted her nose and poked it through the bars of her loose-box to see what he was doing who had not carried her master that sweltering afternoon, and seeing that he was awake, she snorted lightly, to tell him there was thunder in the air. All else in the stables was deadly quiet; the shrubberies around were still; and in the hushed house the master slept.

But on the edge of his wooden chair in the silence of his pantry the old manservant read: 'This bird is a voracious feeder,' and he paused, blinking his eyes and nervously puckering his lips, for he had partially understood. . . .

Mrs. Pendyce was crossing the fields. She had on her prettiest frock, of smoky-grey crepe, and she looked

a little anxiously at the sky. Gathered in the west a
coming storm was chasing the whitened sunlight.
Against its purple the trees stood blackish-green.
Everything was very still, not even the poplars stirred,
yet the purple grew with sinister, unmoving speed.
Mrs. Pendyce hurried, grasping her skirts in both her
hands, and she noticed that the cattle were all grouped
under the hedge.

'What dreadful-looking clouds!' she thought. 'I
wonder if I shall get to the Firs before it comes?'
But though her frock made her hasten, her heart made
her stand still, it fluttered so, and was so full. Suppose
he were not sober! She remembered those little
burning eyes, which had frightened her so the night
he dined at Worsted Skeynes and fell out of his dog-
cart afterwards. A kind of legendary malevolence
clung about his image.

'Suppose he is horrid to me!' she thought.

She could not go back now; but she wished—how
she wished—that it were over. A heat-drop splashed
her glove. She crossed the lane and opened the Firs
gate. Throwing frightened glances at the sky, she
hastened down the drive. The purple was couched like
a pall on the tree-tops, and these had begun to sway
and moan as though struggling and weeping at their
fate. Some splashes of warm rain were falling. A
streak of lightning tore the firmament. Mrs. Pendyce
rushed into the porch covering her ears with her hands.

'How long will it last?' she thought. 'I'm so
frightened!' . . .

A very old manservant, whose face was all puckers,
opened the door suddenly to peer out at the storm, but
seeing Mrs. Pendyce, he peered at her instead.

'Is Captain Bellew at home?'

'Yes, ma'am. The captain's in the study. We don't use the drawing-room now. Nasty storm coming on, ma'am—nasty storm. Will you please to sit down a minute, while I let the captain know?'

The hall was low and dark; the whole house was low and dark, and smelled a little of wood-rot. Mrs. Pendyce did not sit down, but stood under an arrangement of three foxes' heads, supporting two hunting-crops, with their lashes hanging down. And the heads of those animals suggested to her the thought: 'Poor man! He must be very lonely here.'

She started. Something was rubbing against her knees: it was only an enormous bulldog. She stooped down to pat it, and having once begun, found it impossible to leave off, for when she took her hand away the creature pressed against her, and she was afraid for her frock.

'Poor old boy—poor old boy!' she kept on murmuring. 'Did he want a little attention?'

A voice behind her said:

'Get out, Sam! Sorry to have kept you waiting. Won't you come in here?'

Mrs. Pendyce, blushing and turning pale by turns, passed into a low, small, panelled room, smelling of cigars and spirits. Through the window, which was cut up into little panes, she could see the rain driving past, the shrubs bent and dripping from the downpour.

'Won't you sit down?'

Mrs. Pendyce sat down. She had clasped her hands together; she now raised her eyes and looked timidly at her host.

She saw a thin, high-shouldered figure, with bowed legs a little apart, rumpled sandy hair, a pale freckled face, and little dark blinking eyes.

'Sorry the room's in such a mess. Don't often have
the pleasure of seeing a lady. I was asleep; generally
am at this time of year!'

The bristly red moustache was contorted as though
his lips were smiling

Mrs. Pendyce murmured vaguely.

It seemed to her that nothing of this was real, but all
some horrid dream. A clap of thunder made her cover
her ears.

Bellew walked to the window, glanced at the sky,
and came back to the hearth. His little burning eyes
seemed to look her through and through. 'If I don't
speak at once,' she thought, 'I never shall speak at
all.'

'I've come,' she began, and with those words she
lost her fright; her voice, that had been so uncertain
hitherto, regained its trick of speech; her eyes, all
pupil, stared dark and gentle at this man who had them
all in his power—'I've come to tell you something,
Captain Bellew!'

The figure by the hearth bowed, and her fright, like
some evil bird, came fluttering down on her again. It
was dreadful, it was barbarous that she, that any one,
should have to speak of such things; it was barbarous
that men and women should so misunderstand each
other, and have so little sympathy and consideration;
it was barbarous that she, Margery Pendyce, should
have to talk on this subject that must give them both
such pain. It was all so mean and gross and common!
She took out her handkerchief and passed it over
her lips.

'Please forgive me for speaking. Your wife has
given my son up, Captain Bellew!'

Bellew did not move.

'She does not love him; she told me so herself! He will never see her again!'

How hateful, how horrible, how odious!

And still Bellew did not speak, but stood devouring her with his little eyes; and how long this went on she could not tell.

He turned his back suddenly, and leaned against the mantelpiece.

Mrs. Pendyce passed her hand over her brow to get rid of a feeling of unreality.

'That is all,' she said.

Her voice sounded to herself unlike her own.

'If that is really all,' she thought, 'I suppose I must get up and go!' And it flashed through her mind, 'My poor dress will be ruined!'

Bellew turned round.

'Will you have some tea?'

Mrs. Pendyce smiled a pale little smile.

'No, thank you; I don't think I could drink any tea.'

'I wrote a letter to your husband.'

'Yes.'

'He didn't answer it.'

'No.'

Mrs. Pendyce saw him staring at her, and a desperate struggle began within her. Should she not ask him to keep his promise, now that George——? Was not that what she had come for? Ought she not—ought she not for all their sakes?

Bellew went up to the table, poured out some whisky, and drank it off.

'You don't ask me to stop the proceedings,' he said.

Mrs. Pendyce's lips were parted, but nothing came through those parted lips. Her eyes, black as sloes in her white face, never moved from his; she made no sound.

Bellew dashed his hand across his brow.

'Well, I will!' he said, 'for your sake. There's my hand on it. You're the only lady I know!'

He gripped her gloved fingers, brushed past her, and she saw that she was alone.

She found her own way out, with the tears running down her face. Very gently she shut the hall door.

'My poor dress!' she thought. 'I wonder if I might stand here a little? The rain looks nearly over!'

The purple cloud had passed, and sunk behind the house, and a bright white sky was pouring down a sparkling rain; a patch of deep blue showed behind the fir trees in the drive. The thrushes were out already after worms. A squirrel scampering along a branch stopped and looked at Mrs. Pendyce, and Mrs. Pendyce looked absently at the squirrel from behind the little handkerchief with which she was drying her eyes.

'That poor man!' she thought—'poor solitary creature! There's the sun!'

And it seemed to her that it was the first time the sun had shone all this fine hot year. Gathering her dress in both hands, she stepped into the drive, and soon was back again in the fields.

Every green thing glittered, and the air was so rain-sweet that all the summer scents were gone, before the crystal scent of nothing. Mrs. Pendyce's shoes were soon wet through.

'How happy I am!' she thought—'how glad and happy I am!'

And the feeling, which was not as definite as this, possessed her to the exclusion of all other feelings in the rain-soaked fields.

The cloud that had hung over Worsted Skeynes so
long had spent itself and gone.   Every sound seemed to
be music, every moving thing danced.   She longed to
get to her early roses, and see how the rain had treated
them.   She had a stile to cross, and when she was
safely over she paused a minute to gather her skirts
more firmly.   It was a home field she was in now, and
right before her lay the country house.   Long and low
and white it stood in the glamorous evening haze, with
two bright panes, where the sunlight fell, watching,
like eyes, the confines of its acres; and behind it, to the
left, broad, square, and grey among its elms, the village
church.   Around, above, beyond, was peace—the sleepy,
misty peace of the English afternoon.

Mrs. Pendyce walked towards her garden.   When she
was near it, away to the right, she saw the squire and
Mr. Barter.   They were standing together looking at a
tree and — symbol of a subservient underworld — the
spaniel John was seated on his tail, and he, too, was
looking at the tree.   The faces of the rector and Mr.
Pendyce were turned up at the same angle, and different
as those faces and figures were in their eternal rivalry
of type, a sort of essential likeness struck her with a
feeling of surprise.   It was as though a single spirit
seeking for a body had met with these two shapes, and
becoming confused, decided to inhabit both.

Mrs. Pendyce did not wave to them, but passed
quickly, between the yew trees, through the wicket-
gate.

In her garden bright drops were falling one by one
from every rose leaf, and in the petals of each rose
were jewels of water.   A little down the path a weed
caught her eyes; she looked closer, and saw that there
were several.

'Oh,' she thought, 'how dreadfully they 've let the weeds—— I must really speak to Jackman!'

A rose tree, that she herself had planted, rustled close by, letting fall a shower of drops.

Mrs. Pendyce bent down, and took a white rose in her fingers. With her smiling lips she kissed its face.

SOME OTHER TITLES
AVAILABLE IN POCKET CLASSICS

(A full list can be obtained from
Alan Sutton Publishing, 30 Brunswick Road,
Gloucester, GL1 1JJ)

Elsie and the Child & Other Stories

Arnold Bennett

In 1924 Arnold Bennett was moved to complete the novella *Elsie and the Child – A Tale of Riceyman Steps* re-introducing Elsie from the original novel now working with her husband Joe in the household of Dr Raste.

There are twelve other stories in this collection mostly set in the London of the nineteen twenties. Tales of high and low life, of humour and tragedy, the London theatre and business world, of yachts and yachting. *Last Love* tells of Miss Osyth and her cottage on an Essex inlet with Thames barges moving ghostlike to the quay.

For the final story the author returned to his Five Towns and a row of reddish houses on the east side of the municipal park of Bursley. The inhabitants were mostly alike but the Furber family at No. 41 were different. . . .

A treat for all Bennett fans.

The Haunted Man and The Haunted House

Charles Dickens

Everyone said he looked like a haunted man. His was the voice of a haunted man; slow speaking, deep and grave. He had the manner of a haunted man. His lair was solitary and vaultlike and anyone who saw him in his inner chamber, part library and part laboratory, on a winter's night before a flickering fire, trembled.

Conversely, the narrator of the other story first saw the haunted house in daylight with the sun upon it. There was no wind, no rain, no lightning, no thunder, no awful or unwonted circumstance of any kind, to heighten its effect.

And yet it was an avoided house, shunned by the villagers half a mile away.

Two of the best from the master of the ghost story.

Lady Anna

Anthony Trollope

Lovel Grange was a small house, the residence of a rich nobleman, lying among the mountains which separate Cumberland from Westmorland, about ten miles from Keswick. To it came Josephine Murray as a beautiful young bride who considered it quite the thing to be the wife of a lord.

She had not lived with the Earl six months before he told her that the marriage was no marriage – she was his mistress. Her unborn child, the Lady Anna, could make no claim to his title. Threats were issued by the Murray family, a duel was fought, but years of suffering were still to come. The stage was set for high drama.

The West Indies and the Spanish Main

Anthony Trollope

In 1858 Anthony Trollope was selected for the job of reorganising the decrepit postal system in the West Indies. He was in London on November 1st making his preparations and by the 17th was outward bound for the Spanish Main.

The West Indian journey lasted until the following summer and besides the islands included extensive journeys in Central America and British Guiana. He began the book of his travels aboard a trading brig between Kingston, Jamaica and Cien Fuegos on the southern coast of Cuba and from then on the reader is treated to a racily humorous account of his doings in one of the most beautiful regions on earth.

The West Indies and the Spanish Main is full of personal anecdote and all the detail and colour of which Trollope was the master. Long unobtainable, it is sure to delight his many readers.

On Horseback through Asia Minor

Colonel Frederick Burnaby

(Author of *A Ride to Khiva*)

Armed with a single Henry Express rifle, a
No. 12 smooth-bore, a small stock of
medicines and a faithful servant, Burnaby
set off in the winter of 1876/7 to ride 2,000
miles across Asia Minor.

War between Turkey and Russia was
imminent, the whole area was a hotbed of
intrigue and speculation, and reports of
atrocities and massacres were widespread.
His journey was to take five months and
bring him into contact with Turks, Arme-
nians, Greeks, Circassians, Kurds and Per-
sians of all classes from pachas to farmers,
from peasants to soldiers and nomads.

It was a ride of high adventure in wild,
inhospitable country, through snow-drifts
and over mountains, and Burnaby succeeds
in sharing with his readers all the excitement, hardship and humour in this vivid
account of Victorian travel.

Paris and the Parisians

Fanny Trollope

After the abortive attempt to open and run 'Trollope's Folly', her Cincinnati bazaar, Fanny Trollope returned to England to write *The Domestic Manners of the Americans* which brought overnight fame. But not consolation from her personal misfortunes – this was only achieved by travel and writing.

In 1836 appeared *Paris and the Parisians* which paralleled her earlier book in describing the domestic scene as it was in the French capital of 1835. Fanny was fifty-five with a gift for wit and satire and the ability to amuse some of her readers and infuriate others. With her pen she cut through the many layers of Parisian society to expose every facet of this glittering jewel. From her apartment in the rue de Provence she sallied forth on social and sightseeing expeditions. It was the Paris of Chateaubriand, George Sand and Franz Liszt, and Fanny Trollope brings it all to life.

The Black Monk and Other Stories

Anton Chekhov

Chekhov's pages are peopled with psycho-paths, degenerates of genius and virtue and satirically comic characters who succumb in feeble revolt against the baseness and banality of life. They are quite unfit to combat the healthy, rude, but unintelligent forces around them.

Kovrin, Likharyóff and Dr Andréi Yéfimitch, three heroes in this collection, are characteristic of Chekhov's outlook.

With the other stories and characters in this collection we have the best of Chekhov.